SPARKS

This book is dedicated to my brother and my friends, who had to hear me talk about these characters for years before it ever got to this point. Thank you for putting up with my nonsense.

Sparks

KENDALL FLETCHER

CONTENTS

vii

A Content Warning:

There are references to transphobia, ableism, past suicidal ideation, and a scene where torture is implied off page in this story. It's mostly hinted at and not addressed directly in this book, but this content can be easily upsetting, and I believe no one should be exposed to it without warning.

On that note, I hope you enjoy this story, dark content at times included.

Issac Riley and Anna Kahale
@ lostximagination on tumblr

~ One ~

Issac
September 5th, 2018

I grab the corner of the page between my thumb and fore-finger, rubbing it slightly before flicking forward in my book.

Something touches my head, pushing it down lightly and I gasp, every muscle in my body tensing up before my rational mind catches up with me, and I realize it's just my boss, Ms. Powel. I turn a nervous smile up to her as I relax somewhat again, and I pull out one of my ear buds.

"*Issac,*" Her tone is one of what I can only assume is mock disapproval, since we're the only two here this late at the library. I was the last employee working with her tonight- and most nights for that matter- and no guests have been in for nearly twenty minutes since a girl that I checked out left, and with only ten minutes left until the library closes, it's not likely anyone else will come in.

At least I *hope* she's not actually disapproving. The library is one of the few places I feel even remotely comfortable, and I'd hate for the Librarian to be upset with me for any reason. Ms. Powel is an old family friend though, so I *sincerely* doubt I have anything to worry about.

I'm sure my forced smile looks very awkward, but she doesn't seem to mind, and I pause my music. "Yes, Ms. Powel?"

My voice is more relaxed than I feel, with her stare and the rolling thunder doing a lot to set me on edge. My book is clutched so tightly in my hand that my knuckles are white, betraying my anxiety that my voice isn't showing.

She continues staring sternly at me for a moment, before breaking her facade and laughing, the warm, friendly sound doing wonders to relieve my anxiety. She pulls the chair out next to me and sits down.

"So," she says, "What are you reading?"

"Oh," I chuckle slightly, sticking a bookmark in my book and carefully closing it. "It's just," I run my fingers across the stretchy polyester book cover I have on it. What I'm actually reading is a collection of old letters that my father put together between Vincent Riley and Leilani after Vincent had moved away to found his school.

It's hard to make sense of, since most of the letters are actual complete nonsense, written in a pidgin language of sorts that the two of them had just between each other. I *think* I'm starting to figure it out, but it's slow work. I've made frustratingly little actual progress over the last two years.

I *need* to follow this stuff through to its conclusion though. For my dad. It was his life's work, and I won't leave it unfinished. I *know* these letters are the last piece of the puzzle for figuring out their story. It has to be...

But I can't tell Ms. Powel any of that. She's a *Non*, after all. I'm not allowed to talk about anything even relating to magic to her.

"It's just school stuff." I finish after probably too long of a pause. "I'm trying to get my reading done for class. Lord knows I don't get any quiet time to do that at home. Ethan and Lexi are, you know... I love them, but they can be an absolute nightmare at times. *Teenagers*, you know." I laugh faintly.

I'm just glad that they both care enough about their grades that I don't have to give them a hard time about doing their homework.

"Oh, like you're one to complain about teenagers." Ms. Powel laughs. "You were one *three days ago*."

"I was an adult!" I throw my hands in the air, huffing in frustration. "Yes, *nineteen* is *technically* a 'teenager' but not in the cultural sense that people mean when they *say that*. Honestly. You *knew* what I meant."

"Oh course I know, dearie, I just like giving you a hard time." She stands up. "I'll leave you to your studying, then. I wouldn't want to take up your last ten minutes of quiet time."

I ducked my head, hiding the blush I feel heating my face. "How did I up with the best job in all of Seattle..."

She pauses in walking away, chuckling under her breath, and turns back around. "You've been coming here almost every day since you were six, that's how. Silly goose."

"I suppose you're ri-" I flinch, curling forward on the table slightly as thunder cracks, cutting me off and I lose my train of thought entirely, staring over in the direction of a window that I know lays out of view beyond the bookshelves around me.

"... How badly is it raining?" I ask, more than a little troubled, thinking about the walk home and how unpleasant it would be. I *could* teleport, but I try not to when in Non areas, just in case.

Ms. Powel gently puts a hand on my shoulder, squeezing it slightly. "It's raining cats and dog out there," she pauses as thunder rolls again, a little more distant than the last time. "Issac, dear, I could drive you home. I'd really rather you not walk in this weather..."

I smile faintly, but shake my head. She's always so kind, but I really don't want to be any imposition.

"It's just a few blocks away, but thank you for the offer, Ms. Powell." I clasp my hands together, flashing a smile at her. "It means a lot." I twist around in my chair, and shove my book into the old beat up messenger bag that I've been toting around since high school.

"Well, I mean, It's just a bit of rain," I chuckle slightly, forcing a smile at her. "I've lived in Seattle my entire life. It's not like it is anything new. I'm used to it by now."

She just smiles slightly at me and nods, walking away and out of sight behind a bookshelf.

The moment she's out of sight, I grimace, listening to the sound of the pouring rain outside and the distant roar of thunder. Being used to it doesn't even remotely mean that I like it. No matter how long I live here, I'll never be comfortable with it. Thunder is just too loud and unpredictable.

Thunderstorms always just make me want to hide under the covers with my music blaring in my ear buds until it's over. But... It's still home and I've never lived anywhere else but Washington state.

There's another loud boom from a close lightning strike, and I wince. I'm about to put my ear buds back in to drown out the storm, when Ms. Powel walks back over to me, her umbrella in hand.

"*At least* take my umbrella, Issac," Her tone makes it sound like she's fretting, presuming I'm reading it right. I really wish she wouldn't, but I suppose I should appreciate having someone who worries for me. "You'll be soaked to the bone by the time you get home otherwise," She shoves the yellow and purple umbrella, one of those old-fashioned non-tele-scoping kinds, into my hands, whether I want it or not.

I force a smile, hating to take her things. She's *so* kind, but I really don't need the help. Just a subtle waterproofing spell and I'd be good to go, and if I *was* really worried I absolutely *could* just teleport...

Not that she knows that. Not that she *can* know that.

"I *really* shouldn't." I force a laugh, still stiffly smiling at her. "Odds are one of my siblings will break it before I can get it back to you. Umbrellas never last more than a day or two in our house."

"*Issac*," she gives me that stern *look* that she always gives people that are too loud in the library. "I *insist*."

I sigh, and look at the umbrella in my hands, realizing that she won't take no for an answer. "It's just a bit of rain..." I mutter, wishing I could just tell her *why* I don't need it, but

Nons aren't allowed to know. It's the law, and it's for the safety of every single person in the magical community...

She tucks a loose strand of Gray hair that escaped from her bun behind her ear and smiles, making the lines around her eyes crease. "I truly insist." She pats the top of my head. "Now why don't you head on home?"

I idly light up my phone screen to check the time. The library doesn't close for five more minutes, and my shift doesn't end for another twenty. Before I can protest about the time, she's pulling me to my feet and ushering me to the door.

"Nevermind the time, dear." She pushes my navy blue sweater into my hands and my bag. "No one else is coming, and there's not much in the way of closing to do today. I can handle it on my own. You just hurry home through this rain, alright? And have a good night. Do try to get your studying done *despite* your siblings."

"Alright, alright," I lean the umbrella against the wall to pull the sweater on over my lilac button down, and adjust the shirt collar to be over the sweater. "... Thank you, Ms. Powel. You really are too kind..." I sling my bag over my shoulder and pick back up the umbrella. "See you tomorrow?"

"Only way I wouldn't is if the library burned down. Now, hurry on home and say hello to your sister for me!"

"You *do* realize that Lexi barely remembers you, right?"

She laughs and shoves me out the door. "Then bring her around! I haven't seen the girl since your mother used to bring her about."

The mention of my mother is painful, and I have to force a smile at Ms. Powel because I know she means well. It's been two years; it shouldn't hurt this much every time one of my parents is mentioned. I quickly dart away from the door before she could tell anything is wrong, opening the umbrella as I go.

"See you tomorrow," I shout back at her.

Even with the borrowed umbrella, I wish I had cast a waterproofing spell. I'm soaked by the time I reach the corner. Puddles splash up and soak my feet and ankles, and the wind blows the rain clean past the protection of the umbrella.

Thunder cracks from somewhere very near, and I trip at the cacophony, landing on my knees in a puddle in shock.

"I *hate* thunderstorms." My voice is barely audible even to me as the wind takes it away, and I clamber back to my feet, ignoring the seeping cold. "I just want to get *home*."

I should have just let Ms. Powel drive me. *God*, I *should* have checked the weather forecast and drove my own car. I rarely do, but I *could* have.

"*FUCK!*" A high-pitched female voice shouts- quite *loudly* for how audible it is over the storm- and I spin around to see who, almost slipping back into the puddle for my trouble. A brown-skinned girl is struggling to her feet, her black hair pulled into a very soggy ponytail, and her flower-patterned leggings are mud stained and soaked.

It takes her a few attempts to get up, her pink sneakers sliding in the puddle she clearly fell in, but she does and steadies herself before seeming to notice me watching her.

I think I've seen her before, but it's hard to tell through the storm, and at this distance...

"Do you want something?" She shouts, now barely audible over the storm, and she rather pointlessly tries wringing out her ponytail.

I stifle a laugh with my free hand. "Just trying to make sure you're okay! Falls into puddles suck, and you don't exactly look like you're from around here!"

She's not dressed for the season at all, wearing a *sundress* of all things and very light sneakers and leggings, and a thin-looking zip up hoodie. Not something most people from Seattle would wear in *September*. It's not freezing usually, but the weather can get chilly- and wet- enough that clothing like that just... isn't wise.

"Worry about yourself stranger!" She shouts, still barely audible over the storm. "I'm just freaking *dandy*. If soaked and muddy could be counted as dandy that is!" It looks like she laughs, though I can't hear it. "Either way, I'm fine." She nonchalantly waves goodbye, and walks down off down the street, the same way I'm going.

She... doesn't get very far.

The next few moments seem to play out in slow motion, with everything going eerily silent to my ears as all the hair on my arms stands up, and I instinctively brace myself. The light is *blinding*, zigzagging down from the sky, and making contact with the girl's shoulder. In that exact moment, a soft green glow wraps around the girl, making her look hazy and indistinct as the lightning flashes around her, her silhouette standing out.

With the roar of the thunder, time seems to return to normal and sound rushes back in with my ears ringing. Imprints of the lightning still cloud my vision, but I see the girl pitch forward, her knees collapsing under her. That glow is still there. Getting my bearings, and trying desperately to ignore the ringing my ears, I dash cross the street, sliding to my knees next to her, or as close as I can get, the green glow acting as a barrier, even as it fades away.

Frowning, I lean as close as I can while that aura is still there, cloaking her and pushing me back, and I try without much success to blink the spots from my vision.

Why is it that I see a random stranger get struck by lightning, and by chance is another mage? I mean, what even are the odds of something like that? There's only one mage for every three thousand people in Seattle or so, for God's sake.

The glow finally vanishes completely, and after making sure she's still alive, I hurry her to a hospital.

I sit silently in a chair next to her bed in the Emergency Room, with my soaked sweater hanging over the back of the chair, leaving me in just my slightly damp lilac button down. I ring my blue beanie in my hands; the water seeping out of it and dripping to the floor as I fidget with it.

The storm seems quieter in here, just distant rumbling and the muffled patter of rain. The constant steady beeps and chatter of the hospital environment is a much more immediate sound, and it's sitting me on edge to still lingering ringing in my ears.

I *hate* hospitals.

The girl- Anna Kahale, according to her ID- isn't badly hurt. Just some superficial burns feathered across her skin like Lichtenberg figures. The doctor said she's lucky, not being hurt worse, at least in a way that is immediately clear. Some lightning strike victims immediately go into cardiac arrest. Or stop breathing.

But, of course, it wasn't luck. At least not entirely.

She must have had some passive protection on her for that to happen. Good for her, I guess. She was smarter than I was, walking unprotected in a thunderstorm...

I'm honestly surprised I never met her before. She's only a year younger than me, according to her ID- a Hawaiian driver's license- and I really thought I knew most mages around my age in the area. I checked her books out at the Library- she's easier to recognize up close... and also I saw the books she *got* in her bag, but I don't think I'd ever met her before that. She *had* to have come to Seattle very recently.

Anna Kahale. I've never even heard of that mage *family*. It's strange. Am I just forgetting something? I thought I *knew* all the major family names, especially from Hawai'i, given that Leilani's school is a sister school to Vincent's...

I'm not great with faces but I *think* I would have remembered her. Not a whole lot of Polynesian girls in Seattle. She's pretty though, her dark wavy hair a rich brown in better light and a soft round face with full lips and a wide nose.

This *Anna Kahale* is a mystery to me.

With a sigh, I wring out my hat one last time and put it back on. It doesn't feel right if I'm not wearing my hat.

A tall black girl skids into the room, her thick brown coils pulled back into a ponytail. She's a little bit familiar, but I don't have time to dwell on it as she starts to panic over her friend.

"Anna! Oh God! Oh God! Oh God!" She whirls around to face me, and I look away from her intense gaze at once. "You there! Ginger! Is she going to be okay!?" She clutches her head, groaning slightly. "Oh God, oh God. I *knew* I should have picked her up from the library! I *can't* believe I let her walk home in a thunderstorm!"

I sigh, staring at the white floor, where small puddles have pooled around me from the dripping water. Of *course* she has a friend who wants to ask me this stuff. Could she not just ask the nurses, or aids, or even bother the doctor instead of me?

"She's going to be fine. It's just superficial burns, she'll wake up any minute now."

The girl visibly calms down. "Good, good..." She trails off and frowns at me. "Wait, who are you anyway, Ginger?"

I glance at Anna and back her friend. "Issac Riley." I pause, my brow furrowing. I really do *know* this girl from *somewhere*. "I... We go to the same college!" I realize suddenly, "Lorraine, right?"

She blinked several times, then gasps, clapping her hands to her mouth. "Oh!! *Right*! I know you! You are in the same major as me and, like, *never* talk to anyone!"

Yeah, because she definitely had to point that out... Lorraine talks to *everyone* now that I think about it. She's the social butterfly of the class. Everyone knows and likes Lorraine. I'm basically her opposite in our major.

She pauses, tilting her head to the side. "Wait just a sec. Why were you with Anna?" A wide grin crosses her face. "Is it nerd love? I bet it's nerd love! You two were on a date, weren't you?"

I scowl, glaring at the wall behind Lorraine. Why would she jump to *that* conclusion...? "I've never even met her before today, Lorraine. We were just walking both walking through this stupid storm. I was across the street when it happened and got her to the hospital."

Lorraine frowns, walking over to me and leaning on back of my chair, and I move forward away from her immediately. "I believe you for now, Ginger. But it seems like too big of a coincidence if you ask me."

"You're telling me..." I glare at the floor, and then Anna groans slightly. Her big dark brown eyes flutter open, and she starts blinking quickly.

A fellow mage from a family I've never even heard of, who knows someone I go to a *Non* College with, just *happens* to get struck by lightning right across the stress from me? There are coincidences, and then there's *that*...

"Unnnngh... what happened?"

Lorraine launches into all the stuff the hospital undoubtedly told her on the phone, meaning she didn't need to ask *me* at all. "You were walking home, soaking wet through this *terrible* storm when BOOM! Lightning struck you! Then Issac here- he goes to the same school as us BTW- got help for you, and now you're here!"

Anna's gaze flit over to me, and I look away. After a moment, she speaks up. "I... I was struck by lightning?"

I can practically feel her gaze fixed on me despite not looking at her, and I bristle uncomfortably, keeping my gaze fixed firmly on the floor.

"Yes... You were..." I mumble. I should have just left before she woke up, but that would have been beyond rude.

"What about the green light, though? Lightning isn't green?"

I jerk up, staring wide-eyed at her for a moment, before managing to get a handle on my surprise and mask it, returning my stare to the now soaked hospital floor. How could she not know about her own magic? I suppose *hypothetically* some other mage could have cast the protection spell, but that's *illegal.*

And not likely.

"Wasn't there a green light?" She continues, "I swear I saw a green light..." She closes her eyes slowly, shaking her head.

I sigh. *Great*, I have to lie. I *hate* lying. "I didn't see any green light, Anna." I force the sentence out in an even tone, but I'm worried it sounds stiff and awkward. *Deceit* has always been difficult for me. It just feels so unnatural to *lie*.

She stares at me for a long moment before sighing. "Great. So I was struck by lightning and hallucinating. How *delightful*."

I stay out too late-

I pull my phone out quickly before the ringtone gets too far into the up-tempo Taylor Swift song, answering the call from my brother.

"What the hell do you want Ethan?!" I snap, staring off at the wall rather than at either of the girls, both of whom snickered slightly at my ringtone.

"To ask where the hell you are! Lexi is driving me up the wall!" His voice is sharp and I have to bite back an exasperated sigh. "Your shift ended like, an *hour* ago. You should freaking be home by *now*."

It's hard to not just hang up on him, but I have to be the *responsible* one. I'm in charge of him and Lexi, so I really can't lose my temper with him.

But *god*, it's hard to stay calm. I hate phone calls. This entire night suddenly became *very* stressful, and *my ears are still ringing.* I just want everything to *stop* for a minute.

But that's not how the world works, so I just take a few deep breaths before responding to him.

"*Well*," I say slowly, trying my best to keep an even tone. "Maybe, Ethan, you should stop *antagonizing* her. Just *go to your room.* You're sixteen. She's fourteen. Be the bigger person."

"Way to just assume it's *my* fault." He says in a way that all but assures me that it *is*. "But seriously, where are you?"

I sigh. "I'm at the hospital. A girl got struck by lightning across the street from me on the way home, and I got her here."

He's silent for a moment before exhaling heavily. "... *Seriously?* Also, uh, bro you're shouting a bit."

I wince, glancing at the girls, who are both staring at me and *smiling* for some reason. "*Sorry*," I hiss at what I *think* is a much lower volume. "My ears are ringing from the thunder, okay. It's even harder than normal to judge volume right now. I- I'll talk to you when I get home, okay?"

I don't wait for his response, just hanging up and shoving my phone back in my pocket and hiding my face in my hands.

"Younger siblings?" Lorraine says that like a question, and I sigh, my hands dropping back to my lap.

"Yes. He's... difficult, sometimes. Likes to pick fights with our sister. I think he does it for attention though, since he didn't act like that before, but..."

Ever since our parents died, he's been like *this*. I can only *guess* he's doing it for attention. It's so hard to keep on top of everything, so I have to leave him to his own devices a lot because he's more *able* to take care of himself than our sister is.

And he's *angry* as well, of course. He thinks they were *killed*. That it wasn't the accident that it was ruled. I can't say I disagree, but...

I don't know what he expects me to do about it.

"Oh, I *get* it." Lorraine laughs. "My sis is a *nightmare* sometimes. I'm glad I don't live with her anymore. You can't really blame them though, teenagers. Their brains are still developing."

"You say that like ours *aren't*," I say. "I'm the oldest person in the room, and I only turned twenty-*three days ago*."

"Oh-" Lorraine laughs. "Happy belated birthday then."

Anna pushes herself to sitting and grins at me. "Good thing this didn't happen three days ago, then. That would have been a *shitty* birthday." She laughs. "I love your ring-tone, by the way."

My face gets hot, and I look away, smiling slightly despite myself. I really need to *change it*. We're in a new era now, after all.

"Thanks..." I mumble. "Most people just laugh at it. Ethan, my brother, finds it *hilarious*."

"Well, this girl-" She points her thumb at her own chest, "happens to *like* TayTay so *Ethan* can shut up."

I muffle a laugh into my hand and grab my bag, pulling out a small notepad and a pen. "I really should get going," I say, jotting down my number and a note for her. "I don't trust my brother and sister home alone much longer."

I shove the scrap of paper into her hands and force a quick smile at her as I jump to my feet.

"Uh, call me later."

~ Two ~

Anna

September 5th, 2018

I'm intrigued by the redhead who got me to the Hospital. Issac, I guess.

He's... *cute*, honestly, if nothing too impressive in his awkward, fidgety demeanor. Dark auburn hair, pale skin smattered with freckles, a cute little snub nose, and... okay *wow*, *vivid* violet eyes, even if it's really hard to catch them as he seemingly tries his hardest to look anywhere *but* at me or Lorrie.

I've never met anyone else with purple in their eyes, and his look *entirely* purple. I can't fathom that it's his *actual* eye color, but at the same time... why would he be wearing color contacts?

But before I can *ask* him about it, he's excusing himself to leave because of his siblings and handing me a... piece of paper with his phone number. Huh.

I look down at the paper as Lorrie squeals with excitement while practically jumping into the seat he just vacated.

Sorry about lying. The green light was there.

Call me if anything else odd happens. - Issac J. Riley

Two things. **What the hell** and *who the hell signs a note with their first name, last name, and middle initial...*

My eyes trail down to the phone number, and I sigh softly as Lorrie chatters about how he was DEFINITELY was flirting with me.

I... don't think he was. It's a shame; he was kinda cute, but... Well, something *else* is clearly going on if he felt the need to *lie* about the green light to Lorrie.

What did he see?

AUUUUUGH. Why can't things be *normal*? I just want my life to be **normal**.

September 16th, 2018

"Aaaaannnnnaaaaaaaaaaaaaaaaa!" Lorrie shouts from the bathroom, right off our living room. "You left your phone in here, and your dad is calling!"

"Decline the call!" I shout back from my spot on the floor where I'm laying on my stomach in front of the couch, peering under it. I am so not taking a call from my dad right now. I don't want to talk to him. Like, ever. Besides, I have more important things to worry about. Like my missing outline and the notebook it's in. I need to check it to make my sure I don't go off track in my story this late in. I have to get it right.

Where is that stupid notebook?

I groan, rolling over onto my back and glaring up at the ceiling. Oh. One of the bulbs in our light fixture is out. Going to have to replace that later. After I find my notebook.

"I'm not declining a call from your dad." Lorrie says firmly as she comes into the room, wearing nothing but a bath towel, having clearly just come out of the shower, and she sits the still vibrating phone on my forehead. "Answer it." She commands,

With a sigh, I sit up, my phone falling into my lap and I tap decline on my phone screen. "No, Mom." I roll my eyes. "And go put some clothes on. I'm too bisexual for this. And you're too straight."

I'm teasing, of course, and I follow the words with a grin and a barely repressed giggle.

She snorts, shoving my shoulder before skipping to her room. "Trust me, honey, I wish I was available to you. Straight men are absolutely *tragic*. I'd love if girls did it for me. But *alas*, that's not the case."

"You know Lorrie, College is a very normal time for experimentation with sexuality."

"Oh, *hush*." She sticks her tongue out at me over her shoulder. "Girl, why don't you just call Issac? You know, he's *really* nice, if shy. *And* he works at a *library*. Perks!" She giggles. "If you don't go for it, I might at this rate. He's cute."

She goes into her room, but almost immediately pokes her head back out. "You really should talk to your dad, though. Pushing him away like this isn't healthy. He's *worried*."

"Don't go all psych major on me. I have my reasons for not talking to him, alright..." I turn my head to the side, spotting the metal glint of the spiral binding of my notebook, clear against the wall under the couch.

I stretch my arm out, trying to reach it, but it's just beyond my fingertips, and I sigh. I don't want to have to get up and move the couch to get it.

In a sudden flash of green light, the thing hurdles towards me and *whacks me in the face*.

In the eleven days since I was struck by lightning, things have *completely failed* to go back to normal. The only physical evidence that it happened at all are the mostly healed feathery burns down my back and arm, but downright *bizarre* things have been happening. I *wish* it would just *stop*.

Issac's note flashes through my mind, and I grimace. I don't want to admit any of this is happening, and calling him would like... *giving up*.

Lorrie skips out of her room, wearing a yellow sundress that is several inches too short for her, and a little loose, with the waist belted to make up for it, thick orange leggings, and a white jean jacket.

"Is that my dress?" I ask, pulling myself up onto the couch. "It doesn't exactly fit you."

"Yeah, yeah, You're curvier than me, but I belted it, so it's fine. It looks good on me, and you don't wear in anymore. Besides, yellow is my color. *You* should wear more purple. It makes that bit of purple in your eyes *pop*."

"... Sure, whatever. Freeze if you want. Don't blame me if it rains and you regret your decisions."

"It's not supposed to rain today." She sits down next to me on the couch. "I see you found your notebook."

I glance back down at the notebook in my hands, then back at Lorrie. "Oh, yeah. It *was* under the couch. No idea how it got there."

"Clearly Isa dragged it under there." She laughs, shaking her head. "Silly cat."

"Your cat drives me nuts, Lorrie. She likes to steal my stuff."

"She likes *paper*." Lorrie pauses for a long moment, pulling her feet up onto the couch. "You know I had a long chat with your dad yesterday."

I groan. Not *this* again. What was I *thinking* being roomies with a psych major?

"He's just worried about you. He just wants to know you're okay. I mean, you were struck by lightning 11 days ago and you haven't spoken to him once since then! Anna!" She leans towards me. "That is so not okay!"

"*Look.* I'm fine." I insist, waving her down from emphasis. I know that the thing she's calling *'not okay'* is the fact that I'm not speaking to my father, but I'm choosing to focus on lightning thing since she brought it up.

"*Frankly*," I continue, "I just want to forget the whole thing ever had happened!" I hug my notebook to my chest and sigh. "I mean, it was a freak incident, but I mostly got out unscathed. It was freaky, and weird, and I just want to *forget the whole thing.*"

"Even Issac?" She nudges me. "He gave you his number. You *should* call him. You must have made a hell of an impression for him to give his number. He's *waaay* shy, Anna. So he *definitely* liked you. And like I said, he's cute."

I close my eyes, exhaling slowly. Yeah, I especially wish I could forget him and his dumb note. *Issac J. Riley.* I've seen him around school too. I feel like I've been looking for him unconsciously, whether I want to or not.

He seems like he keeps to himself. I've never seen him talking to anyone, and when he's not in class, he seems to just sit in corners reading. And oddly, his books always have those stretchy reusable book covers on them.

Why does he have to be so damn mysterious?

"Cute or not, he didn't seem like my type."

To that, Lori just starts laughing. "I'm *sorry? Not your type?*" She shakes her head. "The guy was wearing vans, dress pants, a sweater, a button-down shirt, and a beanie. *Classic* nerd. The only thing he was missing was the glasses, and I'm not even going to mention how he acts in class. So your type. Oh, and Anna sweetie?" She puts a hand on my shoulder. "Don't think I haven't noticed you staring at him on campus. You. Are. Interested. In. Him." She giggles and ruffles my hair. "Besides, where the hell else you gonna find another boy who actually has good music tastes?"

I feel my face get hot. Was I really that obvious about staring?

"You can't judge people based on their clothes like that!" I open my notebook to a random page and hide my face behind it. "*Look*, I'm sure you mean well trying to set me up with him here, but I'm not currently interested in dating him, no matter what you think." I lower the notebook slightly, peeking over the top at Lorrie. "Besides, the *last* thing in my life is *another* Psych major."

"If you say so." She says in a singsong voice, clearly not believing me, and I sigh.

"*Whatever.*" I lean away from her. "*Anyway*, like half my outline is missing. I swear I'm going to kill your cat if she doesn't stop tearing pages out of my notebooks."

"Isa's a little weirdo." Lorrie shrugs, a silly little smile on her face. "What's this story about?"

"Gay alien detectives, based on Sherlock Holmes and Watson, solving murders throughout the galaxy as the only intergalactic consulting detectives."

I've always had a soft spot for Holmes, and I thought he'd be interesting in a SciFi setting. And of course, give him and Watson the romance they've always deserved.

"You sure are weird, Anna." Lorrie laughs, getting back to her feet. "Gay alien Sherlock. Sure. Why not?" She shakes her head. "Not sure how you could turn that into a six-page outline, but you do have your thing with making sure everything makes sense scientifically."

"I write hard science fiction. Excuse me for liking accuracy." I stand up, hurrying to my bedroom.

"You're excused!" Lorrie shouts after me, laughing as she does so.

I roll my eyes at her, and quickly strip off my t-shirt and pajama bottoms, putting on a blue sweater, jean skirt, and one of my many pairs of flower print leggings. I throw my purse over my shoulder and walk to the front door. "Hey, Lorrie, I'm going out. Do you need anything from the store?"

Lorrie, who is laying on the couch working on homework, blinks slowly. "Uh. We're out of milk, and I'd appreciate if you got a pint of rocky road ice cream, but that's about all I can think of. Bread maybe?"

"Bread. Milk. And Ice Cream. Gotcha. Don't touch my Shakespeare. All the pages are specifically marked." I leave, snapping the door closed behind me.

I dash out the door and down the street, smiling at the sunny sky. "No rain today." I sing to myself under my breath.

I get to the store with no bizarre incidents- *thankfully.*

Unfortunately... My shopping doesn't go near as smoothly, since as I was scanning the freezers for rocky road ice cream a pint of it flew off the shelf and hit the inside of the glass doors. I looked furtively around to make sure no one saw that, and then hurriedly grabbed it, finishing my shopping as quickly as I could.

"Stupid psych student screwing with my head..." I mutter, walking back to my apartment, reusable grocery bag clutched tightly in hand. "Stupid green lightning and stupid weird things flying at me..."

I'm going to *have* to call him. I really, really *don't want to*, but his stupid weirdness won't *leave me alone.* I just wanted to move on and pretend it *never happened*, but noooooo! I'm not allowed any peace apparently...

The first time in my life I felt like I was actually settling down and then this bullshit happened.

If I thought any gods existed, I'd want to punch them in the throat for screwing me over.

Before I even round the corner on the way back home, dark clouds have started to roll in over the previously clear blue sky, and I scowl up at it. *Goddamn Seattle.*

I should have chosen to go to college somewhere *sunnier.*

Huffing slightly, I continue forward, adjust my grip on the bag... when I notice a faint green haze around my hand, and I drop the bag on instinct, wildly waving my hand to try to make it go away.

"Nononononono! No! Go away!!" I close my eyes, shaking my head quickly. "I don't want any weirdness! No!"

Thunder cracks, drowning out that last *No!* and I open my eyes, the green glow from my hand fading just as rain starts to *pour* down in ice cold sheets.

Muffling a frustrated scream into my hand, I kick angrily at the sidewalk a few times, before picking my bag back up and sprinting the rest of the way to my apartment.

Leaning against the door I just slammed shut, I exhale loudly and drop the bag to the floor. "It's official. I hate Seattle."

"Did it rain, after all?" Lorrie asks, not even looking up from her homework. "I thought I heard thunder."

"Yes! Out of nowhere!" I run my fingers through my soaked ponytail, and then glare at my own hand, like it and its stupid glow are somehow responsible. "Look, just, *you* put the stuff away. I'm going to change clothes."

I stomp over to my room, roughly yanking my drenched sweater off and throwing it haphazardly at my hamper, before I fall backward onto by bed, not yet stripping anything else off.

Why me? Why is this happening to *me*? I just wanted to be a normal college student. I thought the worst I'd have to deal with would be like, stupid racist frat guys asking me to *hula* for them or something. It's *not normal* to go from a cloudless blue sky to a storm that quickly...

I sit back up, watching the rain pelt my window for a moment before sighing and grabbing my phone. I have to call him.

It's picked up almost immediately when I call. "Hello?" He says, his voice raised slightly over some sort of commotion in the background.

"Uhh, hi? Issac, right? This is Anna, the girl who was..." I trail off, more than a little uncomfortable with this. What do I *say*?

"Anna!" he says sounding downright cheerful, and there's a loud crash in the background on his end. "I was wondering if I was going to hear from you! I was beginning to doubt it, honestly."

"I, uh, didn't want to call you. But this *bullshit-*" I glance at the window again and sigh. "Weird stuff keeps happening and I want it to *stop*."

Issac sighs, and I distinctly hear *"LET GO OF MY HAIR ETHAN!"* in the background. "What's been happening?" He says after a moment, and calmly like his siblings *aren't* clearly having a fight or something where he is.

Nevertheless, I can't believe he's actually asking me what's happening? Like, he's the one who told me to call *him*. There's *no way* he doesn't **know**.

"Like you don't know!" I snap, pulling the phone away from my ear to hang up when a different also male voice shouts "stop!", and I find myself freezing in place. The commotion on the other side seems to have stopped entirely.

"Hello Anna. I'm Ethan, Issac's brother. He really has no idea what's going on, at least not precisely." His voice is steady, almost hypnotic, and I'm frozen in place with the phone held to my ear. "He figured something odd might be happening, but he needs you to tell him *what*. I'm going to hand the phone back to him now. Please don't hang up."

Quietly from the other end I hear Issac say *"Ethan, that was not okay,"* and Ethan muttering *"She would have hung up otherwise."*

After a moment Issac clears his throat, and I blink, rather dazed. "Uh, sor... sorry about that. My brother can be rather... ah, pushy."

"Oh... no..." I murmur, still blinking quickly as the real world catches up with me. "It was fine. Uh. It's like, mostly been things just flying at me when I'm looking for them, but I *swear* I just made it rain. Because I was angry about things flying at me."

The other end is silent for a moment. Dead silent.

"Okay," he finally says, his voice a little shaky. "Can... can we meet up in person? I know this is all very strange, but it's not something to explain over the phone."

I let out a slow breath. "Tomorrow. Coffee shop on campus. Four o'clock. You better be there."

"... Uh, sure. See you then, I guess?"

"Mm." I hang up, and sit on my bed silently for a moment as the world comes completely back into a sharp focus, and I sigh, finishing changing clothes and going out to join Lorrie in the living room, a copy of the Scarlet Letter in hand.

Tomorrow I have to deal with this all. But the rest of *today* is just going to be a lazy Sunday with my book.

~ Three ~

Issac
September 17th, 2018

3:45 PM.

I came here right after my last class ended at 3:30, and I'm tapping my fingers impatiently on the table to the beat of the song playing in my ears.

"One Two Three, Let's Go Bitch..." I mumble under my breath, towards the start of the song, a wry smile on my face, humming to the tune quietly.

I slowly flip to the next page of my book, rubbing the paper between my fingers a moment before flicking it forward and continuing to read. I turn the volume up slightly on my music, trying to drown out the din of the campus coffee shop, namely the rowdy group of freshmen that are shouting and laughing loudly for no discernible reason.

I throw another sideways glance at the door, my eyes glazing over the other coffee shop patrons, which just seem to be other students hanging out between classes, and one older gentleman in a fedora and long coat, and I sigh impatiently.

Okay, so maybe she's not supposed to be here for another 15 minutes, but I have this knot of anxiety in the pit of my stomach that won't go away and she needs to just get here so I can get this over with.

I *really* don't like people, in a general sense. And people don't *usually* like me much either. I put them off, somehow. Even here on campus, I know I have a reputation as a loner. I *really* can't see this going well.

I shut my eyes tight, ducking my head. Just... try being straightforward. *You haven't been able to get the girl out of your head Issac. You've played out this conversation out a million times in your head. Having it for real won't be **that** different.*

Right. It's never that easy.

I wonder if she's been thinking of me as much as I've been dwelling on her... I've caught her eyes a few times here on campus, but only ever for a moment. I don't know if it's by coincidence, or...

Even if she *has* thought about me **at all** since then, it doesn't change the fact that this conversation seems *impossible* to have. *And* she explicitly said she *didn't* want to call me. My brother practically *coerced* her to be here...

But, even putting that aside, how does one explain to someone that being struck by lightning somehow triggered latent magic?

It did *definitely* did do that, since she's practically leaving trails of quintessence behind her. I've seen them crisscrossing campus. I was going to *have* to talk to her whether or not she called me, since she couldn't more obviously have *no* control over her magic... This is *unprecedented,* and she needs to know what's going on.

But I don't know how to *explain* any of it... I sigh, staring blankly at my book, not really able to process the words on the page right now.

"Hey!"

I jerk back in my seat in surprise, not having noticed Anna sit down across from me. Exhaling slowly, I pause my music and pull out my earbuds.

"Hi. Uh. Ah, you're- you're early."

"So are you." She replies, crossing her arms and leaning back in her chair. "*Now*, explain the weirdness, Ginger. And *make it stop.* Please."

"I..." pausing to collect my thoughts, I gently fold the corner down on my page and close the book, my gaze fixed on the table. "I... I have a few questions for you first, because this doesn't make much sense to me either."

"Could you at least look me in the eyes when talking to me." She mutters, and I wince, forcing myself to meet her eyes.

I don't get why neurotypicals are so insistent on eye contact, especially since they tend to get annoyed by too much eye contact too. But I can force myself to *conform*, if just to get through this conversation...

Looking in her eyes now, I notice something I missed back at the hospital. While her irises are predominately a deep brown, there's a halo of dark purple around her pupils.

Bingo. If I wasn't already sure that she's a mage, I certainly am *now.* But that doesn't explain why her magic is only manifesting *now...*

"Uh," she frowns. "First you're not looking at me at all, now you're *staring.*"

Exhaling hard, I scowl, staring at the table again. My point *exactly.* What am I expected to do? "It doesn't matter. Just, ah... *okay*, this is going to sound strange, but what do you know about your family history?"

"My... My *family*?" Her voice quickly goes cold, and I quickly look up to see her glaring at me. "What the *hell* does my family matter to you?"

"Just..." I groan, pulling down on my hat. This is already going *horribly.* This was a mistake. I should have *known* I'd screw up something so *sensitive.* "Let's just," I take a deep breath. "Let's just start simple here; and I *promise* this is important... What's your mother's maiden name?"

The glare she gives me is sharp and *very* angry, and I instinctively flinch back, watching her warily. I really can't get a read on this girl. She was... nice, for the few moments I interacted with her at the hospital.

Ah, maybe she's just... upset from the chaos she's been dealing with since then, so she's coming into this already in a bad mood...

Or maybe I just touched a nerve.

"Don't even *mention* my mother." She hisses darkly. "And you're staring again. *Stop it.*"

I break my gaze, my face flushing with color. I never know what the line for what counts as *staring.* "Look," my voice shakes a little, and I grip the edge of the table tightly. "I'm *sorry* if I've touched a nerve. I don't know anything about your family, or *you*, for that matter. I'm just trying to make *sense* of this. I don't know how to explain this if I don't know how it's *possible*..."

"*Try*," she says firmly, and I dare a glance up at her. She's still glaring at me, but with a bit less... malice. "Try and I *might* answer your question."

I sigh, pulling down slightly on the edges of my hat again. "It's... complicated." I say after a moment of silence. I need some reference point- she needs some way to understand...

"Do- do you read fantasy novels, by any chance?" I ask faintly.

"... No, not really. I'm more of a sci-fi person. Unless Harry Potter counts, I guess. I read those as a kid."

"... Harry Potter. *Okay*. I can work with that." I exhale. I've never much *liked* Harry Potter, but it is a decent cultural touchstone for this. "So, you know how in those books, the *Wizarding World* is just like, a secret society hidden within the normal world?"

"Yes?" She says slowly. "What are you about to tell me it's all real and that I'm secretly a witch, and my Hogwarts letter is just eight years late?"

"Uh, not exactly." I laugh nervously. Oh God, what am I doing. This is a mistake. I should have had Ethan talk to her. He's good at this sort of thing. "But, ah, something similar."

My heart sinks even more as disbelief crosses her face. This could not be any worse. It's a *disaster*. This is so *so* sensitive, and I *screwed it up.* Even though she hasn't left my head since we met, I feel like I've said everything *exactly* wrong...

Why does she have to be so *difficult?* I was hoping that the things she experienced before she called me would leave her more open to this...

"You *have* to be screwing with me." She crosses her arms. "This *can't* be real."

"I-It is." I stammer, disheartened by her disbelief. How am I supposed to explain magic to someone who won't even believe it exists? *How am I supposed to do this?* This is just... too much for me, isn't it?

I put my head down on the table, trying not to scream in frustration, and I hear her sigh.

"Okay, okay, *fine.* I'm listening; what do mean by *something similar?*"

I sit back up, staring at her moment as she looks back at me, with her eyebrows raised.

"... Alright... There's a secret world of magic hidden in plain sight." I say quietly, wary that she's not going to believe me. "Those with magic are wizards or *mages*- and there *is* a distinction- and those without are rather uncreatively called *non-magics*, or nons for short." I shrink back at her still doubtful gaze, but I force myself to continue. "I'm convinced *you* are a mage, and your magic was inexplicably latent until the moment you were struck by lightning."

"... What does that have to do with my mother?" She says softly.

"Ah, well, see... I was- I was asking about your mother's maiden name because being a mage is *inherited.* I wanted to know if she was from a mage family, because that could have at least made a little sense..."

"... Keahi." She says flatly after a moment. "Her maiden name was Keahi."

Keahi. *Keahi...*

Oh, *wow.*

"I don't know anything about her, or her family." Anna keeps talking, but it reaches my ears as if I had a glass bowl over my head as my mind spins, trying to get a handle on what she just said. "It was just me and my dad for most of my life."

Keahi. It's *Keahi.* What are the *chances...* The surname that Leilani's children were forced to take with the Act to Regulate Names because it was their father's name...

That was *not* a mage family by the time they had that name, but based on all my father's research... Leilani? Definitely was.

Leilani, who was probably the very last nature mage. *Leilani* who is possibly the ancestor to this girl across from me. This girl who said... who said she thought she controlled the weather?

This can't be a coincidence. It's so implausible for it to just be a coincidence. Because *Leilani* has been thoroughly researched by my father, right along with Vincent Riley. The last nature mage, and the last Master, both of which some believe *never* existed now.

My father wanted to prove that they did.

And now? Now me, a descendant of Vincent Riley and this girl, a potential descendant of *Leilani*... it stretches belief for this to just be *chance*.

"Earth to Issac?"

I shake myself and focus back on her, laughing faintly. "Sorry, sorry. I just. I think I know that surname, yeah." I pause, taking a deep breath, moving on from the subject because it's *way* too much to get into right now. "You said you think you made it rain yesterday?"

She groans, putting her head in her hands, and mutters, "It sounds so *stupid*, but I *swear* that's what happened. I was angry, and the sky filled up with storm clouds out of *nowhere*."

I laugh brightly. There it is. This girl is *living proof* that nature mages existed, and *still do*!

I'll prove you right yet, Dad.

"No, no. That's not stupid. Untrained mages tend to do magic accidentally, and highly influenced by emotion. If you think you made it rain, you probably did."

"I didn't want to!"

"I didn't say you did." I grin. "*Influenced by emotion* is the key detail there. You're going to need to learn how to control your magic so you don't accidentally blow the masquerade, but that's doable, even if it's at a later age than most mages get trained."

"Well, your mood turned around fast." She grumbles, scowling at her hands. "And, you know what, I still don't buy any of this. This isn't a freaking urban fantasy novel. This is real life."

"So you're going to need tangible proof, huh?" I sigh, rolling my eyes. "OK, is the rest of your day free? Because I'll give you tangible proof."

Anna frowns, but pulls out her phone and texts someone. "Fine. I just told Lorrie I was hanging out with you and if I vanish tonight, you should be suspect Number One. Got it?"

"What?" I laugh slightly. "Do you think I'm a serial killer or something?" I roll my eyes, getting to my feet. "Come on."

Slowly, she stands as well, staring at me with guarded eyes. "Lead the way."

I throw my bag over my shoulder, my book returned to it, and walk out of the coffee shop, weaving off campus with her following me.

After several minutes she snaps at me, walking stiffly with crossed arms. "Where the hell are we going now?"

I grin at her. "Oh, just the magic district of Seatt..." I trail off, looking over her shoulder, my gaze focusing on a figure across the street. An older man, with chin length brown hair, dark eyes, and tanned skin. He's wearing a fedora- an *actual* fedora; not a trilby- and a brown long coat.

He was in the Coffee Shop.

Is... Is he following us?

I quickly look him over, taking note of the hand hidden in his pocket, when he locks eyes with me, a chill running down my spine.

And there's a jolt of familiarity.

He...

He's being tracked as a Hunter by enforcers. How did I not recognize him sooner!? I never expected being bad with faces to put me in *physical danger*.

Shit.

Without a word, I grab Anna's wrist, and I take a sharp turn down the nearest street, running as fast as I can.

"Woah! Wait! *Issac-* Where are we *going?*"

I should have seen the risk of a Hunter coming. *She leaves a trail everywhere she goes.*

"Sorry!" I gasp, already struggling a bit for air. *Augh.* Running in a binder *sucks.*

"Why are we running!?" She tries to slow down, but I just speed up to counteract her, and I sweep my arm behind me to break the tessence trail she's leaving, pushing a lot of it aside and scattering it. I *hope* that's enough to at least make us *harder* to track...

"Hunter!" I gasp. "I'll explain later! Just run!"

"You are the most infuriating person I've ever met!" She picks up her pace despite her words, though, making it easier to run.

"Noted!" She doesn't seem to like me much. Fine. That's fine. Not any different than most people, really. I can deal with it.

I suddenly turn, ducking into an alley, and I break her tessence trail again before looping around to the residential area where I live with my brother and sister. I'm still sprinting for dear life as we get to my house and I pull Anna in, slamming the door and locking it behind us.

I slide to the floor, struggling to catch my breath, and stare up at the ceiling.

"Master be damned..." I gasp between breaths, curling forward to hold my head in my hands. I can't believe that happened...

Well, my siblings will give her a crash course for sure. Not how I *intended* for her to first see magic, but it will do. *It will do*

~ Four ~

Anna

September 17th, 2018

"Master be damned..." Issac mutters, clearly *very* out of breath with the way he's practically gasping for air.

I am too. We just ran like freaking crazy for no good reason! I mean- *okay*, I can *tell* that this is hard for him. He clearly has *no clue* what he's doing, but he does want to *help*. I can appreciate that much. But could he possibly be anymore *oblique* about all this!?

"What the *hell* was that?" I ask, crouching down next to him on the floor. "If you're going to take us sprinting through the streets to some random house- is this *your* house?- I'd like an explanation."

"It... It was a H-Hu-" He holds up a finger, taking slow deep breaths and seeming to struggle a bit in doing so. How out of shape is he? I'm hardly fit and I've *mostly* caught my breath.

A girl drops down from... the *ceiling?*... somersaulting in midair and sticking the landing in front of me with a huge grin on her face.

She looks maybe fourteen or fifteen, with long hair with messy curls, about the same color as Issac's- a lighter red than my first impression while it was wet, and green eyes with... purple rings around the pupils like mine. Huh. She also has the same nose as Issac and a smattering of freckles.

And she's dressed like a punk rock hipster. Must be Issac's sister, if we're at his house... And she just... fell from the ceiling?

"Hiya!" She crouches down, too, beaming at me. "I'm Lexi! You must be Anna!" She laughs and punches her brother's shoulder. "He didn't say he was bringing you *home*."

"I wasn't *planning* on it." He manages to gasp out between breaths. "There wa-was a *Hunter* tracking- tracking us."

Lexi's expression momentarily falters. "All our spells are still secure, right? And cloaked?"

"Y-Yes..."

Lexi stands up and pulls her brother to his feet. "You go on upstairs and, uhhh, check them. Me and Ethan will keep Anna company for a few minutes." She pauses. "And maybe change clothes. You're all sweaty." She laughs lightly, but Issac looks thankful for some reason.

Isaac hurries out of the little hall room thing the door is in, walking past a boy who almost looks like a younger version of him, but with shorter, curlier hair, a slightly stronger jawline, and blue eyes rather than violet.

This must be Ethan.

"Hey. Ethan right?" I stand back up straight, leaning back against the door. "We talked briefly on the phone."

"Oh, ah, yeah. We did. Briefly." He crosses his arms, looking away. "Sorry."

"Sorry for what?" I cross my arms, looking at him expectantly. Like, is everyone in this family weird?

"Ethan is a Social Mage." Lexi answers quickly for him, beaming at me. "He cast a spell to make you listen to him, and mind control spells are *frowned upon*." She shrugs. "Like, they aren't just straight up *illegal*, and what he did was more of a suggestion than actual mind control, kinda like what the *fey* do to people, but it's still super frowned upon. Social mages have it hard that way."

"... Thanks, Lexi, for not even letting me talk." Ethan mutters, crossing his arms.

"Okay, so wait, now there's different types of this mage lunacy?" I shake my head incredulously. "This gets weirder every second and I'm still not sure I believe any of it."

Lexi shares a look with Ethan, who shrugs, and then she giggles, and *jumps*.

Well, it sort of looks like jumping, but the bottom of her feet are glowing a vibrant green and it's very relaxed... and then she doesn't come back down.

With a laugh she begins to float and swim through the air like *gravity* doesn't exist, ending by somersaulting midair over my head, and sticking the landing on my other side.

She leans on my shoulder, grinning. "So, how about that Little Miss Skeptic?"

That... That was undeniably the coolest thing I've ever seen, and I don't know how to react to it. She just turned off gravity for herself.

This is actually freaking magic, isn't it?

Holy shit.

Holy shit. I can't- I can't even. How. *What.*

Ethan laughs and walks closer. "You've blown her mind, Lexi."

He steps right up in front of me, face to face, and my eyes immediately lock on his, a light ring of purple on the outside of his otherwise baby blue irises clearly visible in this close.

"*Calm,*" he murmurs softly, his eyes briefly taking on a blue glow.

My disorientation and shock vanish almost instantly, and I take a deep breath. "Wow. So, uh, what's with this type thing?"

He laughs. "Why am I surprised that Izz didn't say anything about that to you?" He shakes his head. "Always been a sore spot for him."

Lexi rolls her eyes. "Issac worries too much. He's the best mage I know. Who *cares* if he doesn't know his specialty..." She shakes her head. "But yeah, every mage has a magic thing that they're naturally predisposed to. For me that's the field known as 'Air' magic. As I already said, Ethan's is 'Social' magic, which would really be more fitting for Isaac, since he's gonna be a psychiatrist and whatnot. "

"Oh, uh, so what's mine?" I ask slowly, looking between the two of them.

"Oh, well, you've got to look at your icon for that, and Izz is the only one of us that can reliably cast that spell." Ethan shrugs. "So you've just got to be patient."

"Okay," I move on, not willing to wait for Issac to get all my answers. "*Fine*, what's a '*Hunter*'? And why did Issac make us sprint for several blocks because of one?"

The two share a look, both seeming uncomfortable with the question.

"A Hunter is just a modern day Witch Hunter with a lot more tricks up their sleeves." Isaac says, leaning against the doorway, now wearing a loose blue hoodie rather than the light blue sweater he was wearing earlier.

"Hunters are the entire reason there still a masquerade at all. They are out for the death of all mages because they view it as an unfair advantage." He walks further into the room. "Never mind the fact that these are abilities we're born with, and literally cannot be rid of."

He sighs, doing the weird thing of pulling on his hat like he kept doing at the coffee shop. He seems to have a lot of nervous ticks. And generally seems nervous over all. I almost feel bad for him. This must be *horribly* difficult for him.

Just from the short time I've known him, I can make a *guess* that he's studying *psychology* for personal reasons, even if I can't be completely sure. He just seems very... *anxious.*

"I don't know if he managed to follow us, so it's best if you stay here a little while." He smiles stiffly. "You uh, don't know how to contain or control your magic at all, so you leave a trail, and you'd be easy pickings for him."

I'm silent for a moment at his grim wording, and then I sigh. Are people really so irrational that even now actual witch hunters exist? Why am I even surprised that people can be so awful after the last *election*...

"Okay," I murmur quietly. "I don't want to be murdered by some backwards, irrational asshat, so I'll stay here as long as I need to."

Issac smiles slightly. "Come on, we don't need to hang out in the mudroom."

He leads me to a small but cozy living room, and sits on the sectional, which has a ton of pillows and heavy looking blanket draped over the back.

I sit down next to him, pushing a pillow out of the way. "So. About this specialty thing?"

He smiles, laughing slightly. "I was about to bring it up." He sighs. "I doubt my siblings explained it very well."

"Rude Izz. Just, rude." Ethan says, leaning in the doorway.

Issac growls slightly and throws a pillow at him. "What did I say about calling me Izz! Goddamnit, Ethan! It's not that hard!"

Ethan laughs and walks past the living room and presumably up the stairs off the mudroom.

Issac sighs, then focuses back on me, actually staring at a point over my shoulder. "*Anyway.* Well, all mages have specialties, and-"

"Do you really not know what yours is?" I cut across him. "It just seems weird, since Lexi said you were the best mage she knows, and some icon spell or something can tell you it? And like, that you're the only one here you can cast it? Is it a spell you can only cast on other people?"

He sighs, pulling on his hat again. "I'll get to the icon spell. Just be *patient.*" After a moment, Issac continues. "All mages have specialties, well, er, maybe with one exception, but that's not important." He takes a deep breath. "There are nine remaining specialties that can reliably be identified, and that are officially recognized. Air, fire, water, earth, life, sensory, social, change, and protection. Mages have been known to have up to three specialties, though the more specialties they have, the less skill and power they have in all of them."

"And the icon thingies?"

"I was getting to that!" he says, pinching the bridge of his nose. "Every mage has an 'Icon' that is fundamentally linked to them and their magic. A Magic Signature as it were. *Well,* every specialty has a motif that constantly recurs in the icons of mages with that specialty."

"How do you not know your own then?"

He frowns, staring at the floor and fidgeting with his sweatshirt sleeves. "Uh, well..." After a moment, he raises his hands up, cupping his hands together in front of his chest, an aura of blue light forming in them. A second later a twirling image of a five pointed blue star surrounded by smaller twinkling stars appears.

"Stars and sparkling are a universal motif in Icons, but mine *only* has the stars and no signifiers of any specialty. So, yeah. I've got nothing. I thought I was a sensory mage for a while because my father was, and the first few spells I cast when I was little were sensory, but... I just... I don't know honestly."

"... Weird." I shrug. "What's mine?" I lean forward slightly, grinning at him, and he smiles, looking sidelong, away from me.

Okay, I think he just doesn't like eye contact. He's not trying to be rude, he's just... uncomfortable. Hm. I can accommodate that. It's not like eye contact actually matters that much, I guess. And I can tell he is *genuinely **trying*** to help me with this nonsense...

Again, he holds his hands cupped, but closer to me this time. A faint blue aura surrounds his hands again, but the deep forest green light that's been haunting me forms within that, where a dark storm cloud spewing lightning surrounded by twinkling stars appears.

"*So*," I grin at him. "What does that mean? What specialty am I?"

Issac looks up, his expression totally dumbfounded. "I'll be frank, I'm not *sure*. I was expecting some variety of *leaf*..." He lets out a slow breath. "Your Icon barely makes more sense than mine. Welcome to the club." He laughs bitterly. "Though, I actually do have a fairly solid hunch on what your specialty is, even if you're lacking the *normal* motif. Nature. It's one that died out centuries ago... with the last ones known being in the Kehai family. Or more so the family that *became* the Kehai family, since Native Hawaiians at the time didn't have surnames..." He pauses, frowning slightly. "The actual last nature mage's full name is lost to history, since most accounts of her we have are in English writings, but we know her as *Leilani*."

"Leilani? So she was a chieftess?" I ask curiously, not at *all* surprised that the *English* failed to get her full name. I try to stay connected to my heritage, even if so much of my culture was just... destroyed by colonization, so I know a bit about Hawaiian naming practices. And -*lani* is reserved for chiefs.

"Uh, yeah." He laughs slightly. "She was. I'm going to assume there's something I don't know about that told you that?"

"Don't know anything about the naming practices of ancient Hawai'i, do you?" I giggle into my hand. Silly white boy.

"... I know a bit?" he says slowly. "I know they were unisex, and every child got a *new name*. They might be changed through life, and they might get new names. And I know that in 1860 they were forced to start taking Christian names, and all living Hawaiians at the time were given their father's name as a surname."

"Well, more than I expected you to know, white boy." I grin. "*Lani* is reserved for chiefs. It means sky."

"... Oh." He laughs slightly. "I try to do my research given how central Leilani is to some historical research I'm working on and I don't want to be like... every white historian, misrepresenting indigenous people, but there are still definitely gaps in my knowledge."

"You're a *historian* too, Mr. Psych Student?" I raise my eyebrows. "You're barely twenty years old, so that seems a little weird."

"Oh hardly," He shakes his head. "My father was though, and I want to finish his work because no one else ever would."

"Oh. I-" I hesitate. Asking someone you barely know what happened to their clearly dead parents probably isn't wise, so I just bite my tongue. "So, uh, what would the normal motif for nature be? And what made you think I was nature, be-yond the whole *Leilani* thing?"

"Huh, oh. Well for the later, you having accidentally con-trolled the weather. That's fairly advanced magic, so to do it accidentally it would have to be in your specialty, and weather control fell under the Nature specialty." He sighs. "And the normal motif is *leaves* of some sort. A storm cloud still... thematically makes sense for Nature, but... it's not what all records indicate the motif *should* be."

"Huh. Interesting." I tilt my head. "So, like, am I staying the night here because of this hunter guy, or what? And if I am, where am I *sleeping*?"

He blinks a couple times, then stands up. "We, ah, we have a guest room. I guess I should show you around."

He gives me the house tour, and I can't resist the tempta-tion to stop in his very blue room- must be his favorite color- and look over his bookshelves. I'm a bookshelf snoop. I judge people based on their collections. What kind of English Lit. Major would I be if I didn't?

"Not a bad selection." I smile over my shoulder at him. It's a little YA heavy, mixed with old classics and textbooks, and he must *really* like Taylor Swift since he has physical copies of all of her albums lined up neatly on the top shelf of one of his two large bookshelves, but still. Not bad. "Do you actually *like* Hawthorne or do you just have a few of his books to look smart?"

"Oh, well, I like him well enough, but I'd read almost any-thing, so it's not really saying much." He shrugs. "I steer clear of smut and books I know where the writing is bad, but other than that..."

"Mm, let's see what else you have, Taylor Swift- which are *not* books, how dare you sully a bookshelf with CDs-" He scoffs and I giggle, continuing. "Fahrehheit 451, Carry On, The Female Man, the Hunger Games series, Brave New World, the entire Series of Unfortunate Events and All the Wrong Questions, An Abundance of Katherines, The Hobbit..." My eyes catch on a familiar title, and I pull it off the shelf. "Ooo, 1984. Can I borrow this? I haven't read it since I was four-teen."

He shrugs, and I open the front cover.

"Property of Steven Riley and..." I laugh. "Is that supposed to say Issac? It looks more like Isabc with a few scribbles. And It's written in blue crayon."

"Uh... Well, I was *three*, so..." Issac scratches the back of his head.

"You were reading 1984 at *three*?" I skip back over to him in the doorway. "Sounds like you were a bit precocious."

"*No.*" He looks away, his face flushed. "I didn't actually read it until Middle School, but I had just learned how to read and I was claiming all of my father's books as my own."

"You sound like you were a cute kid. So can I?" I beam at him. "Borrow it, that is?"

"Yeah, just don't damage it." He weaves his fingers to-gether, staring at the floor. "It used to be my dad's."

Okay, so his dad is definitely a sore subject. As much as I'd like to know what's going on to get this weird living situation where someone who just turned twenty seems to be the guardian of two teenagers, it's... probably really personal.

So, I'm not gonna pry into it.

"Uh, the guest room is this way." Issac says, clearly wanting to move on from the mention of his father, and he shows me down the hall.

The guest room is nice, decorated in nautical theming, but I spend little time there, instead bugging Issac for things to do, and he eventually sighs and takes me down to his basement where he has... quite the collection of board games.

"We can get Lexi and Ethan to come down if you want to play a game that requires more than two players." He says quietly, rocking on the balls of his feet with his arms behind his back, and standing several feet away from the shelf. "If you, uh, have questions about any of them, I'm happy to answer them. I know some of them are pretty obscure to more casual players."

I nod, but my attention is more focused on the books that are on the same shelves. *Dungeons and Dragons.*

I grab one of them, and he bites back a laugh and shakes his head. "As fun as *that* game is, I wouldn't advise picking it. It can be a little unwieldy for just playing it once, and more than a little complicated."

I turn a grin towards him and shake my head. "I just wanted to see what edition you had. I usually play in 5e anymore, but 3.5 is still good." I put the book back. "So do you have a group?"

"Mmhm." He nods. "Online. I actually have another mage in my group, though he lives out in D.C. It makes me wonder how many of us like fantasy like that despite it not really... being magic in the *same* way, you know?"

"It's an interesting thought," I say, grabbing a game box at random. "How about this one?"

He takes the box from me and smiles. "Ticket to Ride? Let me go get my siblings, okay?"

I nod at him, and he sits the box down on the table in the middle of the room and runs up the stairs to get Lexi and Ethan.

Well, I didn't exactly plan on not going home today, but I think it's going to be an enjoyable night, at least.

~ Five ~

Issac

September 18th, 2018

I sit at my kitchen table, my fingers weaved together under my chin, just trying to *process* recent events, and pointedly try to ignore what day it is.

- exactly two years since they died-

By total *coincidence* I stumbled into a girl who's very existence backs up half my father's research, affirming that it wasn't all just wasted effort. But the whole situation is totally improbable. And her bizarre icon doesn't exactly... *back up* my hypothesis. It doesn't *mean anything*, unless the centuries dormant somehow radically changed the representative motif of the Nature specialty...

It's *infuriating*.

And how *the actual hell* did being struck by lightning awaken dormant magic?

I force myself to breathe slowly, humming softly to try to keep calm despite how *stressful* this all is.

"You *liiiiiiike* her, don't you, Issac?" Lexi throws her arm around my shoulders, leaning on me as she laughs.

Augh. First Lorraine, and now my sister. I push Lexi off my shoulders and shoot a glare at her. "*No.* Why does everyone *think* that? Her roommate Lorraine was *convinced* we were on a date the night she was struck by lightning."

She was the same with Evan, too, but that doesn't *mean* anything. Just the same old thing of her (and *everyone else*) assuming how I feel about anything... Being right once doesn't mean anything.

"Well, you two *would* be cute together." She teases. "Besides, you're basically stuck with her *now.* You have to be her guide to the magical world." She takes off my hat, ruffles my hair, and puts my hat back on, pulling it over my eyes. "You and your socially awkward self have to be someone's guide. That'll be fun."

I groan, putting my head down on the table, not even bothering to fix my hat aside from pushing it out of my eyes. I hadn't even *thought* about that. I mean, she seemed to warm up to me last night at least, so hopefully this won't be as frictious as our first proper conversation, but *yikes.*

She pats my head. "Hey, I'm sure it'll be fine, Issac. She seemed nice, and a bit nerdy like you." She gently shoves my shoulder, and I sit back up. "I'm just teasing." She grabs one of the other kitchen chairs and spins it around to sit backward on it, facing me, with her arms resting on the back of the chair. "You're smart, and you know more about magic than anyone else I've ever known. You'll be fine."

"I guess..." I say slowly.

"You can talk for *hours* about magic, just like Dad could, and he was one of the best teachers Vincent's Academy of

Magic ever had." She pauses, a frown briefly on her face, but she quickly flashes another smile. "So like, don't sweat it. You'll do fine."

"He really was..." I slide my fingertips around on the wood of the kitchen table, staring at the swirls of the grain. She's being very nice, but I could never measure up to our father. He'd know how to handle this so much better than I ever could...

Two years to the day since he died. Does Lexi remember that it's *today*? It's hard to tell. We don't talk about it ever. It leads to too much friction with Ethan and usually tears with Lexi. Either way... I'd rather avoid it, even as I can't forget the fact that *it's two years to the day since they died.* Two years to the day, and I'm going to be working on his research today.

"Speaking of Vincent's, I'm actually going to be headed there soon, for the library."

It's been two whole years, and this is the first time I've felt like I could make *any* progress. It took two years, but I'm finally going to get somewhere.

"What, going to try to research Anna's Icon?" She chuckles, resting her chin on the back of the chair. "And here I was thinking you have every book on Icons memorized."

I scowl at her. "Hush up, Lexi." I sigh, crossing my arms and leaning back in my chair. "I also want to cross reference some of Dad's research on Nature Mages, and see if there's *any* trace at all of Nature mages after Leilani, or even a hint of *why* they would disappear and then *come back now.*"

"... Good Luck, Issac." She sighs. "Be careful, though. You know how much Harris wants to get his hands on Dad's research."

"Harris won't get anywhere near his research." I shake my head. "He hasn't been able to at all in the last two years, no matter how many times he tries to claim it's the school's property. He's not going to get it *now*."

I stand up, and grab my bag from where it was hanging on the back of my chair, and sling it over my shoulder. "Now get *dressed*, or you're going to miss your bus."

I head out the door as she grumbles about school, and I walk towards the nearby magic district.

It's a short walk to the school and people tend to give me a wide berth on my way. Everyone knows who I am, and they leave me *alone*. Steven Riley's *crazy* and *queer* eldest child. I'm treated with begrudging tolerance for my family name and nothing more. Everyone expects *Ethan* to carry on the family legacy, and I'm just... here, tarnishing the name.

Not that they treat Lexi much better, since she's *extremely* open about being a Lesbian. I think she enjoys pissing homophobes off.

Whatever. I don't care what people think, not *here* anyway, and at least they leave me *alone...*

For as much as Mages like to think they're *better* than Nons, they tend to be a few steps *back* in terms of societal advances, always playing catch up.

Civil Rights movements don't hit as hard when it's not *your* government or society being fought against...

I step into the busy front hall of the school, weaving between the mingling students, heading to their first classes for the day to get to the library.

I wish the school didn't have the best magic library in all of Seattle, but... it's thanks to my dad that it *does*. He donated almost his *entire collection* to the school in his will, only leaving a small selection to *me*. It's an amazing thing that he did that. Most teachers donate *some* of their books to the school library upon leaving or passing, but rarely as *many* as my dad did. And they don't usually have as substantial of collections as my dad did.

My hands are on the handle of one of the glass double doors to the library when two near identical girls materialize from the crowd, standing on either side of me, and leaning back against the doors to hold them closed, and I nearly stumble backward as the door doesn't give thanks to them.

If I didn't know better, I'd have assumed they'd teleported there, but teleportation is very restricted on school grounds.

Why *today*- Today of all days, the Harris twins-

"Hi Issac!" Kaitlyn Harris smiles at me, twirling a lock of her dyed black hair around her finger.

Her sister Carrie, with her equally dyed hair- now *vibrant red*; it was green the last time I saw her- also smiles at me, but it a very fake way, and she waves cheerily.

I shrink back, nearly backing into someone, and I just freeze up, hovering on the balls of my feet. I'm stuck between the crowd and the two of them blocking my destination, and there's just... too many people around.

And these two *especially*... Dealing with the Harris twins always takes far more energy than it's worth. Talking to people unplanned usually does, but *especially* with these two.

Why can't *they* leave me alone like everyone *else* does...

"*So*, Issac," Carrie puts a hand on my shoulder, staring directly into my eyes.

The shining green of her irises draws me in almost hypnotically, and for a brief second my discomfort with eye contact is quieted.

... Then, almost immediately, my passive protection spell kicks in, cancelling out her Captivation Spell.

I look away, glaring at the floor to her right. "*Honestly*, Carrie. I have a pure social mage as a younger brother." I mutter angrily. "Did you *really* think that your basic captivation spell would work?"

Her sister giggles into her hand. "It's the only way you ever talk to us, silly!" She gently pushes my shoulder, and I tense up even more, crossing my arms tightly. "You're always in such a hurry when you come here!"

"That's because I only ever come here *for the library*." I growl under my breath. "I'm here for a *reason*. I'm not just *visiting*. Please leave me alone."

I'm sure *they* don't remember that it's two years to the day since my parents died. Why should they? *Their* lives weren't completely uprooted that day.

Though Carrie did stop even pretending to be my friend after that. I was glad for *that*, however. I've never liked Carrie. Not even when we were little.

It's quiet for a moment, and Kaitlyn giggles girlishly and takes a step closer to me. "Oh, come on, you can't be in *that* much of a hurry. Don't you have all your dad's old books at home? What do you need our humble library for?" She puts a hand on my shoulder, and slowly slides it around to the back of my neck, and I hold my breath, trying to stay calm despite the undesired touch and her physical closeness to me. "Please, just spare us a minute."

Kaitlyn never stopped pretending. I'm not sure she's pretending at all. I think she might *genuinely* like me, in her own weird... possessive way. Doesn't mean I like it.

Forcing myself to take a deep breath, I brush her hand off and step to the side to get away from her, shaking my head quickly. "If you *recall*, my father left most of his collection to the school. Please, just let me through. I have work to do, and only so much time to do it before I have class this evening."

I was intending to skip class today, to go to the cemetery, but they don't need to know that.

"Forget your Non school." Carrie snaps, digging her claw like manicure into my arm, and I whimper slightly. "We actually have something important to say."

"Let-" I jerk my arm away from her, staring wide eyed at her sour expression. "Let me go! I really am *busy*. I'm sure whatever inane nonsense idea your dad has to get a hold of my father's research can w-"

"Shut up Riley!" She cuts me off, the cruel tone of her voice stopping me in my tracks, and I duck my head, taking several shaky breaths.

Why can't they just leave me *alone*?

"I wasn't *done*, Riley. We come with an *offer* from our dad."

I look up at her warily, holding my breath. All Godfrey Harris has wanted from me recently was to get ahold of my father's research at all costs, so this *can't* be good. "I-I don't particularly care what your father wants to *offer* me, Carrie." I force the words out, trying to seem outwardly calm, but it's hard with the knot of anxiety that's getting tighter and tighter in the pit of my stomach and it's hard to not just run away from them.

"He's offering you a *job*. He wants you on as a Student Teacher for the general magic class." Carrie spits. "I don't get it, wanting some homeschooled weirdo who doesn't know his specialty, but I don't pretend to understand my father."

"Hush up Carrie. Issac is a *great* mage, and he has a place at this school, even if he doesn't want to teach. He does have a position on the board by inheritance already. There's no need to be nasty." She giggles. "But Daddy wants you on staff because he thinks you have the potential to be just as good of a Mage and a teacher as your dad was."

I don't trust this. He would never offer this sincerely. He *has* to have an ulterior motive...

The Library doors behind the twins call to me, and they aren't *leaning* on them anymore...

Carrie suddenly shoves me, and my skin crawls where her hands made contact as I stumble backwards, almost falling over.

"Do you accept or not!?" she snaps. "Don't just stand there like a twit not saying anything! It was bad enough when you did this as a kid!"

"N-No!" The reference to our childhood just makes this all worse, reminding me that I grew up with these girls, and they turned on me just as fast as their father did. Though Carrie has always been kind of mean.

I weave my fingers together, rocking my hands back and forth and I stare at the floor, trying to collect myself despite all the stress from this conversation.

"You can inform your father that I already have plans for my future, and that if he's interested in hiring a student teacher, he should try talking to my younger brother, as Ethan is actually interested in teaching and I'm sure he would love to work here after his school hours." I take a shaky breath. "Thank you for the offer, but I must decline. *Goodbye.*"

I push past them and into the sweet respite of the library. The doors click shut behind me, and I'm enveloped by the wonderful and familiar smell of old paper.

Much better. At least it's quiet here.

I deposit my bag at a table off in the corner. It's nice and quiet here, with most students being in class right now. Which is good. Fewer distractions.

I pull an overstuffed binder from my bag, quickly flipping through my dad's painstakingly researched and well-organized work, until I get to the start of the specific info on Leilani.

I trace my fingers over the page, written neatly by my father years ago in blue pen.

Leilani [Keahi Family]

The name is written in careful print at the top of the page, with a star next to it to denote its importance.

Icon (unconfirmed): A flower that looks to be blowing in the wind. Appears to be a na'u flower (or Hawaiian Gardenia), always with three leaves (nature sign?) on the stem. Surrounded by twinkling stars as normal.

Yeah. As I remembered. Plants, specifically *leaves* as the signifier for nature mages.

Born in 1698, Leilani is the very last Nature Mage I can find any record of (last Nature mage on record before her having died ten years earlier in Siberia; see section 10 page 8). She lived an astounding 120 years, eventually dying by her own hand (see section 3, page 11 for details on her death) and she had three children, none of whom displayed any signs of inherited magic. Two of them went on to study Quintessence Flow Wizardry. Neither of them had children, and her third child had two sons. Beyond that, I am unable to trace the family line.

I wonder if Anna has access to her mother's family tree anywhere... I'll have to ask next time I see her, though the chances are rather slim, given that she didn't ever really know her mother.

Leilani was an important magical figure, having worked with Vincent Riley (see Section 1 page 11) when they were teenagers to stop a global magic war, however there is much debate on whether she was a Mage of the Nature Specialty, or a Quintessence Flow Wizard.

Around three hundred years have passed since then. So *much* information was lost in that time, with the colonization and annexation of Hawai'i. But even aside from that, accurate information on *Vincent* can be scarce, and that was just eight generations ago in my family.

Eight generations since Vincent Riley, and no one can even agree whether he was *The Master* or just a particularly well studied Sensory mage, though his *Icon* wouldn't make any sense for that, being the *sun*. It sometimes feels like I'm *missing something*, or there was an effort to obscure the truth of this all at some point in the past.

It's *frustrating*.

I skim over the rest of the page, having read it dozens of times before, and not really gleaning anything *new* from this. I didn't expect to, but it's a good starting point for trying to dig into *Anna*.

Leilani and Vincent were as close as siblings, with Leilani's family doing more to raise Vincent than his own father did, and the two worked together to trap and destroy the *Great Evil* and saved the world, and pulled the whole global magic community back from the brink of war in the process.

Everyone who's ever had a magic history lesson knows the basics of that story, though my father documented it in more detail than anyone else ever had before.

Every detail points to Leilani having been a *Nature Mage*. Plant growth and control, weather manipulation, and a particular affinity for animal kind. Everything we presume a nature mage would *do*. And that's just *not* what Wizards do.

But those accounts are *disputed*, because even at the best of times nature was likely a *rare* specialty, which combined with a scarce historical record has resulted in many mages believing that they never existed.

But even considering that, Leilani is the *last one* that we have any record of at all...

And for her family to have the same surname as Anna's mother... Anna, who demonstrated *Weather Control*... Anna *has* to be a Nature Mage.

I have to dig deeper.

I sweep the binder up, and carry it with me- not willing to leave even one binder of my Dad's research unattended here- to go grab several books on Icon symbolism, returning them to my table, and combing them for *anything* about storm clouds.

But there's nothing. *Nothing.*

Yes, Icons tend to stray from normal patterns *a little* if they skip a few generations, and this was eight generations in my family, and who knows how many in Anna's, but... But there still should be *something* identifiable in it. And there's *not*. It's like... somehow the act of getting struck by lightning imprinted itself onto her magic itself...

Which makes *no* sense.

I groan, putting my head down on the table. This makes even less sense than my *just stars* Icon. She has a somewhat clear specialty, but not the icon to back it up. *No*, her icon is just... pure nonsense.

I *need* to ask her about her mother's family, to see if she knows *anything* about it, before I start stressing myself out over this.

But in the meantime I should at least keep digging, to see if I can find *anything* else. There's nothing about Leilani's de-scendants, Nature Mages, or iconography of magical signatures that I don't already know, so I'm really just reviewing for the off chance that there's something that I've missed...

I idly flip to the next page in my Dad's binder, only half reading it at this point, not really expecting new information, but a particular line catches my attention, and I practically dive to pull the book of letters between Vincent and Leilani from my bag, flipping through to where I was last working on translating it.

- those darkened skies will return one day with us, and I fear that the world will be unprepared for it, no matter what we do, and I find it difficult to go on when things seem so hopeless -

My translation so far is scattershot, and I find it easier to translate Vincent's letters since his writing is a little more grounded in *English* rather than Hawaiian, but I have started to make progress, and that *phrase*...

There's one description of Vincent and Leilani's defeat of the "Great Evil" that crops up time and time again in contemporary sources. "Through the darkened skies with twisting vines and pure magic, the Great Evil falls, leaving only a stain on the hearts of those who fought it". It frankly reads as nonsense with today's knowledge. I'm not certain if it's intended to be metaphorical or a literal description of something people saw, but it is rather consistent to some degree in contemporary accounts.

Darkened Skies. Vincent isn't one for metaphor and tends to be very literal and straightforward in his writing- something I'm very appreciative of- so that means it's... probably a *literal description.*

Twisted vines. *Leilani.* If that's not the clearest evidence that she definitely was a Nature Mage, I don't know what else could be at this point.

I've read that somewhere else before too, I *swear...*

I jump to my feet, darting across the library to grab a specific book before returning to my table quickly.

History of the Master: Pg. 67.

"It's been said that through *darkened skies and twisting vines,*" I read aloud softly, "the Master performed their last great act of heroism until such time that they were needed again, and with them went magic as we know it...?"

Oh my god.

Something- *something* to do with how they defeated The Great Evil explains why the Master stopped reincarnating... and maybe why Nature Mages disappeared too.

Went Magic as We Know It.

I just need to figure out what they *did*, and it will all tie together. And maybe, just *maybe*, Anna could give me the answer to that. If Nature Mages are coming back...

September 21st, 2018

"*This is Anna Kahale. I'm probably busy, hence why I didn't pick up the phone. If it's important, please leave a message.*"

I groan, and hang up, falling back on the couch, and staring up at the ceiling.

"Got her voicemail again?" Ethan sits down on my feet, and I scramble to sitting, pulling my feet out from under him, and shoot a glare at him before yanking my weighted blanket from the back of the couch and pulling it over my head. "I'm going to take *that* as a yes?" he chuckles. "Maybe she's busy or something."

"For *three days* in a row she's too busy to even call me back?" I shake my head. "Doesn't seem likely. I think she's ignoring me."

It hurts, honestly. I thought... I thought she at least *kind of* liked me after she stayed the night here, and now she can't even be bothered to call me back. Or even *text* me or something...

Ethan sighs. "Look, Issac, is it like super important that you talk to this girl again?"

I nod slightly. "Yes, even putting aside the fact that she could be relevant to Dad's work... she's *completely untrained.* She needs to get a handle on her magic or she's going to get herself killed. *And* she *sheds tessence* wherever she goes, Ethan. It's not a matter of *if*, but *when* a Hunter goes after her."

Again. When a Hunter goes after her *again.*

And all that aside, I just... wanted to talk to her again. She was *nice.* I thought... Was I totally out of line in thinking we might be able to be *friends*?

I should have known better.

"Don't you have classes with her roommate?"

"Lorraine, yeah." I pull the blanket down onto my shoulders to look at him. "Why?"

"*Dork.* Ask her roommate." He reaches forward, pushing gently on my knee. Laughing, he stands back up. "For someone so smart you can be a bit dense some time, Izz. See you after school!"

"Don't call me that!" I snap at him as he leaves the room, and I pull the blanket back over my face. Why does he find it so *hard* to call me the right name...

But talking to Lorriane *is* probably a good idea.

I catch her after class later that day, running up behind her before she can get too far from the classroom. "Wait! Lorriane! Could you, could you wait a second?"

She stops and turns around toward me, her hands on her hips. "Oh, so lover boy *can* speak on campus. With how mute you are in class I'm genuinely surprised." She pauses. "It's just Lorrie, by the way."

"Social Anxiety..." I mumble by way of explanation for her comment on my silence in class, and I exhale hard, staring at the ground. "I, uh, I haven't been able get ahold of Anna, and I needed to talk to her. Do you know why she hasn't been picking up her phone?"

"*Anxiety.*" She murmurs. "*Oooooh,* that explains a lot. But," She laughs. "Yeah, she's been busy. Some local small publisher that likes to work with student authors reached out to her, so she's been working herself to death and ignoring everything else to finish this draft of her manuscript. I'm sure she'll call you back later tonight; she's got a meeting there today."

Small... Small local... Small local publishing company?

Alarm bells sound in my head, and I take a shaky breath while blinking quickly at her. "Is it Trial Publishing?" My voice sounds surprisingly calm for the panic screeching in my mind right now.

*Please say no- Please say **no**-*

"Hey, yeah, how did you know that?" Lorraine grins. "It's like, *super* cool, honestly. I'm thrilled for her."

I shake my head slowly, my breath caught in my throat. No no *no.*

Three days, and she's noticed by another Hunter.

Trial Publishing, owned by one Kevin Anderson, the most dangerous Hunter this side of the country.

~ Six ~

Anna
September 18th, 2018

The door clicks shut behind me, and I slowly slide to the floor, my back pressed flat against it. Yesterday doesn't even feel *real*, now that I'm back in my quiet normal apartment.

It's like, the whole damn world changed, but nothing changed here and it's extremely dissonant.

But I just left Issac a couple minutes ago after he drove me home. It was just moments ago that I was still in his strange world. As abnormally *normal* as things seem here in the living room of my apartment, I know that *nothing* is normal.

Magic is real. Magic has *always* been real, just a secret. It's really hard to wrap my head around, but I can't *deny* that it's true.

"Where have you been!?"

I wince at Lorrie's voice, and look up at her standing in the kitchen doorway in her soft yellow nightgown, leaning in the frame with her hand on her hip.

Augh, I was hoping she was still asleep. It *is* like, 5:30 in the morning. "I just hung out with Issac longer than I expected, and it was *late*, so I stayed over in his guest room. It was no big d-"

"Oh my *god!*" Lorrie darts forward, grabbing my hands and pulling me to standing whether I like it or not. "Tell me all about it, girl!"

"Don't get any weird ideas, Lorrie." I roll my eyes. "We were just hanging out."

"Anna, sweetie, you stayed the night at his house." She throws an arm around my shoulders. "In what *world* is that *just hanging out?*"

"Ugh, stop," I grumble, ducking out from under her arm. "Stop making it weird. I was in the *guest room.* And we just played board games with his younger siblings most of the night."

"Whaaaatever you say." She says in a singsong voice, before twirling away from me, her nightgown skirt flaring out as she does. And she twirls right into the couch, falling backward onto it, and promptly bursts into a fit of giggles. "You'd be cute with him you know."

My face heats up, and I scowl at her. "Shut *up.* I'm going to get a few hours more sleep." And I go to my room without another word.

I really didn't want her to be awake. That felt *weird*, to not at all mention the *crazy magic stuff.* I wanted more time to process it all before seeing her.

I fall back on my bed, closing my eyes. Should I be writing fantasy novels if I want to accurately reflect reality? Would I even be *allowed to* if the secrecy stuff is like... a law? I guess I'll have to ask Issac later. He is really nice, if absolutely *painfully* shy...

The next thing I know, my phone is ringing, and it's daylight.

Bolting upright, I look around groggily for the sound, finding my purse where I discarded it next to my bed earlier, and fishing my phone from it, half expecting it to be Issac calling.

It's my Dad. I can't say I haven't been thinking about him, with Issac's questions about my mother. I was *so mad* at him for being dishonest about my mother's death. For not telling me the truth about her *suicide*...

But *maybe* I've been too hard on him.

I hesitate, staring at my phone screen for a long moment. Augh. At the last second, I tap to answer the call, putting my phone to my ear.

"Anna!" He's surprised, and I don't blame him. I've dodged so many calls from him. "I-I," he stammers, sounding like he's about to cry, and I wince.

Yeah, this is at least part of the reason I was avoiding this. I *knew* it was hurting him, the way I was shutting him out. I don't want to *deal* with that. And I'm still *mad*, but... augh. This doesn't help anything.

"... Dad," I say softly, not sure what else *to* say.

"Baby girl, I love you, you know that, right?" He's talking quickly, like he expects me to hang up, and he still sounds on the verge of tears. "And I'm *sorry*. I know I should have told you the truth about your mom. You have every right to be mad at me, but I'm just- I just wanted to hear from you that you were okay."

"... I'm okay. Sorry for worrying you." I don't know what to say to the apology. It doesn't really change how I feel about it, even if he *is* genuinely sorry.

"I don't expect you to forgive me, but just... please remember that I love you."

"I know, Dad." I say, my voice shaking slightly. "I... Uh, actually about Mom, do- Did you ever know anything about her family?"

He goes dead silent, and I hear the faint crashing of the ocean in his background noise, before he takes a shaky breath. "Uh, why?"

"Nevermind," I quickly hang up, regretting having asked, and flop back onto my bed with a groan.

I can't do this. I can't just turn off how *furious* I still am at the fact that he lied to me my whole life about how my mother died and that I had to find out she took her own live from finding her *obituary* when I was seventeen... I miss him so badly it hurts sometimes, which I *know* is why Lorrie pushes me on it so much, but I'm still *mad*.

And I really should have pressed about Mom's family, for Issac, but that's beyond uncomfortable.

"Anna!" Lorrie smacks on my door. "It's almost 10:30! Get your lazy butt out here!"

Heaving myself off my bed and to my feet, I trudge over to the door and open it so quickly that she almost knocks on my face.

"Not all of us are okay with getting up before six in the morning, Lorrie." I grumble. "I got woken up at five in the morning, and was driven home by Issac, who I'm 90% sure was driving for the first time in *months*." I fake a yawn. "Cut me some slack. 'Sides, I don't have a class until noon today."

"Yes, and you still have to tell me all about your night, missy!" She waggles her finger in my face before giggling and skipping over to the couch. "I'm *dying* to know all the details."

"... I told you *earlier*, nothing happened. We just played board games. His siblings are weird." I walk over and sit down next to her. "Oh, and he has quite a few D&D books on his game shelf. I tried to talk him into joining our campaign, but he's got a group online, I guess."

"Oh *no*, he's joining. You keep trying to talk him into it. Lover Boy *will* face my DM wrath!" She pulls her legs up onto the couch and sits on her knees, leaning forward towards me. "But weird how?"

"Weird, like I think his sister is destined to be an Olympic gymnast and his brother a conman." I answer, ignoring the fact that she called him Lover Boy. "His sister literally *back flipped* into our meeting. And she stuck the landing."

"Ha, I always had a feeling that nerd had a loud family. He's just too *quiet*."

I chuckle. I don't really understand her logic, but she isn't wrong, so who am I to question it?

"I should get showered and changed before class." I say, standing back up. "Stop being weird about Issac. We're nothing more than *friends*, you hear me?"

"Oh *sure*. For now." She grins at me, and I growl, grabbing a pillow from the couch and hitting her with it before walking away as she breaks into a fit of giggles.

When I get out of my shower, I wander into the kitchen where Lorrie is making grilled cheese.

"You've got mail, by the way," she says, glancing over her shoulder at me. "It's on the table."

I pour myself a cup of coffee, and sit down, looking at the two envelopes she sat down on the table. One of them is from my dad, and I sigh slightly, sitting it aside. I'll look at it later. The other is from...

Trial Publishing?

I immediately pull out my phone and search the name, coming up with a small publishing company in Seattle that frequently works with student writers.

Oh. Oh *wow*.

I tear open the letter quickly, my coffee completely forgotten as I'm quite suddenly *wide awake*, ripping the letter out of its envelope.

"*Dear Ms. Kahale, you've been chosen for...*" I jump out of my seat, squealing excitedly. "Lorrie! Lorrie! This *publisher* wants to work with me, as a student author, to publish a manuscript!!!!"

"And, like, is the company legit?" She sits a plate down at my seat and sits down with a plate for herself.

"From a quick search? Yeah. Seems to be." I can't stop grinning. This is *incredible*. I never expected a publisher to reach out to me, but from what my quick look online, it *seems* like they seek out and publish a student author from Seattle once every year, and I'm just the lucky person who was picked...

A big smile flashes across Lorrie's face. "Congrats! I mean, I'd look into them a little more to make sure, but that's *great* if it's legit."

"*Ah*, I don't even want to go to class today. I need to finish my Sherlock Manuscript, and type it up..."

"Don't skip class." Lorrie rolls her eyes. "You can work on it later today."

I definitely *will* work on it later today. Every free moment I have will be dedicated to it now, for *sure*. Magic stuff can, like, *wait* to be dealt with.

September 21st, 2018

The next three days are spent *entirely* on typing up my Sherlock Manuscript and exchanging emails with Trial Publishing. I need a good title for it... A Study in Dark Matter, maybe?

No... No, that's a little extra, and barely fits the story.

Issac calls again, but I ignore it. I don't have time for magic stuff now. I'm sure he'll understand once I can actually talk to him again. I have a meeting with one Mr. Kevin Anderson this evening. I can talk to Issac after *that*. I'm sure he can *wait* a few more hours.

"*Annaaaaaa*," Lorrie squeals, running around in front of me after having just french braided my hair, and she starts fiddling with the longer side of my bangs, brushing it back to tuck behind my ear, and clipping it back with a sparkly pink barrette. "You're having a meeting with a *publisher* today."

I crack a smile, though I'm mostly just nervous at this point. I have a class before I go to the meeting, but Lorrie wanted to do my hair, so I'm be going to class looking *much* nicer than usual, because I'm going straight from there to my meeting with Mr. Anderson.

A *publisher*. And they're interested in *me*. In publishing my silly space mystery with queer romance elements. It's nothing short of incredible.

"I'm a bit nervous." I admit weakly. "This guy is like, *forty*, and he wants to publish *me*. Like, me specifically. How could I possibly be so *lucky-*"

She looks up from straightening my collar. "Mm? Oh, don't go getting cold feet on me now, girl!" She playfully shoves my shoulders, and I laugh weakly. "You're going to kill it. That Anderson guy will be *super* impressed, and then you're going to come home and write a long happy entry for your blog about it! Got it!?"

I giggle, shoving her back. "Alright, alright! No need to be so pushy!"

I leave for class before Lorrie, and it's the *longest class of my life*, and I practically run out when it's over to get to the offices of Trial Publishing, and wait for Mr. Kevin Anderson to call me into his office.

Ahhh, this is going to be incredible.

I pull out 1984 as I wait, laughing to myself again at the very cute handwriting of three-year-old Issac, and start reading the borrowed book.

His secretary keeps sending me weird looks. It's starting to make me uncomfortable. Is there something wrong with the way I look? I self-consciously fiddle with my hair and clothes, the secretary still giving me strange looks.

Ugh, what did I do to upset this dude!?

I quickly use my phone's selfie cam like a mirror to make sure I look fine, and I shoot a dirty look at the secretary.

He flinches back, even rolling his chair back a little bit, and stops looking at me all together.

Good. Weirdo. He was probably perving on me. This pencil skirt Lorrie picked out for me feels way too tight to me. It's just not my style.

At least I have my own sweater and floral print button down under it.

Shifting uncomfortably, I start reading my book again when Mr. Anderson pokes his head out of his office. "Anna, right?"

His voice is deeper than I expected, and I hop to my feet, grinning at him. "Yessir! That's me, Anna Kahale!"

He smiles warmly, beckoning me into his office, and I start walking towards him, when I'm suddenly jerked to a stop by someone grabbing my wrist in a vice grip.

The suddenness of it wrenches my shoulder, and I glare over my shoulder ready to chew out who I *assumed* was the creep of a secretary, but the retort dies on my lips as I see it's... Issac, who's gasping for breath and looking like he *ran* here, his face red and his bangs damp with sweat.

He's not looking at me, but at Mr. Anderson, his expressions a strange mix of fear and anger, and he's holding onto my wrist so tight that his knuckles are white and he might be cutting off my circulation to my hand.

After a moment, his violet eyes flick to me, and he says "*Anna*," breathlessly.

He *ran* here. He definitely ran here. *Why would he do that?* What could be *SO IMPORTANT* that he *ran* here and stopped me before I could go into possibly the most important meeting of my life?

"Issac," I say slowly, "I have *no idea* what you're doing her, but *please* go away." I smile slightly to try to convey that I'm not mad at him or anything like that. "I'm in the middle of something."

He throws a glance towards the creepy secretary, who nods at him. It...? Seems like they know each other?

"Anna, please, just, leave with me. It's an emergency with... uh..." He glances warily over at Mr. Anderson. "Lorrie, it's an emergency with Lorrie."

He's a *terrible* liar, but he seems genuinely afraid... And while he tends to act first and explain later, he *has* been fairly rational up to now once he *does* explain, even if his world is pure craziness... So if he's *afraid*, it's probably for good reason.

"What, did she eat a peanut?" I ask, feigning worry. Lorrie is allergic to peanuts, so it seems like a good lie.

"Y-Yeah!" He nods quickly, just going along with it.

I look back at Mr. Anderson, who, to my shock, now has an absolutely *furious* look on his face.

"I'm *terribly* sorry, Mr. Anderson, but I think we need to reschedule. My roommate is having a medical emergency."

He smiles stiffly, his eyes flicking to everyone in the room before he answers. "Very well, Ms. Kahale."

Before I can say another word, Issac is pulling me out of the room, picking up the pace the further we get away, to the point where we're outright running by the time we get out of the building, and a little ways from it, before he slows down, gasping for air, and throwing a worried glance over his shoulder at the empty street.

"That was close..." he mumbles, still tugging me along at a brisk walking pace.

"And what exactly *was* that!?" I snap, and he winces, looking over at me wide eyed. I don't know why he's so surprised. Wanting an explanation right away is *fucking reasonable*.

"Anna..." He frowns at the ground, swallowing audibly, and fiddling with the collar of his sweater. "That- That was- That was Kevin Anderson, the most infamous and dangerous Hunter on the West Coast."

"*What?*" I say sharply, jerking my wrist from his grip, and he stops walking, turning to face me. "You expect me to believe that he's one of those Hunter things? The *secretary* was more suspicious than him."

"His Secretary was Bryan Cole, a Quintessence Flow Wizard who volunteered to put himself at risk to keep an eye on one of the most dangerous men this side of the country. If he seemed suspicious, it's probably because he was trying to figure out how to *save your life* without blowing his cover. Anderson is responsible for the deaths of no less than *ten mages*, and we can't seem to wipe the memory of Magic from his mind like the protocol is for most Hunters. The most we've *ever* been able to do is make him forget *specific* mages." He whimpers, pulling down on his hat.

"Look, Anna, he has you in his sights now..." He trails off, wincing. "Probably me too, after that. It's not going to be easy to stay *safe*."

"Wait, are you *seriously* telling me that he's going to try to hunt down both of us to try to *kill* us?" I shake my head slowly. "*No* way."

"*Anna*," he says, his tone *pleading*. "He was probably intending to kill you *today*." He crosses his arms, seeming to fold in on himself a bit. "So, *yes*, he probably will try to hunt *both* of us down since I came to rescue you...

~ Seven ~

"

Issac

September 21st, 2018

The words hang in the air, and Anna exhales loudly. "*Fucking hell...*"

"I'm sorry. I- I wish I had better news. I'm sure you don't like me much, since I really only bring *chaos* into your life..."

"Don't be stupid." She says, shaking her head quickly. "It's not *your* fault. You just saved my life."

It's a relief to hear her say that, and a faint ghost of a smile flickers across my face, but it's hard to really be happy about the reassurance given the current active threat to our lives, and I look around warily again, before offering my hand for her to take it.

"We really need to keep moving." I say quietly, and she looks at my extended hand and sighs softly before taking it, and I start walking again at once, trying to make it to my house.

The Wards should keep up safe for a short time, but I don't know how long. Oh *god*, I don't know how I got myself into this mess. I'm usually so *careful...*

"Issac, where are we going?"

"My house." I respond quickly, glancing over my shoulder at her. "The wards will keep us safe for a short while... I mean, I live in a Non Neighborhood, he'd eventually notice the faint magic of the wards even if he couldn't see *us* through them, and from there he could tear them down... so we can't stay indefinitely, but it'll be safe for a bit..."

"Is there any way we could be safe *permanently?*" She asks. "I don't want to be on the run for the rest of my life!"

I slow down for just a moment, looking back at her. "Oh, it wouldn't be *forever*. While the normal protocol of just making him forget Magic entirely doesn't *work* on Anderson for some reason, the enforcers can make him forget *us specifically*. It could be as quick as tomorrow, or as long as... I'd say two to three weeks. It all depends on when they can catch him clandestinely."

"So if your house wouldn't work for very long, how the *hell* are we supposed to stay safe for up to *three weeks*?"

"Oh," I shake my head slowly. "There's a place we can hide indefinitely, but..." I groan. "I don't *like* it..."

"You don't *like it*?" She scoffs. "You're kidding, right? You've made it very clear this is a life or death thing, and this place is *safe*, but you *don't like it*? If it's safe, we need to go there."

I groan, ducking my head, clutching her hand tighter for a moment. "I *never* said we wouldn't end up going there. I just said I don't like it."

Vincent's Academy for magic is one of the most secure magical places in the whole State, and I can guarantee us safe lodging there, but that means bringing *Anna* in close proximity to Harris.

It will be *fine*, but we're going to have to be careful while were there, lest Harris get suspicious of her origins. I'm allowed lodging anytime there, due to my family ties to the institution, so I have the grounds to insist she stay as my guest, with Harris having no right to question it. We would be *fine*, it's just...

Taking a deep breath, I look over my shoulder at her again. "We'll be going to Vincent's Academy of Magic. It's the most well protected and warded place in all of Washington State, and it's within the magic district, so it'd be next to impossible for Anderson to even get to it." I pause, picking up my pace slightly.

"*And* I'm always welcome to stay there, because an ancestor of mine founded it. Also, my father was a professor there, before..." I shake myself. I can't dwell on my father right now. "The point is that we can take shelter there as long as we need too, even if I don't like it."

"Why don't you like it?" She pulls her hand out of mine and speeds up to walk next to me. "I mean, your dad worked there, right? Can't be so bad a place." She giggles slightly, like this is *at all* funny... "What, just don't want to go back to your old school?"

"It's not the place itself..." I mutter, staring at the cracked concrete of the sidewalk as we hurry along. "And I didn't attend that school. My father homeschooled me and my siblings in magic."

"So, what *is* your problem, then?" She grabs my hand, and I look at her, startled. I figured she didn't want to hold my hand, given that she pulled away just a moment ago... "Oh, don't look at me like that," she says sharply. "I just thought it would be smarter if we stayed in contact until we were *safe*. That's why you wanted me to take your hand before, right?"

Right. It *is* why, but still. I thought she didn't want... Shaking myself; I take a few deep breaths before answering her question.

"It's, ah, it's the Headmaster." I say after a moment, staring pointedly ahead of us, my gaze focused on the horizon as we walk. It's weird, to try to explain my personal family drama to her. I don't want to bother her with it... but she asked.

"He... He, uh, was like *family*, acting like my father's best friend for years, but after..." I clear my throat, glancing sideways at Anna before quickly turning my gaze to the ground.

"After he almost seemed *glad* that my father was gone, and he's been trying to force me to give him my father unfinished research, which he *explicitly* didn't want shared until it was *finished*. He's been making respecting my father's memory a living hell, frankly. And every time I've been at that building in the past two years, he or his daughters have harassed me, and it's just... miserable, frankly. But it's *safe*, so I can deal with it..."

And none of that is even considering how painful it *can* be to be there sometimes. It can feel like I'm haunted by my father's memory there...

Anna squeezes my hand gently. "That... I'm sorry. That sucks."

I dare a glance sidelong at her, and she's smiling slightly at me, like she... actually cares. I'm surprised she cares. *Touched*, certainly, but surprised. We barely know each other, so I wouldn't expect her to care about my family drama.

Though I could just be reading too much into a smile. I have done things like that plenty of times in the past. I'm really not good at reading people like this.

We finally get to my house, and I pull her inside. This is *twice* now I've brought her home to hide from a Hunter. She needs to come here under better circumstances at some point...

If... If she wants to, of course. I'm not sure she would. I've done nothing but make her life hectic.

"We... We'll wait for my siblings to get home, so I can send them to our Gran's, then we'll go to the school, okay? The wards should protect us until then at least..." I close the curtains on the windows by the door, carefully checking out them to make sure that Anderson didn't follow us as I do so.

Looking back towards Anna, she nods at me. "Okay." She's silent for a moment, biting her lip. "Hey, you called me a bunch over the past few days. It wasn't about the whole Hunter thing, was it? Were you trying to warn me the whole time, and I was just dumb and ignoring you?"

"Oh," I shake my head. "No. I didn't even know about that until Lorrie told me today. I *ran* there from Campus." I sink to the floor, my back against the door. "I had been researching things, and I had some questions."

She sits down on the floor in front of me and smiles. "Ask away then."

"It's about your mother." I say immediately. "If that bothers you..." I look away from her, fixing my gaze on the rough fibers of the mat just inside the door.

She's silent for a long moment. Long enough for three cars to pass by, all rattling the manhole cover down the street just a bit.

"I don't know much," she finally whispers, staring at the floor, "but go ahead..."

"Do you know of any relatives she had?"

Anna shakes her head slowly. "She was an only child, and both her parents died before I was born."

"Mm." I frown, running my fingertips lightly across the mat, focusing on the sensation of the texture. "Anna, I'm *really* sorry to ask this, but how did she *die*?"

"W-What?" She stares at me with wide eyes, and I duck my head. Yeah, I anticipated *that*, but the answer... might be important... "What does *that* matter?"

"Ah, well," I exhale hard. "You don't have to answer if you don't want to, but there's... potentially something relevant there."

Both Vincent and Leilani died by *suicide*, and I know that depression runs in my family, even beyond my *personal* experiences with it. *Leaving only a stain on the hearts of those who fought it.*

If that means what I think it does... God, I don't know, but I feel like it has something to do with the disappearance of both Nature Mages and the Master. A stain on the hearts of those who fought it, and went magic as we know it. There's something *there*. I just need to figure it out...

She frowns at me, crossing her arms. "I will, but you tell me how your parents died first."

I suck in a sharp breath, closing my eyes. "That's fair." I say weakly. I asked a very personal question, with little justification as to *why*. I need a minute though, and I hold up a finger to indicate for her to wait.

It's so hard to even *think about* two years out. I've never had a chance to really just *grieve*, because I had to step up to take care of Ethan and Lexi...

I had only turned eighteen two weeks before they died, and I was in Tacoma for college, and I just... dropped everything to come back here.

"It was a magical... A... Accident." I force out quickly, my voice cracking. "As in it was- it was *ruled* an accident, l-legally. Supposedly resulting from my father experimenting with s-something and it going very wrong. I was at my own apartment in *Tacoma* at the time, and my siblings were at our Gran's house."

Anna is silent for a long moment, and it seems like she is going to try to pull me into a hug, but I jerk back so quickly that my back slams into the door.

Holding out a hand to keep her at arm's length. I shake my head. "I-I don't like being touched much."

I know she means well, and that hugging me would have been intended as a kind gesture, but it just... makes my skin crawl for someone to touch me without warning. I can't stand it.

"... Oh," Anna says softly. "I'm sorry. I'll be sure to keep that in mind." She takes a shaky breath. "To- to keep my end of the bargain. My mother... she well, uh, she took her own life when I was just a year old." She pulls absently on the edge of her skirt. "She left a note, and my dad showed me last year, but it was like, in another language, sorta like, I don't know an English-Hawaiian creole but... not the one that people actually speak in Hawaii, so I don't know what it said."

I exhale hard. There it is.

Wait... A *note in another language*? Could it be... "Another language?" I pull myself up to standing with the doorknob. "Hold that thought." I run upstairs, grabbing the bound book of letters and coming back to Anna, who's standing at the foot of the stairs when I get back.

"Now, I don't expect you to be able to read this, but was it perhaps similar to *this*?" I hand her the book, open to one of Leilani's letters. "Because if so, well, I've been working on *translating that*. It seems to have developed from a, well, *an English-Hawaiian pidgin*. Which made sense for Vincent and Leilani, since, well, Vincent was English and Leilani was from pre-colonial Hawai'i. And he lived with her family for ten years, so there *was* time for it to *develop...*"

Anna stares blankly at it for a long moment, and sighs softly, handing the book back to me. "It might be. It would be a weird coincidence if it wasn't the same... Just as unintelligible though."

I nod slightly, hugging the book of letters close to my chest. This... this is all a lot to process and work out. I've read every bit of my father's research probably *hundreds* of times in the past two years, and I *think* I understand it as well as he did by this point, but... honestly, I only half know what I'm *doing* in finishing his life's work like this...

Plainly speaking, I'm not as good at this as him. I'm not a *scholar* or a *historian*. Just a pre-med student, with a with my major in psychology. My every intention is to become a psychiatrist, and not work in academia *at all*. I'm not cut out for it. But I *have* to finish *this*. For my dad.

I'm sure if he had all the same pieces of information before him as I do, he'd connect all the dots lightning fast, while I feel like I'm trying to think through a thick haze.

"What does my Mom's death have to do with all this?" Anna asks softly. "I-I can see why the note might matter, but you didn't even know about the note, so..."

I look up at her and exhale hard.

"... There's... Well, I wasn't *surprised* by that answer, if that tells you anything..." I murmur. "Both Vincent and Leilani... well, you know, died by their own hands..."

It's little... awkward to talk about this for me, given my own history with... well, *suicidal ideation*, but she deserves an explanation...

"*And*," I continue, forcing the words out. "There's a... history of that in my family. My current working hypothesis is that in Vincent and Leilani's defeat of something only known as *The Great Evil* is connected to both *why* Nature Mages and the Master disappeared, and also... well, that trend of suicidal tendencies in... likely both of our families..."

"What would make you think that? And who's Vincent? What's the *Master*?"

"Oh." I laugh nervously. *"Right.* Sorry. I forgot I hadn't explained Vincent to you. First, uh, the Master is a Mage with no specialty. They aren't limited the way all of other mages are, so can hypothetically cast *any* spell. And they're much more powerful than most mages are. They're *supposed* to reincarnate... but haven't for nearly three centuries now. *Vincent Riley* was the last Master, before the cycle stopped." I take a deep breath.

Vincent was actually the *third* Master on record, born into our family. The Master tended to reincarnate into the most magically powerful families, which ours *is.* One of seven of the old magic families left. Us and the Harris family are all that's left of old European magic families, in name at least. In *name,* Me, Ethan, and Lexi are the last Rileys left. We have a second cousin on our dad's side, Ilene, but her last name is *Whisper.*

"As for *why* I think that... well, that idea is mostly built on the way that their heroism is described in contemporary sources, and a bit I've already managed to translate from the letters..." I trail off, not sure how to explain this without getting into the phrases that repeated time and time again, or my reasoning for taking it literally. "In short, it's just... implied something *dark* affected them in sealing the *'Great Evil'* away, and it *'changed magic as we know it'*..."

"And he saved the world with Leilani?" She asks, leaning forward on the balls of her feet. "And *Riley*? Based on what you were saying before... I assume there's a relation there, then?"

"Directly descended, eight generations back." I answer, smiling faintly. "He founded the school we're going to take shelter at, actually."

"I guessed as much." Anna responds, smiling slightly. "How'd they even meet?"

"Not sure." I shrug. "There's no record of it. Vincent disappeared from his home in the colony of Pennsylvania when he was nine, and he wasn't seen again until he was sixteen, and he seemed to have been living with Leilani's family in the intervening time, and continued to do so for two more years, refusing to go back to his father."

Records show that, though Christopher Riley involved himself in Vincent's school, the two had a less than good relationship, especially given that Vincent had made a point of requesting his sister Dorothy and his wife Lydia handle his funeral and estate when he killed himself, and he father was to have *no* part in it...

"... Huh." She says slowly, breathing out and leaning back against the wall. "So our families were connected in an inexplicable way a few centuries ago, with some weird magic stuff along with it?" She pauses, biting her lip. "*Probably?*"

"Probably." I echo.

Tired of just standing in the mudroom, I gesture towards the living room as I walk to it, sitting down on the loveseat, and I absentmindedly pull my weighted blanket off the back, onto my shoulders. She sits down next to me on the loveseat, almost too close for comfort, but it's not the worst, so I don't say anything.

"Sooo, the Master just doesn't have the specialty thing? What do *their* icons look like?"

"Oh, well," I pause. "We don't have a clear record? Vincent's had a rising sun surrounded by sparkles. It's uh, incorporated into the logo of the school in a simplified version, actually. But beyond Vincent, I'm not sure."

"A sun? So, like, a star? A star surrounded by stars?" She giggles and reaches forward, pulling my hat down over my eyes. "Maybe you're the Master!"

Righting my hat, I shoot a glare at her. I can see the logic that led her to that, even if she clearly meant it in jest. My infuriating inability to figure out my specialty could easily be interpreted as *not having one*, but... Well, I'm nothing extraordinary. I understand magic theory really well, is all. That's from *hard study*, not any sort of innate natural talent. I've worked so, *so* hard to be a decent mage despite not know my specialty.

It wouldn't have been so *difficult* if I were the Master.

"Don't be silly," I mutter. "Even if the Master *was* back, they've never been born in into the same family twice *in a row.*"

I wouldn't be too surprised if the Master *does* turn up soon though, since Nature Mages *just* came back... Probably a kid with no specialty will show up in a few years...

"Well, maybe you're the first," she teases, and I roll my eyes.

I hear the front door unlock and swing open, followed immediately by the sound of my siblings bickering as they come inside.

With a sigh, I get to my feet, taking a moment to return my blanket neatly to the back of the couch, and meet them in the mudroom. "You two need to stay at Gran's for a little while."

They both go dead silent, staring at me for a long moment, before Lexi frowns, floating up into the air slightly to look over my shoulder at Anna in the living room behind me.

She touches back down gently, her brow furrowed. "What happened, Issac?"

Ethan snickers into his hand, also looking past me at Anna. "I bet Izz just wants some time alone with his girl-friend. He *has* been calling her like, constantly."

Lexi hits Ethan with her backpack, sending him stumbling back slightly. "Be *serious* Ethan! I think something is wrong!"

Anna follows me into the mudroom, stopping once she's standing next to me. "We have to hide from someone who wants to kill us, apparently."

I sigh, fiddling with the bottom of my hat. "I had to rescue her from Kevin Anderson." I take a shaky breath. "In person. He saw us both."

Lexi gasps through her teeth, wincing, and Ethan's eyes widen. "Not *Anderson*..." She shakes her head, closing her eyes. "That might take *weeks* to fix. How did *that* happen?"

I look at Anna, then back at Lexi. "He would have killed her, Lexi. I had to do *something*." I exhale softly. "But how long this might take to fix is why *you two* will be staying at Gran's." I cross my arms, staring at the ground. "Now go get your stuff together."

"... What are you going to do?" Ethan asks quietly, kicking at the floor, while Lexi flies up the stairs. "It won't be safe here indefinitely. You can't just protect yourself and let yourself be in danger."

"We're..." I shut my eyes tight, taking a shaky breath. "We won't be in danger. We'll be staying at Vincent's until it's no longer a problem."

"At Vincent's..." He echos, and sighs. "Are you sure that's a good idea, Issac? You and I both know that Harris can't be trusted. I'm not sure it'd be much safer there."

"It's the only option we *have*, Ethan. And yeah, Harris is *unpleasant* but I don't think he's actively *dangerous.*"

I look up at Ethan, and he sighs, but nods slightly and heads up the stairs.

"It must be strange," Anna says quietly. "To have to parent your siblings like that. I mean, you're not that much older than them, and you have to be responsible for them *and* yourself?"

"Ah, yeah, it is." But I don't have any choice in it. They need *someone* to take care of them as they finish growing up, and our grandmother isn't an option, because she's a *Non.* "It is what it is, though..."

I lean back against the door frame to the living room, staring up at the ceiling. "I should probably *call* Gran before they go there, so she knows they're coming. She wouldn't *mind* them showing up without warning, but... I just... probably should call her." I sigh, standing back up straight. "I should also probably lessen all the wards, to stop him from noticing the house while we're gone. I'd rather him not ransack my home..."

"I'm sorry." Anna blurts, and I stop and look at her as she stares at me wide-eyed. "If I just- If I had just answered the phone any of the times you called me this wouldn't have happened. You could have warned me before he ever knew you were involved."

I shake my head slowly and hesitantly put a hand on her shoulder. "It's not your fault, Anna. You can't blame yourself for knowledge you didn't have." I smile faintly at her. "Besides, it will be fine. They *will* catch him, and he'll be made to forget us entirely. He won't even know we exist."

She puts a hand over mine on her shoulder and smiles back at me. "Thank you, Issac, for saving me. You really didn't have to do that. You put your own life at risk to save mine."

She leans forward slightly, seeming as if she's going to do *something*, but thinks better of it, rocking back on her heels and taking her hand off mine.

"I guess we'll be going soon, huh?" She says quietly after a moment.

I nod slightly. We'll be going right after siblings leave for Gran's. It's best not to linger here for too long, especially since I don't know if or how well he might have tracked us on foot on the way here. I didn't clear Anna's tessence trail this time because I was just focused on getting away, so it should be somewhat easy for him to find this street, even if it'd be lost on the street itself thanks to the ley line under my house...

Which means it's just a few minutes more before I have to face Harris again. I'm not looking forward to that, and I'm *definitely* not looking forward to having to explain Anna to him.

~ Eight ~

Anna

September 21st, 2018

Issac's younger siblings are out the door, and he comes slowly down the stairs, an old but clearly well taken care of brown messenger bag slung over his shoulder. Now that I think about it, he's had that bag with him every time I've seen him.

"Come on..." He sighs, adjusting the bag on his shoulder. "Let's just, go..."

He seems tired, just staring blankly past me at the door, and I can't help but wonder if he sleeps enough. I know the one night I stayed here before; he went to bed rather late, and got up obscenely early, so based on that- admittedly very small- data set... no, he probably doesn't. *And* he said he *ran* to save me *from campus*, which was like, five blocks away. That had to have been exhausting, especially since he's hardly *fit*, given how quickly he seems to run out of breath. Or maybe he's asthmatic, I don't know. But he's probably exhausted right now.

Shit, I'm just making things difficult for him, when he's *clearly* already got a difficult life, with his parent's deaths and having to take care of his siblings, and this nonsense with the Headmaster. And he's barely older than me. My squabbles with my dad seem like... nothing in comparison.

I mean, he's a white guy so at least the country isn't systemically against him, but *still*. I wish I could do something to at least fix the problems *I've* caused him.

I gesture him forward, past me. "Lead the way, Magic Man."

Issac rolls his eyes at me, and I suppress a giggle as he walks past me and out the door, his hand taking on a faint blue glow as he casually waves it back at the house.

It's actually not a far walk to the school, but I'm *fascinated* as we cross into the magic district, the air seeming to ripple as a whole new city block appears out of nowhere. I don't have time to stop and marvel at it though, because Issac grabs my wrist to tug me forward when I do slow down, so we get to the school rather quickly, and it's... Well, it looks like a private school. Not a castle or anything dramatic like that, but like an American Private School. Stone buildings, with ivy climbing up the wall and an ornamental fence and gate. Pretty, but really quite ordinary.

We walk in the front double doors, entering into a crowded hall with what looks like kids from like eight to eighteen milling about and chatting with their friends. Friday classes probably just finished.

I lean towards Issac, still looking around. "Does *everybody* go here?" I ask incredulously.

He chuckles. "No, no, not *everyone*. There's a different elementary school. But just about every magic kid from middle school to high school age in the area, yes." He shrugs slightly. "Come on, we can talk to Professor Gif-"

"Oh! Hello Issac!" a loud booming voice says from behind us in the doorway, and Issac flinches at the sound, as do a number of students who *quickly* hurry along.

I glance over my shoulder to see a tall man with pale pinkish skin, greying shoulder-length brown hair, pointed nose, and a neatly trimmed beard hurrying towards us. He's dressed in a navy long coat, navy pants, a white button-down shirt, and a light blue tie.

Issac slowly turns to face him as well, a very forced, uncomfortable smile on his face. "Heeeaaaaaadmaster Harris." He stretches out the word Headmaster uncomfortably. "Hi..."

So, this is the Headmaster that totally turned on Issac's father after his death. Gross.

"Who's this?" He smiles warmly at me, and I return the smile, internally thinking about how much of a sleazebag he is. I wonder how much of a brat I can be in this conversation? I'd love to annoy him.

"Th-This- This is An-Anna." Issac stammers nervously, crossing his arms and staring pointedly at the floor to the Headmaster's right. "She's n-no one special. Just a mage who moved here from H-Hawai'i."

Oh, so he's lying? I guess I should follow his lead; he knows more about what's going on than I do.

"Oh, so you attended the Honolulu Academy of Magic?" He smiles cheerily. "That's a good school. It's a sister school to this one, though I'm sure you already knew that." He claps a hand to Issac's shoulder, and he gasps softly, going very stiff, his expression almost *pained.* "The founders were good friends. Vincent Riley and Leilani Keahi. Vincent was actually Issac here's ancestor."

"She *didn't have a surname.*" Issac mutters through gritted teeth. "Keahi was the surname of her *children* that they were forced to take. Leilani was dead before then."

"Oh, don't be so pedantic, Issac." Harris rolls his eyes. "It was the Keahi *family.*"

He closes his eyes, taking very deliberate deep breaths, and I frown. He doesn't like being touched...

My eyes jump to Harris' hand on his shoulder, and I grab Harris' wrist to *remove* his hand from Issac's shoulder, and I practically *feel* Issac relax as the contact ends, and Harris jerks his hand away from me, eyeing me coldly now.

"What did you say your name was again, Miss...?"

"Oh," I smile sweetly, clasping my hands together at my waist. "I didn't; Issac did. But I'm Anna. Anna Kahale."

He grabs his chin, his index finger horizontally on his lips, clearly thinking for a minute. "Kahale? Now, I don't think I've heard of that mage family."

Issac grabs my arm, and I can feel his hand shaking. I glance at him and see that he's biting his lip and staring at me wide eyed. "Anna, we were going to talk to Professor Gifford."

My gaze flits between Issac and Harris for a moment, and judging from how intently Harris is staring at me, I really doubt I'll be allowed to walk away.

"Just a second." I murmur to Issac, and he whimpers slightly, but lets go of my arm and takes a step back away from me.

I look back at the headmaster and smile sweetly. "See, the magic in my family comes from my mother. My Father is a Non."

"And who would your mother be?" His tone is cold, holding none of the cheeriness it held before I forced his hand off Issac's shoulder.

I get the feeling that telling him that it isn't his business wouldn't go over well. *Fine.*

"Oh, just Liliha Ke-"

Issac grabs my wrist and starts to pull me away. "O-Okay! That's enough!" He says, his quivering voice getting a bit sharper. "*Goodbye* Headmaster."

The Headmaster grabs my other wrist, halting both me and Issac in our tracks.

"*Finish that name.*" He hisses absolutely *every* pretense of being nice gone.

I gulp at the sudden *aggression*, looking between him and a very forlorn Issac, who's only tightened his grip on my wrist. I didn't expect Harris to get *aggressive.*

Well, *fuck him.* He's not allowed to treat me that way.

"*No.*" I respond sharply. "And I don't appreciate you touching me without my permission." I try to yank my wrist away, but his grip is too tight, actually hurting for my attempt to pull free.

"No, my dear," he yanks me closer to him, wrenching my shoulder. "I *insist* you tell me at once."

I quickly glance at Issac, who shakes his head, and then looks back to Harris. "And *again*," I say in a mockery of my sweet voice from earlier. "I must decline, Headmaster."

"*Ms. Kahale.*" He almost growls my name, a scowl etched onto his face.

The hall is almost empty at this point; all the students have gone on their way. I wish they hadn't. I doubt he'd be doing *this* if they were here.

I glare at him, my gaze flicking between his face and his hand, still clutching my wrist so tightly that my hand is starting to go numb.

What the *fuck* is wrong with this guy? I grit my teeth and glance back at Issac again, who's staring at the floor rather than looking at either of us.

I look back at Harris, and he tugs on my wrist again to jerk me a little closer to him, and I hiss slightly as he drags me. There's a weird feeling in the air, like lightning crackling around me, but also *not* like that, and Issac lets go of my other wrist.

"*Fuck off!*" I snap at Harris, and there's a loud crack and a green light blinding me, and the next thing I know I'm flying backward off my feet, and into Issac's arms, where he seemed prepared to catch me.

His arms are surprisingly sturdy, and he keeps me upright as my head spins. I realize after a few long seconds that the headmaster got sent flying back as well, slamming into the double doors behind him.

"*Anna,*" Issac groans softly into my ear, as the headmaster storms back towards us. "Way to blow your own cover..."

"Blow my own..." I mutter dizzily, blinking a few times before realizing I'm still in Issac's arms and I quickly stand back up straight, my face flushing.

What does he mean, though? My cover?

"*That*," The Headmaster hisses, stopping back in front of us. "Was the single most unpracticed magic I have *ever* seen, and it was *blatantly* accidental." He glares at the both of us, and Issac shies back from him. "*Explain yourself!*"

Oh. That cover.

I don't know what to say, and it doesn't seem like Issac does either, because he's still silent with his head ducked.

I look back at the Headmaster, who's looking past me at Issac, rather than at me. After a moment he lifts a hand slightly, a faint yellow aura around it, and I feel the air behind me shift, and a gasp from Issac.

Looking over my shoulder at him again, I see Issac suspended about a foot above the ground.

"I'm the most powerful social mage in this *country*." He hisses. "I will take the information I want directly from your mind if I have to."

Issac shuts his eyes tight, and in a quick flash of blue light, he falls gently back to the ground.

"That's *illegal*, Harris." He mutters, not looking up at the Headmaster. "Mind reading of anything beyond surface thoughts and/or feelings is considered a gross invasion of privacy and even *you* could be sentenced for up to six months for it."

"It's permitted in certain extreme circumstances, and I'm *certain* a case could be made for protecting the masquerade."

Issac sucks in a sharp breath and shoots a pleading look to me.

How am *I* supposed to help him with nutjob who wants to poke around his head? *Fuck, oh,* he wants me to be *honest* now, doesn't he? Okay...

"Fine! Fine! Just leave Issac out of it! That..." I pause, taking a shaky breath. "Whatever that was... it happened because I've never had any training in magic. Because I didn't *have* it until recently."

Without a word, Harris does that same thing Issac did before to summon my icon with cupping his hands and whatnot and makes the sparkly storm cloud appear, just as before.

"*What?*" He growls. "This doesn't even make *sense.*"

"Welcome to my world..." Issac mutters, staring at the floor, crossing his arms.

"And *do enlighten me* on how someone just gains the abilities of a mage, Issac?" Harris takes a step towards Issac who... shrugs.

I don't like how Harris keeps talking at Issac about me, like I'm not even here, but he's already proven himself to be *aggressive,* so I'm not sure what to do about that.

"I don't know why you expect *me* to have all the answers. It makes as little since to me as it does you." His stammering is all but gone, but he's quiet and talking slowly and deliberately, so maybe that's a conscious effort.

"And how exactly did you two meet? I know you aren't the most *social* of people, Issac."

"I don't think that's any of your business." I cut across before Issac can answer, and he sighs slightly.

"Can we *go*, Harris? *Please?*" He says. "We came here for a *reason.*"

"This girl can't be permitted to leave this building until she's trained enough to not be a threat to our secrecy." Harris growls, glowering at Issac.

"That's fine!" He snaps. "We were planning on staying here, anyway!"

"*And* given that you're tangled up in this, *you're* not permitted to leave *either.*"

"*Again,*" Issac turns an icy glare up to Harris. "*Fine.* We were *going to stay, anyway.* Now may we *go?* We needed to talk to Professor Gifford."

"Ah, well, I'd like to speak to Ms. Kahale. Alone. *You* may go to speak with Professor Gifford, if you need to, though I am curious as to *why?*"

Issac looks at me, and I nod slightly. He can go, it's... fine, I guess. It's not like either of us are leaving here, and he still needs to tell someone to actually go after Harris.

He seems doubtful, but sighs, taking a few steps back, nevertheless. "I guess- I- You can find me in my father's room, if you need me Anna. Just, just ask anyone if you need help finding it." He adjusts his bag on his shoulder, sending one last scathing look at Harris before he *quickly* walks away.

And I'm alone. With the complete and utter garbage headmaster.

Not that I blame him. I *did* tell him he could go, and he probably *really* wanted to get away from Harris, given that he's the guy who made this school so uncomfortable for him in the first place.

"Let me show you to a room you can stay in for the time being." He smiles at me, all the fake kindness back in an instant. "I could show you Issac's room as well, so you know where it is." He pauses. "It's somewhat sad, that Issac still thinks of it as his father's room. It's been *two years*, but ah, but I suppose everyone grieves at their own pace."

"Uh," I frown, kicking at the floor. "Okay?"

I don't know what to do or say without Issac here. I'm going to just... try to give him as little information as possible, I guess. I just have to hope he doesn't try to fish around in my head.

Harris leads me out of the entrance hall, through a couple more halls, stopping outside a door that has a gold plate on it that has *Staff Quarters* engraved on it in neat serif lettering.

"*Now*, Ms. Kahale," he says slowly. "What *was* your mother's surname?"

"Does it actually matter?" I shrug. "She wasn't actually a mage." I know it matters a lot to him. He probably has *some* inkling of Issac's dad's research, given how much trouble he's apparently been giving Issac over *getting it*... So that's probably why he wants to know. He might *suspect* the actual answer.

"Color me curious still." He smiles warmly, and I roll my eyes, crossing my arms.

"Well, it's not any of your business." I smile sweetly at him, and his friendly mask slips again as he scowls and narrows his eyes at me. "And you can't justify reading my mind again, so you're just going to have to deal."

He exhales hard through his nose before putting back on the smile. "What magic *have* you done? There was that electric burst just now, but before that?"

"Mm. Not much. Mostly just things flying at me." I say vaguely. It's *true*, that *is* most of it, but he doesn't need to know the like, weather thing.

"That's it?" He sounds disappointed, and he exhales through his teeth. "*Well*, that's not really helpful for figuring out your specialty."

He pushes open the door, and leads me past a sitting room with a fireplace, and several more doors with gold plates, these ones with names on them, and he stops at a door with no plate on it.

"This is where you will be staying." He says, barely a veneer of cheeriness left in his voice, and then he strides off quickly, his coat flapping behind him as he does.

After watching him go, I take a deep breath, and open the door to see a... fairly ordinary bedroom with a queen sized bed that has a green bed set, and there's a dresser off to my left, *not* that I had the chance to gather any of my clothes.

I wonder how long me and Issac are going to be stuck here...

September 23rd, 2018

I'm sitting in the library, and it's really quiet. Like, there's no one here. I think all the students must be in class or something. The calm is nice, I guess, but I almost wish there was someone around to help me understand the book in my hands. The librarian recommended it as a beginner's magic book, but the words look like nonsense to my eyes.

I really need some *help* understanding this, but I think I'm supposed to be keeping a low profile still. It sucks that the Headmaster knows about my weird situation, but the entire school doesn't need to.

I hear a chair at my table pull out, and I look up from the book at- *Issac!* Like a knight in shining armor showing up to help me understand this nonsense!

"Struggling a little?" He asks quietly, and I laugh humorlessly and put my head down on the table, pushing the book away from me, towards him.

"Try *struggling a lot.*" I say without lifting my head, and he chuckles.

"Well, it's no wonder." He picks up the book. "You can't really just dive right in with a book if you have no magical experience at all. Not only do textbooks like this *assume* you have a teacher, they assume baseline knowledge from having grown up in the magical community. Mages who *don't* are... *very* rare. They crop up now and then, but it's rare, and they're usually noticed quite young."

"Great." I sigh. "I'm a freak."

"Oh, well, I wouldn't have put it that way..." he says, "but uh, you are quite *unusual.* But, I- I *can* try to help, if you'd like? I'm no teacher, but I do very much know this stuff."

"Yes!" I sit up quickly. "Please! I'm so lost here, Issac. I don't know what I'm doing at all. And I like, think I need to?"

"You... definitely need to." He says slowly. "It's not, *safe* exactly, to be untrained. Magic tends to slip out of control easily with high emotion, and the *older* one gets the more dangerous it is, because your power does steadily increase with age." Issac pauses. "And from looking at your reserve, I'd say... you *are* at about what I would *expect* from nineteen years of passive increase, with no practice. It's unprecedented, but one could *extrapolate* the trends to... Sorry, I'm rambling a little. I- I'll just- I'll just shut up, sorry."

"No, no, it's fine." I shake my head. "You clearly really know your stuff. Bet you would have been top of your class had you actually gone here."

He snorts. "Hardly. I'm not even sure what section of the school I'd have been shuffled off to, since past a certain point it's divided by specialty."

"So, no one else *ever* has had so much difficulty with knowing their specialty before then, huh?" That must be really annoying. These Specialty things seem to be really important, and he just... doesn't *know*?

"I'm afraid not." He sighs. "I'm alone in that struggle, and it's endlessly frustrating. But I wasn't even close to top of my class in High School- not even with honors, so I *really* doubt that I would have been here."

"Not even with honors?" I chuckle. "Here I was taking you as the honor AP student type."

His dad's a teacher, so I would expect him to be an excellent student.

"Uh," He blinks quickly. "AP yes, honors no. My grades were a bit all over the place in school due to, like, personal issues around that time. Th-This is a digression, though!" He sits the book back down. "I'm supposed to be helping you learn."

Ah, well, that doesn't sound good. I probably shouldn't pry into *personal issues,* though, and he was trying to move on...

"How do you even *see* a reserve?"

"Oh, uh, Tessence Sight. It's, it's not usually the *first* thing you learn, more like the third, so maybe... save that for a bit..."

Tessence. Yeah, I saw that word in the book, but I'm not really sure what it means. But I guess there's a way to see it. Is it like... the magical energy they use or whatever?

"Alright, what do we start with then?"

"Not this book." He snorts. "Definitely not this book. It's too specific anyway, even if you had the groundwork of growing up in the mage community. You need ah," he lifts a hand, and with a blue flash, a book flies into his hand. "Probably this one? It's the basics on how a Mage's magic even works."

"You're still going to help me, right?" I take the new book from him, looking at its glossy cover, and the title embossed on it. *Quintessence and Magecraft.*

Hopefully, this one is easier to comprehend than *General Magecraft Book One,* because I got absolutely *nothing* out of that. My eyes kept glazing over every time I tried.

"Of course I'm going to try to help. I'm not about to just leave you all by yourself on this. So... let's just start with the very basics of what magic and *quintessence* is..."

September 24th, 2018

I stare blankly at the book in front of me, trying to comprehend the words printed on it. It's easier than that first book, but this is still really fucking *hard*.

Three days here I feel like I haven't really *learned* anything. I've only seen Issac a handful of times, mostly here in the library, like yesterday. I tried to go see him in his father's room- the name *Steven D. Riley* still on the door- but I felt weird about it, like I would be intruding on a private place, so I didn't even knock.

I wish he was here now. He could definitely help me like he did yesterday.

AUGH. Come *on*, Anna. You're a good student. And this is *beginner* stuff. You can do this.

Magic is the art of manipulating and using Quintessence, or Tessence, as it is often shortened. There are two types of active magic user: mages and wizards. Quintessence exists everywhere in the world, travelling along leylines.

Sure, yeah, okay. I follow. I guess. Issac explained that one well enough.

Leylines are lines of magic circling the globe, that stray tessence produced by mages settles into, pooling most intensely where Leylines cross, and those are called Nexus Points. Tessence spreads back out from leylines like a mist, transporting and spreading tessence all over the world. The closer to a leyline any given location is, the denser tessence tends to be.

Yeah, yeah, makes sense. Issac even grabbed a different book to show me a map of the leylines yesterday. So far, so good. I can keep up.

In the past Nexus points would generate magic, but all Nexus points have been sealed for several centuries, leaving quintessence production to just magekind.

I... guess? Issac did talk about how mages have *sources*, which is what differentiates a Mage from a Wizard. Mages are innately magical because... they produce *quintessence.* Yeah.

All living things contain some amount of tessence within themselves, absorbed from the environment at their birth. This tessence is used but not consumed in the processes of life. If some of this tessence is lost, the creature is weakened and exhausted. Living creatures naturally reabsorb any tessence they lose over time.

Sure, why not, I guess? I'm not going to pretend to understand how that works, but I can follow.

Mages are those born with a source; an innate ability to generate tessence, and have an unparalleled ability to intuitively channel tessence, though what they can channel it into is heavily restricted by their specialty, unlike the limited versatility of wizards.

That totally lost me. I don't know what the hell it's on about *intuitively* because this is far from intuitive to me. This is like the most *unintuitive* thing I've ever tried. Source, yes, *intuitively,* no.

A wispy girl, kinda similar in frame to Lorrie- though that where the similarities end- sits down at the same table as me. She has a thin face, narrow green eyes that have hints of purple, and the same pointed nose as the headmaster. Is this one of his daughters? Her hair is wavy, shoulder length and *clearly* dyed red, given the brown roots.

She smiles, her lips glossy and pink, and I notice she had dark purple eyeshadow on.

"You must be *Anna*." She says sweetly, her tone so saccharine that it's *too* sweet. If her pretty eyes weren't pulling me in so intently, I'd want to punch her. "You're not going to learn anything from that silly old book." She gently closes my book, smiling at me. "You grew up a Non, that book won't be any help to you."

I mean, Issac picked this one out for me because it'd be easier, but... I can't bring myself to voice that protest, just staring into her eyes.

She scoots her chair closer to mine and sits her hand on the back of mine. "I'm Carrie Harris."

In the back of my mind I dimly register that she *is* in fact one of his daughters, but I don't really quite process it, still looking into her eyes.

A near identical girl takes the third seat at our table, the only difference being that her hair is dyed black instead of red. The two are even dressed identically, in a black and purple pleated skirt, purple thigh high socks, with black Mary Janes, and a black sweater.

"I'm Kaitlyn," she says cheerfully, smiling brightly at me, but I barely look away from her sister.

"Tell us a bit about yourself, Anna." Carrie practically purrs, sliding her hand up my arm and onto my shoulder.

"I'm Anna Kahale." The words leave my mouth involuntarily. "I technically grew up in Lahaina, Hawai'i, but my dad is an investigative journalist, so we travelled a lot."

"Do tell me more." She giggles, and I dimly register how *fake* it sounds, but I... can't... *focus* on it.

"Well-" I start to say.

"*Stop.*" Issac's voice rings behind me, a strange quality to it, and it's like a haze clears from my mind. I jerk back from Carrie, almost tipping my chair over in my haste, and I quickly jump to my feet, taking several steps back from her to be standing next to Issac.

"*Carrie,*" he hisses, and I'm genuinely surprised by the *venom* in his voice. "You will *NOT* use your magic to pry information from Anna for your father."

Looking him over, he looks a little frazzled. His clothes are rumpled like he's slept in them, and I *know* he has because it's the same flannel and t-shirt he was wearing yesterday. Also, he has dark shadows under his eyes that make it seem like he hasn't slept at all.

"You stay out of this Riley!" Carrie spits, but she gets to her feet and storms off, and her sister quickly follows suit, but not before giving Issac a flirty wave on her way out, that he ignores.

"Carrie is a dual specialty Social Life mage." He says, staring intently at me for a moment before looking away. "She was enchanting you to make you pliable, so you'd tell her things." He sighs. "Let's just, go talk in *private*..."

~ Nine ~

Issac

September 24th, 2018

I can't believe Harris left me alone in his office. He dragged me up here to chat with me himself about his offer of a student teacher position, and I again turned it down, directing him to Ethan, but he didn't seem dissuaded.

But then Professor Rivera came to get him for something, and he told me to *wait here*. And he left me alone.

As tempted as I was to just *leave*, I know another opportunity to be alone in his office won't come anytime soon, and if could figure *why* he's so intent on getting my father's research when he *claims* to not even believe the central tenets of it...

Furtively glancing at the door to make sure he's not coming back, I stand up slowly and start looking over his bookshelves, my eyes briefly lingering on the Master's Staff mounted to the wall behind his desk. It still makes me mad that he took that out of its place in the entrance hall, where it had been mounted above the door since the school was founded.

He does have quite a few books on the Master, for someone who claims not to believe in it. My eyes land on an unlabeled book, tucked between two books about past Masters, and I pull it out. It's just... a small leather-bound book. A *journal,* really. Why is he keeping it on his bookshelf?

I flip through it quickly, and nearly drop the book at just a *glimpse* of a page of spellwork. I- I recognized that. Flipping back to the start of the spellwork, I take a shaky breath, staring blankly at the pages as I take it in.

This is the spell that killed my parents. Either he painstakingly did what I did and worked it back from the results... or he designed the spell.

And this looks like design work, with all the notes scribbled around it.

I hear footsteps on the stairs before I can read any of it, and quickly shove the journal back on the shelf, darting back to the chair, but... It's just Professor Gifford.

"There was an explosion in the fire dorms, Issac." She smiles slightly. "He'll be awhile. You don't have to wait here for him."

I'd like to stay here to look over that journal more, but I can't very well *say that* to Professor Gifford. She's very nice, but I doubt she'd approve of me snooping in Harris' office.

But that spell being there... Harris had to have been the one who... I look back at the shelf with that journal as I follow Professor Gifford out of the room.

I always suspected that it wasn't an accident, but there was nothing I could *do* about that. A fact that Ethan never seemed to understand, given how many times he's picked fights with me over it, like it's *my* fault.

But what I just saw... Harris... he killed my parents. He killed *his own best friend.*

"Issac, are you quite alright?" Professor Gifford asks quietly at the bottom of the stairs that lead up to the Headmaster's office. "You seem a little dazed? Are you concerned about Anderson? Enforcers are tracking him, so I can't imagine that it will take too much longer. You'll be able to return to your life soon enough."

"Uh, yeah, yeah..." I mumble, blinking quickly. "I know, I know. But, uh, thanks. I'm going to find Anna..." I walk off quickly, just wanting an excuse to get away, and I duck into the Library, just for some *quiet*. I hide behind a bookshelf, just making myself breathe slowly.

Harris killed my parents. I'm in a building under near total control of the man who *killed my parents.*

"Do tell more-" I jump slightly at the sound of Carrie Harris' voice, and I peak around the bookshelf, seeing her and Kaitlyn *'talking'* to Anna, and clearly enchanting her.

"Stop." I say, forcefully ending Carrie's spell, quickly approaching the table they're at. The two of them quickly leave, but I'm not paying attention to them, more focused on Anna, and magically making sure she's *okay.* Carrie tends to life drain a bit while she enchants, because it contributes to weakening her targets.

But she doesn't seem to have done that to Anna. Okay. Maybe it was just... too much of a risk for her to do that in this case, to actually *harm* Anna.

"Carrie is a dual specialty Social Life mage." I say by way of explanation to Anna. "She was enchanting you to make you pliable, so you'd tell her things." I sigh, ducking my head. As comforting as the library tends to be, I don't want to be somewhere Harris or his daughters can just bother us at any time. And the only place in the whole building where I'm confident we could be *alone* is my father's room.

"Let's just, go talk in private..." I mumble, gesturing for her to follow me out, and back to the staff quarters, to my father's room.

It's kind of a mess, because I've just been working from here, with books haphazardly stacked around, and my active work notebooks open on the desk.

Once Anna is in behind me, I close and lock the door, adding an extra warding spell for good measure, to make *damn* sure we're not intruded upon. I sigh, pressing my hand flat against the door and taking a few deep breaths.

Harris killed my parents. Harris killed my parents. And his daughters were just trying to force Anna to talk to them. Ethan was right. The school isn't *safe* either. If- If Harris knew that I saw that...

I hear Anna sit down on the bed behind me. "Uh, Issac are you okay?"

I turn around and go to sit down next to her on the bed, kicking my sneakers off to pull my feet up onto the bed, hugging my knees, and staring down at the rich blue rug that's under the edge of the bed.

"I think I've figured it out." I say quickly, not really wanting to answer her question. She doesn't need to feel as scared as I do now.

"Figured...?" She echoes, her voice pitching up in confusion. "Figured *what* out, Issac?"

"You've always had the purple in your eyes, right?" I glance sidelong at her before turning my gaze back to the carpet, tapping my fingers on the side of my leg.

"Uhh, yeah?"

"And your mother, did she have purple in her eyes?"

She makes a confused sound, and I glance at her as she's rapidly blinking. "Uh, yeah? Dad always said I got it from her."

"Well," I exhale hard, and lay back on the bed, staring up at the lightly textured ceiling. "Then you were *always* a Mage, and so was your mother." I feel her shift slightly on the bed before I continue. "The lightning merely unlocked it somehow. And possibly saved your life. The *how* still eludes me, but *something* had sealed away your family's magic, making your source inaccessible."

"Oh." She exhales hard, and I sit up to look at her. "That's... really strange."

I smile faintly, looking back down at the rug again. Strange is an understatement. I still have no idea *how* any of this happened, but I'm fairly confident on what now.

"I think it explains your icon as well. Since your magic wasn't previously realized, you didn't *have* an icon, so that moment magically imprinted onto you. Maybe it will change with time, or maybe you're the start of a new Nature Lineage with new symbology, we'll just have to wait to see on that..."

I look around the room, and sigh. I still can practically *feel* my father here. If he had just lived to meet Anna, so much of his work would have validated. He'd be so *happy*...

But Harris killed him.

"Issac, are you *okay*?" She asks again, and I look sideways at her, blinking quickly. I realize that I was almost crying, and I quickly wipe at my eyes.

God, I can't just pretend everything is *fine*. I'm not a good liar, but I don't want her to be scared.

"Ah," I look sideways at her and take a shaky breath. "Not really, but it's nothing you need to worry about." I duck my head. So long as I keep it to myself what I learned... and so long as Ethan and Lexi don't come here, because... Harris might have intended to kill them too, or at least didn't care if they died. He wouldn't have known they were at Gran's that day...

"Issac..." She starts to reach out to me, but she stops and retracts her hand. "Issac, whatever's wrong, you can tell me."

I shake my head immediately. It's not her problem to worry about. She doesn't need to feel unsafe here too. It's just not her problem.

"*Issac*," she huffs, and stands up. "Honestly, if you're not going to talk to me, I might as well just *go*. I mean, I thought we were *friends*," I wince, hiding my face in my hands. She shouldn't have to-

"But I *guess*..." She trails off, walking to the door, but she stops with her hand on the doorknob, before turning back around towards me, her back against the door. "*Aren't* we friends? Do you not trust me? I don't get what I'm doing wrong here, Issac. And you're *blatantly* upset about something, and it's *worrying me.*"

I briefly meet her eyes before quickly looking away and exhaling hard. "It's not like-" I groan, pulling my hat down over my eyes, and rocking slightly in place. "Anna, it's- it's not that I don't trust you. I- I'd love to have you as a friend if you can put up with me, but this just- this just isn't your problem to worry about."

She huffs and unlocks the door, and I just barely hear her mutter something like *boys...* and *idiot* under her breath as she goes.

And then she's gone, the door clicking closed behind her, and I gesture to relock it with magic.

A second later the tears come in spite of my best efforts, and I lay back on the bed, pulling a pillow over my face, trying to take deep breaths to calm down. *Don't panic.*

There are no good options here. I... I can't stay here with the man who murdered my parents, but I can't exactly leave with Anderson still after me and Anna.

There's nowhere in Seattle we could go. Harris has too much power in the magical community here, and outside of the magic district, we'd be in danger from Anderson.

I sit back up, twisting my hands in my lap, trying to think clearly. The... the obvious answer is somewhere *out* of Seattle, but I can't very well drag Anna out of the city just because *I* feel unsafe here.

tap tap tap

I flinch, covering my ears at the sudden sharp tapping noise.

God, Issac, don't be so jumpy...

I lower my hands slowly, breathing slowly to try to stay calm as I look around for the source of the sound.

tap tap tap

I wince again, but I find the source at the window... where my little sister is, and for a second, it's like time stops.

She shouldn't be here, and I just blink quickly for a moment as she waves cheerily at me. When I don't move to let her in, she taps on the glass with her nail again and I wince at the sharp sound, but I do get up and open up the window.

She climbs in the window, followed just a moment later by Ethan, and I just stare at the two, struggling to breathe.

Logically, I *know* that it's *probably* fine that they're here. That Harris has no idea I saw his journal, and trying to hurt them now even *if* he tried to kill them before it would be *risky* for him to attempt anything right now.

But *knowing that* doesn't do anything to stop my heart racing at the sight of them. They. They're supposed to be at *Gran's.* They're supposed to *safe.*

They *aren't safe here.*

"What- *what are you two doing here?*" I choke out, and the two share a look.

"Well, we came to see how you were doing?" Ethan says slowly. "We had Hannah trying to keep an eye on you, but she said you've mostly been holed up in Dad's old room, so we just wanted to make sure everything was fine?"

Ah. No, no. They came here because they were worried about *me*. They came somewhere that might be *dangerous to them* because they were worried about me.

I shake my head quickly, and back up until I hit the bed and practically fall to sitting on it. They can't be here. He could hurt them. He probably meant to. He might- he might- he might try again.

And they're just here because of me. They're in *danger* because of me.

What if- What Harris had some kind of spell to track if someone read his journal? What if he *knows*? What if he knows and tries to hurt them here?

No no-

I pull my feet up onto the bed, hugging my knees and rocking in place.

"Issac?" Lexi says quietly, sitting down next to me, and Ethan sits on my other side. "Issac, are you okay?"

I don't say anything, just whimper and hide my face in my hands. They can't- *They can't be here.* It's not safe. It's not safe. It's not safe.

"*You can't be here-*" I gasp out, still hiding my face as I rock in place. "You can't- you can't-"

They gently pull my hands away from my face and place a tangle in my hands, which I start twisting immediately. At least it's keeping my hands busy.

If he knows I know- if he knows I know- he'll hurt them. They- they're supposed to be at *Gran's*. They'd be safe at Gran's! But instead they're here! They're *here*. Because of me.

They put themselves in danger for *me*. Because they were worried about me.

It's- it's my job to take care of them. Not the other way- they're in danger because of *me*.

They need to leave. To- to go back to Gran's. To be *safe*. He probably knows they're here- what if-

They put a blanket around my shoulders, and I drop the tangle, to pull the comforter tight around my shoulders, and I take a long moment to force myself to breathe slowly, and I close my eyes.

They're in the same building as our parent's murderer, and there's nothing I can do about it.

He could hurt them. He might even *get away with it* here, where he nearly has absolute power...

But they don't know that.

I touch my face, realizing that I was crying again, and I wipe weakly at my eyes, and I can feel both of my siblings' eyes locked on me, and my heart is still racing in my ears, but I'm starting to get a grip again, and my gaze trails over to the grandfather clock in the corner, and I exhale hard seeing almost an *hour* passed while I was *panicking*, and I bite back a sob, wiping furiously at my eyes.

Calm down.

I pull the blanket tighter around my shoulders and duck my head. "I'm sorry."

It'd been *months* since I panicked like that. God, why do things keep getting more *stressful*...

Ethan slips his arm around my shoulders, hugging me gently. "Don't apologize. It's not your fault, Issac."

"But I'm the *adult*! You two shouldn't have to take care of me!" I choke out. "It's my job to take care of the two of you!"

Lexi reaches forward, brushing my bangs out of my eyes, smiling softly at me. "Issac, you take care of us all the time. Even before Mom and Dad died, you did." I bite back another sob at the mention of our parents, and she pauses, frowning slightly. "*But*, Issac, that doesn't change the fact that sometimes you just need help, and that's *fine*. We know how it goes by now. It's really not your fault." She pauses. "Are you *okay*, though? What was that about?"

"You two need to leave," I take a shaky breath. "*Now*."

Ethan shakes his head. "No way. Not right after you have a meltdown. We're not leaving you alone here. Just tell us what's *wrong*."

My breath hitches, and I turn my gaze up to the ceiling. "It's not safe." I mumble. "You two could be in *danger* here."

"In danger, how?" Ethan asks, shifting to gently grab my hands. "Issac?"

I turn my gaze to Ethan, locking eyes with him. I'm not sure how he'll react to this news. He's been so short with me whenever our parent's death came up. I know he wanted me to *do something* about it. About how suspicious it all seemed despite being ruled an accident.

"... Harris," I take a few deep breaths, "is the one who killed our parents."

It's silent for a very long moment, before Ethan jumps to his feet, taking several steps away, swearing under his breath, and Lexi throws her arms around me, quickly breaking down into tears on my shoulder.

"That bastard..." Lexi mumbles through her tears.

Ethan starts pacing with his arms crossed, and he looks *furious*. "How did you find this out? *When* did you find this out?"

"Just earlier today." I say softly, following him with my eyes and slipping an arm around Lexi's shoulders. "And I... I found a journal in his office that *had the spell development notes* in it, for the spell that killed them. I was only alone in his office for a few minutes, so I didn't get to study it closely, but that's *undeniably* what it was."

At least he doesn't seem to be mad at *me*. I guess in a way this is what he always wanted. The *truth* about it all.

I pick up my previously discarded tangle, fiddling with it with one hand, as Ethan sighs, stopping in his pacing. "Issac, if- if he just has something like *that* in his office, you need to-" He takes a deep breath. "And I can't believe I'm saying this, *report it to the enforcers*. Get the bastard put away like the murderer he is."

I shake my head slowly. "Think about it, Ethan," I take a shaky breath. "He's the one rushed the investigation and got it declared an *accident* in the first place. Harris just has too much power in the magic community here. We'd never be able to get him to trial, let alone *convicted*."

"*Goddamn it!*" Ethan growls, sitting back down forcefully on the bed. "So, there's *nothing* we can do?"

"*Well*, you two could go back to Gran's so you *aren't* in the same place as someone who probably intended to kill you as well."

"Well-" Lexi pulls back, wiping at her eyes. "What about you? You can't stay here with him either. I mean- What if- what if he tries to hurt *you*? While you're stuck here, and vulnerable."

"I don't know what you expect me to do, Lex." I stare up the ceiling. "I remind you that *Kevin Anderson* is after me out there."

"But- But- There has to be somewhere *else* you can go? You can't- You can't just- *Issac*." Her tone is pleading, and she holds onto my arm. "We're not going to just leave you here in with our parent's murderer. What if- What if he does something to you to try to get dad's research?"

"I... don't even know if that's his motivation. I know he *wants* Dad's research, but *killing* him wouldn't be a good tactic for that. He... He was almost done with it. If Harris had just... Not done that, Dad would have finished it, and *published*. He would have to have some sort of ulterior motive. Harris is a lot of things, but he's not the kind of person who would make mistakes like *that*." I sigh. "But as far as my safety goes... well, I was in *Tacoma* then, and he very well knew that. He didn't expect me to be there, but he expected the two of you to be."

Lexi grabs a pillow and screams into it, before throwing it at the wall. "Augh! Still! You can't stay here!"

"Lexi's right." Ethan says, staring down at the floor. "Whether he was actively trying to kill you or not, it doesn't seem like a good idea to stay at a place under near total control of the man who murdered our parents. Maybe just... get out of Seattle until they wipe Anderson's memory?"

"Anna, Ethan. I can't leave Anna here, and-"

"Then explain what's going on to her!" he cuts across me. "Stop being a selfless idiot for *five minutes* and consider that she might be willing to go with you."

"... Alright, *alright*. But you two need to go first, *please*, for my peace of mind."

"Are you sure you're going to b-" Ethan cuts himself off, springing to his feet and darting across the room, throwing open the door, causing Carrie Harris to *fall* into the room.

She sits up quickly, glaring at me with her teeth bared. "How *dare* you accuse my father of something like *that*! You *monster*!"

Ethan growls, yanking her up off the ground and pinning her against the wall. "Your deception spell doesn't work on other social mages, you *vile* little-"

"Ethan." I say quietly. "Ethan no, no." I slowly get up and walk over to them, putting a hand on his shoulder. "You'll only get in trouble for this."

Ethan slowly lets out a breath through gritted teeth, and he lets her go, taking a step back, but he's still glaring daggers at her as she dusts herself off and smiles at him.

"You can't touch me, Riley. After all, Daddy doesn't *need* you." She shoots a look at me and giggles. "Well, bye-bye for now, Rileys. I need to go have a chat with my dad." And she skips away, humming a cheery tune as she goes.

Did she mean to confirm that? That her father *needs* me for some reason? I didn't know that for sure, but I do *now*.

But that also rather forced my hand. I *can't* stay here after that. Not with Harris *definitely* knowing that I know the truth. I just have to hope that Anna is okay with it.

"Ethan, Lexi. Leave *now*."

"But-"

"*Alexis Joan Riley!*" I whirl to face her, talking over her protests. "That was a *threat*. He doesn't '*need*' the two of you. **Leave.**"

She nods meekly and quickly hurries out the window. Ethan follows her, hesitating right before heading out, and he turns to face me.

"Are you going to be *okay*, bro? This is... you know... a lot. I'm worried about you. I know you can get... overwhelmed..."

"I'll be fine." I say softly. "Just go, please."

"... What are you going to do? You really can't stay here."

"I'm not going to." I shake my head. "I'll be leaving shortly, but *you* need to leave now."

He sighs, but nods and follows Lexi out. I just stare at the window for a long moment after he's gone, before I sigh and gather my stuff back into my bag, and head over to Anna's room.

I knock three times raptly, pause briefly, then knock twice more, and she opens it a moment later, her gaze flitting to my bag briefly.

"Are we leaving? Did they catch the Hunter? Is Headmaster Douche letting us leave?"

"Yes, no, and no." I say quickly. "I'm sorry, something happened and we need to leave rather quickly..."

Anna frowns, her eyes sweeping up and down me, and she exhales hard. "You look like you've been crying." She says softly, stepping out of her room, and closing the door. "What happened?"

She likes upfront explanations, but I don't know if I could make myself talk about it right now. Especially not with the hurry to go, given the potential danger.

"It's- It's a bit much." I say weakly. "Can I *please* explain *after* we leave?"

After a moment, she nods, which is a *relief*, and I gesture for her to follow me, and I head down the hall, to a hidden passage out of the school.

"Uhhh, Issac, the exit is in the other direction?"

"Not the exit we're taking." I mumble, stopping in front of a blank stretch of wall, quickly pulsing tessence into the correct brick to open up the secret passage there, the entire stretch of wall temporarily vanishing.

I gesture her into the now accessible tunnel ahead of me, and it seals back closed behind us.

I speed walk, barely resisting the urge to break into a run. I stop the moment we cross the threshold of school grounds, as the slight magical pressure of the anti-teleport wards lifts, and I hold a hand out to her.

"It's easier to teleport when we're in contact." I say softly, and she looks at my hand then takes it after a moment, and I turn us into tessence, transporting us instantly to our destination.

"That was weird..." Anna rubs the back of her head. "That was... teleportation?"

"My version of it, anyway." I say, glancing sideways at her. "I made my own nonstandard way of teleporting, based loosely on how Wizards teleport. It's a more efficient, if more *difficult* spell."

She looks around the suburban street I took us to, crossing her arms. "Where are we?"

"Issaquah, Washington." I force a smile. "My boss- she's very nice, don't worry- lives out here, and she's been a family friend since I was little, so I thought... maybe we could try to see if we could hide out at her house, and it's... far enough away that we're probably safe from Anderson..."

"Does she know about magic?"

"Ah, no." I sigh. "But she's going to find out *now*..."

~ Ten ~

Anna

September 24th, 2018

Issac leads me to a cute little one-story house, with a one-car garage attached, and he knocks on the door, rocking back and forth on the balls of his feet.

I *knew* something was wrong; I don't understand why he wouldn't just.... tell me. I mean, I could've at least tried to help, right? *Ugh*, boys. Always bottling up their emotions. Like, *come on* Issac, you aren't exactly a super masculine guy; don't hold to the dumb ideas about masculinity and *feelings*...

And he's a psych student; he should know better. But still, here we are. Something having gone wrong, and him *still* having not told me.

The door opens, revealing a nice older... Oh, wait, I know her! She's the main librarian at the cute little library I found. I didn't know Issac worked there! I've always been struck by how *happy* she seems, a lifetime of smiling etched into the lines around her eyes.

She immediately pulls Issac into a tight-looking hug, which he *surprisingly* returns, given how little he seems to like being touched. I guess he did say he's known her since he was little...

"Issac Riley!" She pulls back and gently smacks his shoulder. "Never scare me like that again!" She frets, straightening his jacket. "Get inside and tell what's wrong this instant." His eyes land on me, and she smiles. "And introduce me to your friend!" She turns and walks into the house, Issac following her.

I repress a laugh, since something *serious* is going on, but she's fretting over him like she's his mother and it's sweet. I follow him in, pulling the door closed gently behind me, and locking it. Better safe than sorry.

"*Honestly*, Issac." I follow her voice to a cozy, cute little kitchen, where she's sat Issac down at the kitchen table. "Phone call or not, you can't just miss school and work for three days with no explanation."

"Sorry," he mutters, ducking his head, and running his fingers along the blue check tablecloth. "*Things* came up rather suddenly."

She pulls the other kitchen chair close to him and sits down, taking both of his hands into hers. "What happened, dear?"

"It's- It's... *complicated*..." Issac's gaze looks unfocused, staring down at his hands in hers.

"Issac..." She stares at him, her brow furrow. "Dearie, you know you can tell me anything, right?"

He suddenly sits up straight, looking over at me, and pulling his hands away from her. "I-I should introduce you two! Ms. Powel, this is Anna! I've told you about her..."

"The girl who was str..." She looks over at me, then smiles brightly after a moment. "Oh, I know her. She's a fairly regular visitor to our little library! She usually comes in the mornings."

"She was there late the day we met, since I'm the one who checked her out." Issac chuckles, though it sounds a little forced, looking towards the window next to the table.

I pause. He's the one who...? I was in a hurry that night, wanting to beat the storm home; something I *miserably* failed at, so I don't think I even registered who checked me out at the library. Was it really Issac?

"Really?" I say after a moment. "I didn't remember that *at all.*"

"Well," Issac glances at me quickly. "That night was kind of *a lot,* so you can be forgiven for not remembering."

"Yes, I think a lapse in memory could be forgiven for that night." Ms. Powel laughs. "Are you doing alright though? No lasting effects?"

"Oh," I laugh nervously. "No, no. Just a faint scar. I..." I glance over at Issac, who's pulled a brightly colored twisty thing out of his bag, and is fidgeting with it. He notices my look and meets my eyes for a half second, and just... shrugs.

Augh, he's just as clueless as I am here.

"I was exceptionally lucky." I settle on quietly. "Though if Issac hadn't been there, I still might have *frozen* to death in that storm."

She chuckles, then focuses back on Issac. "*Now,* dearie, no more stalling. What happened?"

He looks vaguely in my direction rather than at her, and he's clearly on the verge of tears, his eyes shining with how wet they are. Looking at them, I'm struck for the first times since we met how *vividly purple* his eyes are. When I first saw them I was sure they were contacts, but like... his eyes are really just that *pretty,* aren't they?

"It's complicated." He repeats himself from earlier. "I-It's *really* complicated."

"Dearie, you can tell me *anything...*" She reaches forward, brushing his beanie off to run her fingers through his hair in a very motherly fashion. "Please, Issac..."

"I don't even know where to start..." His voice is quiet and fragile. He seems so vulnerable, sitting there, hunched over and on the verge of tears.

Seriously, what happened? I mean, everything with the Hunter has me stressed out, but this is something else entirely. He's clearly hurting a lot over *something.* I knew he was upset, but it's like... he's crumpling at her being so gentle with him.

"You started with fantasy novels for me?" I say quietly, trying to help, and he laughs faintly, followed by a sniffle, and wiping at his eyes.

"I *did,* didn't I..."

Ms. Powel laughing seems to catch us both off guard, as Issac's head jerks to face her, and I quickly look at her too.

"*Oh,*" She smiles warmly. "So, you're finally telling me about this, are you? I knew your dad for more than twenty years and not even *once* did he let out a peep that he was a mage."

Issac is silent, just blinking quickly at her, clearly a little bit in shock.

"Sorry, dear," she smiles sadly. "I was just waiting for you to tell me when you were ready to. I wasn't about to press either you or your dad if you didn't feel comfortable with it."

"How did you…" Issac runs his hands through his hair, leaning forward on his knees. "All this time…"

"My Mother was a Wizard." She pats his shoulder. "I chose not to learn it myself, but I grew up very aware of the magic world." She gently strokes his cheek. "Ah, so, this is a magic problem then, dear?"

He takes a shaky sounding breath and nods slightly. "There- There are *two* major problems…" He glances sidelong at me before looking at the floor. "One, there's an extremely dangerous Hunter after us."

"My bad…" I mumble, looking away embarrassed, and Issac sighs.

"It's not your fault, Anna." I look back at him, and he's smiling faintly at me, but his smile doesn't last long, before he's staring back at the floor. "As for the other…" He closes his eyes and doesn't say anything, visibly taking deep breaths.

"Issac, dear, what is it?" She glances over at me, and I shrug, not taking my eyes off of him. He said it was *a bit much*. Whatever it is, he's clearly upset over it.

"I-" Issac, shakes his head, and gets to his feet. "I-I'll be right back- I just need a- I need a minute," and he tears out the back door without another word.

I sigh, staring out the door he just ran out of. What the *hell* is going on?

"Oh, Issac..." Ms. Powel sighs softly, then stands up, turning to face me. "Is there anything I can do for you, Anna, dear?"

"He..." I huff, crossing my arms. "He just *left*. I *knew* something was *wrong*! I asked him about it, and he was just like *this isn't your problem to worry about*, then a little more than an hour later he's having us leave! Augh! And he *still* hasn't told me what's wrong!"

How can someone *so nice* be *so infuriatingly opaque*!? I like him, like *a lot*. He's really nice and seems to genuinely want to help me, but he keeps *doing this*, where he acts without explaining things, and it's starting to get really annoying.

Ms. Powel pulls out the chair Issac just vacated, and gestures for me to sit down, which I do with a heavy sigh. She pours me a cup of iced tea before resuming her seat.

"Issac has a hard time opening up to people." She says quietly, then sighs. "He always has, but it got worse after his folks passed. It's like he thinks he needs to carry the whole world on his shoulders."

I'm quiet for a moment, stirring in sweetener in the tea she gave me. "... For someone so smart, he's an idiot. I get that he needs to keep a brave face with his siblings, since he's their guardian and all, but I outright *asked* him what was wrong, and he refused to tell me... I just wanted to *help*..."

"Give him a little time, Dear. I'm sure he's trying his best. He's not great with people, and he tends to struggle to speak when he's upset. It's better to..." She pauses. "Just, accommodate him on this, and let him calm down a bit."

I narrow my eyes at her. *Accommodate* was an interesting word to use there. It could be nothing, but that word has *connotations* to me. Like, something is just generally *wrong* that leads to these problems. Hm. I mean, ah, he's the one studying psychology, not me, so I *shouldn't* make any assumptions... Though he has seemed really *anxious* since basically the first day we met...

Maybe I'll ask him. If there *is* something wrong, I'd like to know so I **can** *accommodate* it...

"It's really frustrating though," I sigh after a moment. "I don't know what to do if he doesn't tell me anything."

Like, just, *let me care about you, idiot.*

"He'll be back, Anna." She says softly. "But really, is there anything I can do for you in the meantime?"

"Something to read?" I answer after a moment, putting aside my frustration with him leaving. "I only have one book with me, and I think I need his help to understand it."

"Oh," she laughs lightly. "Come on, I have plenty of books for you to choose from."

September 25th, 2018

Drifting off in a comfy chair with a good book is one of the best ways to fall asleep. It's a less than pleasant way of waking up though, since I always end up falling onto the floor.

Like right now.

I sit up, rubbing the back of my head, squinting up at someone in the dark sitting room. After an entirely too long sleep-brained moment, I realize it's Issac.

Looking rather sheepish, he offers a hand to help me up, and I take it, pulling myself to my feet. "Issac," I mutter, more than a little annoyed still at him just leaving like that.

He winces, taking a step back from me. "I'm sorry! I know- I know I said I'd explain once we left the school! I'm sorry!"

"... Why did you leave then?"

"I..." He sits down on the couch and sighs. "I wasn't in any state to explain. I'm sorry. And I needed to go back to get some answers," he pauses, an angry look briefly crossing his face, but it's gone as quickly as it appeared. "I'm okay now, though. And, uh, sorry if I woke you. It's very late..."

I pull out my phone to check the time at his mention of it, and sigh slightly, seeing that it's nearly one in the morning. Did he just now get back?

"This is all ridiculous, you know that, right? I like, barely know you, really, but we're just... stuck together, and you're not communicating much at all..."

Alright, I mean 'barely know him' might be a bit of an exaggeration. I know he's scholarly, and likes to read, and cares enough about psychology to be going to college for it. And I know he likes board games, due to his *extensive* collection. And tabletop RPGs too. And that he doesn't like being touched or eye contact. And that he's a terrible liar. And that he clearly loved his parents *a lot*, and still hurts *a lot* over losing them.

I've payed close attention to him, but most of that doesn't feel *personal*. Anyone could see most of that if they were looking.

"I- I..." He shakes his head slowly. "I'm sorry," he apologizes again. "I... I wish we knew each other better. That things had gone better, and we could just... talk without anything else going on. But, well, circumstances are a bit odd, to say the least..."

I hesitate a moment before getting up off the floor and joining him on the couch, grabbing his hand. I'm ready to let go in a moment if he seems uncomfortable, but he just glances at our intertwined hands for a long moment, before looking up at me and smiling faintly, gently squeezing my hand.

Okay, that's good. He's okay with this at least.

"Well," I say, smiling at him. "Let's just *talk* now, Issac. Odd circumstances or not, nothing is happening this moment, so we might as well. I mean. I already *like* you. A lot. I want us to be good friends, and it *has* to get better than this from now, right? Start with *what happened,* please."

He blinks several times, before looking away with a sigh, and I notice for the first time that his eyes seem to have a faint glow in the dark, and I have to actively stop myself from staring at them. Is that a magic thing? Do my eyes do that?

It's a captivating effect, nevertheless, especially given their vivid color.

"... It was two things that compounded together," he says softly. "Right before I found you in the Library with the twins... I was in Harris' office, and I had been left there alone for a few minutes. I... found evidence that... Do you remember how I said my parent's death was *ruled* an accident?"

I nod slightly. The way he said it came with the distinct implication that he thought the ruling was bullshit, but wasn't outright stating as much.

"Well," His voice shakes a little, and he looks up at the ceiling. "I found evidence that it *wasn't*. And that Harris is the one who killed them. The second thing was... Carrie Harris eavesdropping at my door, and overhearing me telling my siblings about that. I- I didn't think it would be safe there, with him knowing that I... knew... that."

"The headmaster..." I repeat faintly, and squeeze his hand. "I'm so sorry, Issac. That's awful."

"Mm. Yeah. And, well, it's not much help for being... normal friends. Sorry. I don't know how to fix any of this. I haven't made a *real* friend since the first grade, and that's not even factoring in these circumstances..."

I'm silent for a moment. He hasn't made a friend since *the first grade*? I'm a little lost for words, honestly. I'd gotten the idea that he wasn't particularly sociable, but that's a *long time*...

"That's... That's really sad, Issac." I lean back on the couch. "All my friendships growing up were fleeting because I was always travelling with Dad, but at least I *had* friends."

Issac laughs bitterly, roughly running his hand through his hair. "Oh I *had* people who *called* themselves my friends. Even putting aside the fact that all of my Non Friends in high school ditched me, every kid in the magical community wanted to be my friend. They thought they could get in my father's good graces that way..."

All his friends in high school ditched him? "... What happened?"

Issac freezes, and is quiet for a very long moment, looking sideways at me, with his eyes wide with clear fear, and he bites his lip.

He's scared? Why would he be scared of me?

Finally he sighs, ducking his head and covering his eyes with his hands, whimpering slightly. "Issac Riley happened." He says at barely more than a whisper, but it doesn't make much sense.

What is he talking about? "Issac, what do you mean?"

"Why was your dad always travelling?" He asks quickly, his voice shaking. He's blatantly trying to change the subject, but I guess I'll allow it. I don't want him to be *scared* of me for whatever reason.

"Uh. Well, he's an investigative journalist. He was travelling for work, chasing stories and whatnot. And since my mother... you know, wasn't around, I was homeschooled and went with him."

He nods slightly, fiddling with the collar of his shirt. "T-To clarify what I said before, I... I was given the name *Isabelle Riley* when I was born. I transitioned in the ninth grade, and all but two of my friends abandoned me entirely."

Ohhhh. He's trans. That... explains a lot.

"You- you don't think any less of me for it, do you?" He squeaks, clearly very, *very* worried about the possibility of that, and I have to fight the urge to hug him. Even if he *hadn't* just told me that his friends abandoned him, it couldn't be more obvious that he's faced serious transphobia in his life.

It's no wonder, really, that he has a hard time opening up if that happened to him. I'd have trust issues too if I lost almost all my friends for coming out.

I shake my head, squeezing his hand. "Not a chance." Cautiously, I put my other hand on his shoulder. "I'm not some transphobic asshole. What kind of member of the LGBTA Plus community would I be if I were? Some loser lesbian TERF? *As if.* I'll let the white girls keep that exclusionary nonsense." I laugh weakly. "It doesn't change anything, promise."

The tension visibly slips from his shoulders, and he cracks a faint smile. "You're Queer? Or, uh, LGBTA plus, if you'd prefer?"

"Yeah, A is for A-" I start laughing, but force myself to finish my lame joke. "For Ally." I take a moment to calm down and stop myself from laughing. "I couldn't even get through that with a straight face. I'm *hella* bisexual."

"Well, of course you couldn't get it out with a *Straight* face," he smiles. "You're *Hella Bisexual.*"

I burst into giggles, almost falling forward into him.

"I'm *also* bisexual, for what it's worth." He adds. "Or well, biromantic demisexual. If you wanted to know."

"*Noted.*" I say in between giggles, and he stays quiet for a moment as my laughs taper off.

"... What's your dad like?" He asks once I stop.

"Uh, very exuberant and friendly. Our relationship is... a little strained right now because he lied to me for a long time about how my mother died... but I do miss him..."

"... I was always closer to my dad than my mom growing up. I was a bookworm from the first moment I could read, and my dad loved to read with me." He closes his eyes, sighing slightly. It must hurt a lot, for his parent's murderer to just... be out there, free to live his life.

"When I was little, I wanted to be a journalist like my dad. I still keep a blog as an artifact of that." I smile faintly. "I actually got into fiction writing through online roleplay."

"Structured or Freeform?" He asks immediately, and I can tell I've piqued his interest. He does know I'm familiar with D&D, so I suppose it's a fair question. Most people wouldn't know the difference.

"Bit of both. I started with Freeform, but there were a few systems I liked, even if Play by Post frequently crashes and burns." I smile at him. "What'd you say your group does again?"

He leans his forehead onto his hand, groaning. "Augh, *Play-by-Post* is endlessly frustrating. My group plays over Discord. Voice Chat tends to make it go smoother."

I giggle, still clutching his hand, and I tug on it slightly. "Hey, me and Lorrie have an I-R-L group. You should join it."

"See, I was about to ask you to join *my* gro-" I push his shoulder, cutting him off as I burst into laughter again.

"Shut up! I am NOT letting an actual wizard GM for me!"

"*Mage!*" he corrects, clearly trying desperately to not follow me into laughter, and largely failing. "Wizards are something else! And I'm not the GM, anyway!"

Without a word, I shove him off the couch, and what little of his composure that remained vanishes in an instant as he breaks down laughing.

He should smile like this more often. It lights up his whole face and makes him seem like... like he's the most approachable person in the world. It's nice to see him smiling so genuinely.

It makes me wonder how many of his smiles have been faked.

~ Eleven ~

Issac

September 24th, 2018

I stop for a moment as the back door out of the kitchen closes behind me, and wipe quickly at my eyes, I really shouldn't have just left like that, but I couldn't make myself *say it*, and I didn't want to break down into tears in front of Anna.

I'm exhausted, and really all I want to do is curl up and sleep for a year, but... I can't. Not even hyperbolically.

No, no, I have too much to do. I can't make myself talk about Harris and what he did right now, but... It's only a matter of time before he destroys the evidence. I have to *go back and get it* before he does- if it's not already too late.

This is the only chance I have to *maybe* get justice for my parents. I have to take it, and just... hope Anna doesn't mind too much.

I'll just... be exhausted for the next month at this rate, with how much is happening today. I can deal with it.

And... hopefully I'll be composed enough when I get back to actually explain what's going on to Anna. Hopefully.

Despite being mostly out of sight in the backyard, I glance around furtively, to make absolutely certain no one is watching before I teleport out, reappearing on the doorstep of my longtime friend Morgan Peters.

I quickly knock on the door, and it's opened almost immediately by Morgan's girlfriend- my only other friend- Hannah Spencer, blowing a bubble with the gum she's almost perpetually chewing, and it pops when she sees me there.

"Issac!?" She grabs my shoulders and yanks me inside, kicking the door shut behind us. "Dude, you're supposed to be like, gone! It's not like Mor's is much safer than the school for you!"

I sigh, brushing her hands off my shoulders. "I take it then," I say slowly. "That you've already spoken with my siblings?"

Hannah nods quickly, her wild blue and pink dyed curls bouncing as she does. "Yeah! Al stopped back by here on her way back to your Gran's!" She smacks my shoulder lightly. "So, what are you doing here, you Dingbat!?"

Morgan pokes her head into the room, seeming half made up to go somewhere, her hair natural in its thick black coils spilling out of an aqua blue loose knit beanie, with jeans and white doc martins, but just a white camisole for her top, and her normal bright blue eye shadow that contrasts her brown skin only done on one eye, as with her Mascara and eyeliner.

"Issac? Get the hell out! You can't be here!"

I sigh, shaking my head. "It's not like I'm asking to stay here. I'm not brainless, Morgan."

"No," Hannah giggles, elbowing me. "You're just brain different. Soooo, why *are* you here, and where this girlfriend of yours that Al mentioned?"

I step away from her, groaning. "Argh. Lexi needs to not say that." I shake my head. "Anna isn't my girlfriend, and she's somewhere safe." Crossing my arms, I look up at the ceiling, focusing on the popcorn texture of it. "And... I need your help. I need to *get* the journal I found in his office before he has a chance to destroy it. It's the only chance I have to..."

"The only chance you have to put the bastard away!?" Morgan shouts from the next room over.

"Well, I was going to say get justice for my parents, but yes! Basically!"

Hannah glances toward Morgan, then back to me, exhaling hard. "You want to go back into *spitting distance* of the guy who murdered your folks. You want to go to his *office*..." She shakes her head. "I'm willing to help, but this seems dangerous. *Really* dangerous..."

Morgan comes into the room, buttoning up a shirt, and her makeup is done now. "Hannah's right, Issac. Are you sure it's worth it? I mean, Harris *sucks* and deserves to go down for this, but is it worth risking your own safety?"

"*Yes*," I say immediately. As long as my siblings are safe, I don't care. "This is my only chance, Morgan."

And answers as to *Why* might be there too. Why does he need *me*? Why did he kill my parents... I just... I don't *get it*. Harris is an atrocious person, but he's not the type to kill without motive.

"Besides, he *needs* me for some reason, so I should be fine." I add after a moment. "I know this is dangerous, but I wouldn't ever forgive myself if he just... got away with this."

She sighs, closing her eyes. "Fine. We'll help you sneak back into the school and keep Harris off you. It's going to make us miss our date, but it's fine. But for one of our best buds we can cancel *one* date." She pauses. "So are we going all, like, ninja and sneaking into the school, or what?"

I shoot a glare at her. "This is *serious*, Morgan. I was thinking Hannah could just *go in* like a student teacher can, and open a secret passage for us from the inside."

She sighs dramatically. "That's no fun."

I roll my eyes. "Be *serious*, Morgan..."

She gasps, clapping her hands to her face dramatically. "*Me*, not serious? No no, that *can't* be right."

Hannah rolls his eyes. "Ignore Mor. She's just being an adorable, yet annoying twit, as per usual."

Morgan hugs Hannah from behind, lifting her up off the ground. "I'll show you who's adorable yet annoying!" She stumbles backward, and both girls fall to the floor, giggling.

I clear my throat. "Girls? There's a bit of a hurry. I'm worried he might destroy evidence, remember?"

They sit up, and Hannah smiles sheepishly. "Sorry, Issac. Won't happen again." She clambers to her feet and pulls Morgan up with her.

"Sorry," Morgan says quietly. "But you *know* I'm taking you seriously, right? I just don't like things getting dark and depressing, so I'm just trying to keep the mood light." She sighs. "Just... Lighten up a little, Red."

"It's hard to 'lighten up' when a major authority figure in the area murdered my parents and still has ill intentions for me and the rest of my family! *And* one of the most dangerous Hunters in the world is currently after me!" I snap, but immediately regret it, wincing and staring at the floor.

I wonder if Harris is the one who killed Ilene's family too... The timing was close, just three weeks apart, and their killer was never found... Ah, I'll worry about that *later*. Later.

Morgan sighs, shaking her head. "You *do this.* You let yourself get wound up in this tight ball of stress, and never talk to anyone about it." She sighs. "Please tell me you're still seeing your therapist?"

I sigh. I haven't been. I stopped regularly seeing Dr. Everhart a year ago. I was *stable*, and so long as I stayed on my meds, she wasn't too worried. I was supposed to call her if anything *drastic* happened, and I suppose this qualifies but... ah, *later.*

"Not *currently*, no. But that doesn't matter at the moment, Morgan. We need to go."

She shakes her head, but we *do* leave, heading towards the school, and Hannah goes in ahead of us, opening up one of the three secret passages that leave school grounds for us.

Slipping in, I cast a basic invisibility spell to slip up to his office unnoticed, Hannah and Morgan hovering near the bottom of the stairs to stop anyone who might want to follow.

"I know it was around here somewhere..." I say quietly to myself, scanning the bookshelves for the small leather-bound journal.

Ah ha! There it is! I snatch it off the shelf, quickly opening it back up. I didn't get to look at very much before I had to leave before, but...

Has to look accidental

Those words jump out at me as I flip though, and I sigh. Of course, that makes sense. He designed the spell in a very specific way so it would look accidental. That's why he could sweep it under the rug so easily.

Powerful enough to kill at least three people (Non's life is irrelevant)

It's unsettling to read that; the confirmation that he *clearly* intended to kill Ethan and Lexi too. I don't know why he *needs* me, but he intended to kill my entire family.

I wonder if Dad sent them to Gran's that weekend because some part of him knew it wasn't *safe*...

And 'non's life is irrelevant' makes my stomach turn. I *hate* mages like Harris and his daughters. They just think that nons have little to no worth or importance. Why do they have these ludicrous ideas that they're *superior*? They tend to look down on wizards in the same vein, and it's *horrible*.

My mother mattered, no matter what he thinks.

Add Sensory Components [important!!!! Make it work!]

Of course. That would make the spell harder to cast for him, but it would make his accident plan more *believable* as an accident, since Dad was a Sensory Mage. Even just skimming this now, it's clear he put a lot of work and thought into this plan, but I can't figure out *why*. What was his motive?

Why does he need *me*?

I flip a few pages further and pause. The spellwork ended, but... he wrote about more than just the spell itself. *Ah.* That's... even better evidence than I thought.

It looks like these pages were stapled into the journal behind the spell later, being on a slightly different paper, and there's a date scrawled at the top of the page...

Four years ago? A full two years before my parents died?

Riley seems to trust me less every day. Stopped sharing his progress in his research with me at all last week. How much does he know? Does he suspect my intentions? I need to hasten my plans, lest he figure it out. It might ruin everything...

Does this have to do with my father's research after all? Figure *what* out?

Flipping quickly through the haphazard journal notes, it's sickening to even skim through his thought process leading him to a detailed plan of *murder.* Of my dad.

But he never wrote down his *motive.*

I stop, closing my eyes tight once I get to a page dated with my Parent's death. It only said one thing.

It's done. Just wait and see now.

"You almost done?"

I jump, fumbling the journal, barely catching it before it hits the floor, and I whirl around to face Morgan, blinking quickly at her. When did she come up the stairs?

"*Morgan,*" I gasp faintly. "I- Yeah, I have it, I just- Just give me a second more. I just need a second..."

I flip it back open, going to the next page. I have to know what the *hell* he wrote next. Why he did this...

THEY AREN'T DEAD. The kids weren't home. I have to completely readjust my plans.... Maybe I can work with this, though. Having to take care of the two of them would keep the eldest busy and distracted.

If he's too busy, he may not realize the truth, and I can kill all three of them once I have an heir lined up.

Along with that, there's some scribbled spell notes that seem to be based in Life Magic principles, but it's largely incoherent.

Until he has an *heir* lined up?... No... He doesn't think...?

My gaze flicks up to the Master's Staff mounted on the wall, and I exhale hard, turning the journal into tessence and storing it in my reserve.

Somehow, he's convinced that if he eliminates my family that Master's Cycle would restart. Yes, the Harris Family is one of the seven families left that have, on record, had a Master born into them more than once, same for my family, but... That can't be his *entire* motivation.

But it *would* explain why he probably killed Ilene's family, too. She was lucky, to be at a friend's house that day... I wonder how she's...

I shake off the thought. Not right now.

Why would he *think* that, though? It doesn't make any sense... Why would he think that the total eradication of my family would restart the cycle? And why does he need me?

"WELL HEADMASTER, I WAS THINKING THAT THE CLASS COULD GO ON A FIELD TRIP!" Hannah's loud voice reaches us from the staircase, and I exchange a look with Morgan, pulling her back against the wall by the door with me, turning us both 'invisible' by altering the way the light reflect, so it reflects like we aren't there at all. It's a more difficult to cast version of the spell, but harder to detect, and we *really* don't want Harris to notice us here.

The two come in, and before the door can close behind them, I bolt through it, pulling Morgan with me and quickly down the stairs.

"Oh my *god*," I look over my shoulder as we exit the staircase. "I- I, thank you Morgan. And thank Hannah for me. This-" I take the journal out of my reserve, gesturing with it. "*This* is all I need. It's in his own handwriting. I- I can't do anything with it just yet. Not until Anderson is taken care of, but once he is..." I hug it to my chest. "Well, I just need to go over Harris' head with this. It's basically a signed confession."

"I really hope that works out. He deserves to go down." Morgan smiles at me. "And you've gotta introduce me to that girl at some point."

"Oh, yeah, sure, soon as it's actually safe to be in Seattle." I chuckle slightly. "I need to get back to her, though. It's late, and she's probably mad at me for leaving..."

I hurry off school grounds, and teleport out, carefully aiming for Ms. Powel's backyard, and I try the door, but it's locked. So, I knock lightly on it three times, and she opens the door before I can knock twice more, like I was going to.

She pulls me into the kitchen and sits me down. "Tell me what happened, Issac. I've been worried sick!"

I sigh slightly, staring at the floor.

It takes more than an hour to get through the explanation of everything with Anna, and Anderson, and Harris, and she listens intently the entire time as I have to force the painful words out when I get to *Harris.*

Ms. Powel squeezes my hands gently. "Oh, Issac." She leans forward and kisses my forehead. "You've been having such a hard time."

"I'm okay now, really." I sigh. "Just... a bit tired." Or... completely exhausted. I'm not sure anymore. I don't feel like I could sleep, but I don't have the energy to do... anything for the rest of forever right now.

She smiles slightly at me, then ruffles my hair. "You get some rest here soon, dearie. It's nearly midnight, so I think the both of us should get some sleep..." She stands up, and smiles at me one last time before leaving the room.

After a moment, I get to my feet, going into the living room, smiling slightly at the sight of Anna asleep in the chair, curled up around the book, and I sit quietly down on the couch, being as quiet as I can to not wake her.

~ Twelve ~

Anna

September 25th, 2018

Issac is really quite adorable, curled up on the couch in a big t-shirt and pajama pants, sound asleep. It's strange, to actually see him so *calm*. It's in sharp contrast to how he usually seems perpetually stressed when he's awake.

This is actually the first time I've been up before him for any of the days we've slept in the same place. Frankly, I'm not entirely sure he's even been sleeping at the school. He keeps seeming to stay up later than me, and he's up before I am every day, and he seems constantly more exhausted.

He shifts slightly, and after a moment his eyes flutter open, revealing the vibrant purple irises that I now see are specked with blue this close up. He blinks sleepily a few times, and sits up, repressing a yawn and rubbing at his eyes.

"Morning sleepyhead." I chirp cheerfully and he jerks back in surprise, hitting his head on the wall behind the couch.

"Anna..." He laughs breathlessly. "Don't *do* that." He ducks his head, running his hands through his hair. "You startled me."

"You startle easy." I retort, which gets a chuckle from him before he sighs, crossing his arms over his chest and looking to the side.

"I suppose I do." He glances at the clock, then closes his eyes. "Ah, I overslept. I guess I was up *particularly* late, but still..."

"What?" I laugh. "Do you have somewhere to be this morning?"

"No," he breathes out slowly, shaking his head. "No, nothing like that. I just- I always get up at 5AM." He winces slightly. "Augh, and it's almost *nine*..."

"*Five?*" I laugh incredulously. "No wonder you're always up before me. That's way too early." I pull myself up off the floor, up onto the couch next to him. "But whatever floats your boat."

He looks away, his face flushing slightly. "Habit I formed back in high school. Just haven't broken it..."

I laugh lightly, turning to face him, sitting crossed legged on the couch. "Ah, see," I point at myself. "Homeschooled. I never had that kind of schedule. And I am *very* glad for that. Mornings are *evil*."

He smiles faintly, glancing sideways at me momentarily before returning his gaze back to the floor. "I think my mom insisted that we go to a regular, non-magical school. She was a Kindergarten teacher, and just wanted us to have a more normal- from her perspective- upbringing than we would in the magic community. So," He chuckles. "I was homeschooled in *Magic*. Basically, had school twice over because of it."

"Wow." I muffle a laugh into my hand. "Both your parents were teachers." I lean forwards towards him. "Explains why you're such a nerd."

"Hey-"

"It's a compliment coming from me, silly." I scoot a little closer while trying not to burst into giggles, putting a hand on his knee. "I *like* Nerds. Intelligent people just flatly more interesting." I pause, noticing him staring at my hand, and I start to retract it, remembering that he doesn't like being touched, but his hand jumps to mine, holding it there for a second, before he pulls it back, crossing his arms again, his face going red.

"I just- it's fine. It's..." He takes a deep breath, closing his eyes. "It's f-fine. It's actually fine..." He sounds surprised himself, and he smiles faintly.

Huh. Well, I guess he does seem like... more comfortable with the likes of Ms. Powel touching him, so maybe it's just about how close he is to someone. Maybe after our chat last night...

I'm too aware of my hand on his knee now though, and I pull it away, my face somewhat hot.

"So," I say quickly. "What's public school even li-"

He suddenly grabs my shoulders and jerks me down and off the couch, causing us both to tumble to the floor, accompanied by the sound of shattering glass and a loud bang.

"What the-" I start to say, until Issac throws his hands up and a shimmering blue field springs up in front of us, just in time for a bullet to slam into it- I realize that the first bang also probably a gunshot- and the magic barrier dissolves immediately as Issac gasps in pain, but it did stop the bullet, and he magically sweeps the couch to be in front of us.

"*Shit.*" He hisses through gritted teeth. "How did he find us *out here*? We teleported from the magic district, so he couldn't have traced it..."

"Is this the Hunter then?" I whisper, and he nods tensely, raising up slightly to try to peek over the top of the couch, but quickly jumps back down as another bullet soars our way.

"*Shit, shit-*" He swears, grabbing my wrist and pulling me toward the kitchen, keeping us close to the floor. He doesn't stand upright until we're in the kitchen and he's dragging me out the door.

The blue forcefield reappears around us as we run, and it's almost immediately hit by several more shots and Issac winces in clear pain as each one hits, but he keeps running, pulling me with him.

"*Well,*" Anderson's deep voice is immediately recognizable, and I throw a look over my shoulder to see him pursuing us, a gun in his hand. "You must be one *powerful* abomination to be able to hold out like that, boy."

Issac just saved my life. *Again.* But we're still not safe, with Anderson actively tailing us.

"I wonder how I managed to miss someone like you."

"Maybe because you're a blind, fool stuck in the dark ages." Issac hisses, before ripping us apart into tessence to teleport us like he did before. But he doesn't take us far, just around the corner.

It puts some distance between us and Anderson, but...

"Why didn't you take us further?" I say, struggling a bit to keep up with him, even as he's holding my hand very tightly. "We're hardly *safe* yet!"

"He can trace teleports! We have to lose him before we ca-" There's another bang, cutting Issac off as another bullet flies past his head, and he cries out in pain, slowing down for just a moment as he does. It *missed* him though, so what's wrong?

"Oh shit, *oh shit*," he mutters breathlessly, clutching his head with one hand. "A-Anna," he stammers, clearly in pain, though I'm not sure from what? "If- If I walk you through a spell, can you- can you try to cast it? It's n-not a difficult spell."

"I-" I glance over my shoulder, Anderson in sight again, before looking back to Issac. "I guess I can try? But why can't you just cast it?"

"I-" He takes a pained breath, "I'll explain later, once we're, uuh, relatively safe, a-alright?" He tightens his grip on my hand. "Please, just, close your eyes."

"You want me to close my eyes while we're running from a mad-man!?"

"Anna! Just *listen* to me! I know what I'm doing!" He squeezes my hand tightly. "I won't let- let you go. Y-You'll be fine. Close your eyes."

He seems sincere, and I lock gazes with him for a moment. I can tell he's dead serious. So I comply, closing my eyes and clinging to his hand for dear life.

"Okay, try to focus, on, uh, everything. I know you've read about Quintessence, try to picture it, and *focus* on that image in your mind's eye."

I squeeze my eyes shut tighter, trying to do as he asks, but it's *hard,* especially as we keep running and I'm breathing really hard, but I'm not going to give up so quickly.

Focus. Quintessence is like... life energy, right? All living things contain *tessence* within themselves, that book said. So maybe I can try focusing on me and Issac to find it.

Life energy... an *explosion* of color spreads across my black field of view, outlining the world in hazy purple light, with me and Issac being *bright* silhouettes of people, though Issac is *much* bright than me. Like this I can also see that, ah, *yikes,* I seem to be leaving a *trail* of the light behind me as I run. That's not great, if Anderson might be able to see this.

"Do you see him behind us, Anna?" Issac murmurs, and now that he says that, I *do* notice a blob of light behind us, but a lot less distinct than we are, and very fuzzy around the edges, like it's *fizzing* or something, for how little sense that makes even to me.

"Yeah, I see it."

"Good," I can hear the pained smile in his voice. "Now point your free hand, palm open, back at him." I immediately do so, and he continues. "Do you sense the tessence in your hand? It should seem more defined if you focus on it."

"Mmhm." I nod, and I have to resist the urge to flex my fingers to watch it move.

"O-Okay, focus on- on it, it's an extension of *you.* As a mage your t-tessence is inherently part of you and you should be able to move it like you would a part of your body. Will it out towards him."

I try to take a deep breath, even as I'm breathing really hard from the prolonged running, and I do as he says, willing it out, and it stretches out, like a really long arm made of tessence. It makes me slightly dizzy for it to leave my body like this, as it sheds tessence *quickly* once out of my body, making *my* light much dimmer. The dizzy feeling doesn't last though, as warm feeling starting from Issac's hand floods my whole body and our lights seem to mingle together.

"Grab his- his tessence, and just *pull it away from him.*"

I comply at once, partially pulling it away from him, and I hear Anderson audibly gasp in pain, and his light nearly slowing to a stop, letting us put some more distance between us and him.

"Anna, let go now!"

I start to let go, the tessence quickly dissipating as my focus slips, but maybe it was a second too late, since there's a flash, blinding this weird second sight as the line of tessence still tied next to me is burned off, if burning could be ice cold slamming into and down my arm, like arctic water in my veins, and it's *intensely* painful. I instinctively slow down as the pain hits me and makes my head spin.

Issac continues to drag me along, despite my feet's unwillingness to move. "We have to keep moving!"

"What..." I blink several times, and look over my shoulder where Anderson is struggling to get to his feet. "What just happened? That- that *hurt-*"

"You'll be fine!" He gasps. "I- I think we've put enough distance!"

I look over my shoulder again, and he's still on his knees behind us, but he has his gun up and leveled at us.

"Issac, he's going to shoo-" The sound of the gun firing cuts me off, but Issac throws his free hand back in the same moment, creating another forcefield and seeming to brace for impact, but the bullet dissolves it immediately not even seeming to *slow* down. Then it stops in midair and turns around *just* before it would have hit Issac, and he teleports us away without warning.

We land back in Seattle, at a park, and Issac almost instantly hits the ground, falling to his knees and letting out a pained groan. He's breathing really heavily, but... I guess I am too.

"We *need* to find somewhere safe, if just for a day or two. I'm in no state to face him again. We need to..." He leans forward on his knees, closing his eyes tight. "We need to keep moving, though. He'll get to the spot we teleported from soon enough. You aren't trailing now, so if we just... just keep moving, we should be safe for a bit..."

"What..." I crouch down next to him. "What *was* that? Are you okay?" I shiver, still cold from whatever it was he did to *me*. "Issac?"

He reopens his eyes, and they're glowing *fiercely*, the violet light visible even in broad daylight like this. He gives me a pained smile. "Hunters have a number of abilities to harm magic users." He runs a hand through his hair, visibly shaking a little. "What hit *you* was known as quintessence blocking. He basically just temporarily cut off your access to your own tessence. *Immensely* Painful but just momentary. No lasting effects." He winces. "I got hit *twice* by a weakened version of something known as Spellburn." He struggles to his feet with a pained sound. "If either of those near misses hit me, they would have probably knocked me out, and badly, *badly* hurt me magically, in- in addition to being, you know, *shot...*"

I blink a few times, offering my arm for support, as he looks *really* unsteady on his feet. "How badly are you hurt *now*?"

"Ah," he sighs, stepping close to me to accept my help staying upright, leaning on my arm. "I'll be fine by tomorrow. It's just... having your tessence forcibly burned off like that, even in a more limited degree than he *wanted* it to be... it's... not pleasant. And tessence is life energy for *mages* to a much more significant degree than it is for others, so it's... ah. Just, I'm not feeling great..."

"... Well, okay, this park isn't actually that far from my apartment with Lorrie, if we just need somewhere to go *right now*."

He laughs weakly. "Oh, oh, the *audacity* of that... but it... it might actually work. He knows exactly who *you* are, and he knows that we know that, so he- he wouldn't expect us to go there. Could work, for today, at least..."

It's a little awkward to walk, half supporting his weight, since he's a few inches taller than me, but I'm not going to let him fall. It's really clear he's in *a lot* of pain, but we make it to my apartment, and he staggers away to fall onto the couch once we're in the door.

I return the spare key to its hiding place, since my normal key got left behind with all my stuff, then close and lock the door before joining him on the couch.

That was a hell of a way to start the day.

~ Thirteen ~

Issac
September 25th, 2018

I pull my knees up to my chest, sitting on Anna's bed while she talks to a hysterical sounding Lorraine out in the living room. She's giving excuses for her absence, and for why she's just going to be staying in her room for today.

I'm not really listening to what they're saying out there though, as it's hard to process *words* with how badly my head is spinning, and I feel *nauseous.* But at least it doesn't *hurt* as badly, so long as I hold still.

I can barely think though, with black spots floating about my vision, and sharp little stabs of pain from even *breathing.* I know it'd be even *worse* if I were wearing my binder, so I guess I should be grateful I'm not, but in the same breath... I'm *beyond* uncomfortable without it, with Anna having spent so much time around me without it...

It's not like I have any other options right now. We had to run away from Ms. Powel's in our pajamas, without any of our stuff. Ah, I'm going to have to pay to replace her window later, if she'll let me...

I take a deep breath, then immediately have to stop myself from crying out in pain, covering my mouth with my hands.

It's a miracle that I managed to walk here, even with Anna's help.

Twice. Twice I got grazed by Spellburn. I *knew*, in theory, what Spellburn did, but no description in a book does this pain justice. This all-encompassing ache and pounding head... It's hard to even discern the various objects around Anna's room with this. Even so far as I can see, aside from the spots in my vision, I can't process any of it. It's all just... too much. It's hard to not just start crying... but that would hurt too, I'm sure.

Anna creeps back in, and I wince at the creaking of the door as she does. She leans back against the door, exhaling slowly. "Well, she's convinced I'm sick now, but she should be leaving us alone." She comes over and sits down next to me on the bed, forcing me to shift positions slightly, to a fresh wave of head spinning pain, and I almost feel like I'm going to be sick. "... Issac, are you okay?"

I shake my head slightly, causing the black spots in my vision to worsen briefly, and I rest my chin on my knees, hugging them tight.

"Is... Is there anything I can do to help?"

I smile slightly, and look sideways at her, meeting her gaze as she stares at me with her brow furrowed and a frown on his face.

"No, o-only thing to do is wait for it to fade, unless I went to the *hospital*, which, uh, *no*. I just- It's miserable in the meantime..."

"You..." She pauses. "You never explained exactly what *Spellburn* is. It seems really, *really* bad for this to be a *lesser* version of it..."

"Mm, well, Spellburn is the most powerful tool in a Hunter's arsenal, and Anderson is an extremely powerful Hunter..." I hug my knees even tighter, trying to focus on the pressure of that rather than the pained sickly feeling of Spellburn. "It, it... Spellburn, as implied by the name, burns away at the Te- the Quintessence reserve of the magic user it hit. The- the best way I have to put it is that... it- it literally damages the Reserve itself, hurting like *hell*, and that pain *lingers*, and damages the ability to cast spells effectively. I, ah, metaphorically speaking you could picture a tessence reserve as a bag full of liquid, and Spellburn is boiling that liquid to burn a hole in that bag. And that bag is a part of your body that you can feel. It... It eventually it heals itself. It's also a little more severe for Mages than it is for Wizards, because Mages have *sources*, meaning our tessence ends up being a lot more integral to our health than it is for say, Wizards, which makes all the symptoms *worse*."

"That... That sounds painful, I guess, but... you weren't hit?"

"Spellburn is always... attached to a physical attack, but not so... strictly. It's like an aura around it. That first near miss was close enough that you could say I was... singed, metaphorically. It's why I didn't trust myself to jerk his native tessence to stop him. As for the second one..." I sigh, closing my eyes. "I had to take part of it intentionally to get out of there. I couldn't make a strong enough shield to block it again, so I just had to forcibly turn it away, which required magically going around the Spellburn, which, again, metaphorically singed me. And even just... partial affects are... not... good..." I lay back on the bed, wincing slightly as I do, and stare up at her ceiling, dotted with glow in the dark stars. "We can't stay here long."

"Issac, you're *really* hurt. We have to stay here. You can barely walk. You're *wincing* every time you move."

I close my eyes again, sighing. "I know, but he *will* find us again if we stay here too long. Refuge in audacity won't last long. Not if he managed to track us out to Issaquah..."

She sighs, and I feel her shift on the bed. "This is *crazy*. I feel like my whole like has just been *uprooted*. Like I have no control anymore." She sniffles. "I don't like having no control."

"I haven't felt like I've had any control over my life since my parents died." I mumble, opening my eyes to stare up at the ceiling, my eyes automatically trying to find patterns in the uneven paint job.

"Issac..." She mumbles, and I jerk to sitting, ignoring the sharp pain shooting through me as I do, and look wide-eyed at her.

"I-I'm sorry- I shouldn't have said that!" It's so hard to figure out when it's appropriate to try to *relate* versus when doing that is just *making it about you*, but I should have *known* that *that* wasn't good to say...

"No, no... Issac... it's fine. I just... I can't imagine being in your place... I mean... why? You were just *eighteen*, right? Why not your Grandmother?"

"She's a Non." I breathe out, splaying my fingers across my knees. "She's wonderful, but under mage law, Nons aren't allowed to be the Only guardians to mages. It's a safety issue, should something magical happen."

"So... you were left to do it. That can't have been easy."

I laugh bitterly, ignoring the ache from that, and look sideways at her. "You don't even know that half of it. Lexi was only twelve, and she was *shattered* by our parent's death, while Ethan for a solid year thought I didn't care, and hated me for it, while in reality I just- I couldn't afford to let myself grieve. I-I had to be there for *them*..."

My entire life metaphorically blew up. Some of it was self inflicted, but I really couldn't... It was just so much change so fast and I was so easily upset by everything for a solid half a year before I pulled myself together. I'm just lucky I came out of that without Lexi resenting me, and with Morgan and Hannah still as my friends.

Ethan... it's been more difficult with, but at least he doesn't hate me. I'm sure Evan does at this point...

Anna is silent for several minutes. "This isn't right." She finally says, raising her voice slightly, then sends a worried glance at the door, and continuing at a lower volume. "We can't let *either* of these bastards steal control of our lives like this. Harris or Anderson. There has to be something we can do."

"Once Anderson is caught and made to forget about us, I have evidence against Harris. We just have to *wait...*"

"That'll take too long!" She snaps quietly. "There's got to be *something* we can do! Isn't there some way we could, I don't know, speed the process up?"

"Uh, maybe, in theory-"

"Well, what's stopping us?" She cuts across me, and I press on like she hadn't said anything.

"*Iiiiiiif* one of the most powerful magical men in this state- Ah, no, *on this side of the country* wasn't out for my blood."

"Oh." She sighs. "Right..."

We both fall silent for a few more minutes, and I close my eyes, breathing slowly, as I try to relax and will the pain away. I wish I had something better to offer her on this, but... I'm at a loss. I have *no idea* what we can do. If Anderson is skilled enough to track us out to Issaquah, then... I don't know what options we *have.* Leave the *State?* I couldn't force that on Anna...

"Can't we try to get him in trouble with the *regular* police?" Anna says suddenly, and my eyes shoot open. "I mean, I'm no fan of the police, but..."

"You want to get him *arrested?*" I say incredulously. "That's-" I shake my head, ignoring the spinning from that. "I would have never thought of that."

"Well, I mean, it shouldn't be *that* hard. The guy just proved he was willing to *shoot* at us on a residential street." She chuckles. "If we just, I don't know, lead him to someplace that has cops there while he's trying to attack us..."

"That could actually work. And wouldn't just solve our problem, but a major problem for the *entire Washington Magical Community...* The entire Pacific Northwest, honestly..."

"So, we're going to do it?"

"*Later.* We're going to need help with that, and I really probably should rest first. I'm in no state to be anywhere near him..."

"Mm, who exactly is going to help us? Your siblings?"

I push myself back to sitting, holding my breath for a moment until my head stops spinning from the movement. "No, no. Absolutely *not.* I'm not putting them into the line of fire. I... was thinking of two girls who might just be crazy enough to go along with it."

Anna shoots me a look, and I grin at her. Well, Morgan *did* want to meet her.

"We just have to wait for Lorrie to leave for class, and I'll call them..."

It's about an hour and a half later that we're back in the living room, waiting for them. I'm sitting cross-legged on the couch, my arms crossed and staring up at the ceiling. I still feel horrible, but I'm a little giddy at this point. This idea is *audacious* to say the least, but it really could work. And getting Anderson arrested by Non Authorities would eliminate him as a threat to Magic Users in a much more permanent way than anything the Magic Enforcers can do...

Anna flops onto the couch next to me with a heavy sigh. "Are you going to tell me anything about these two or what?"

"I... don't really know how to describe them." I say softly, not taking my eyes off the ceiling. "They're... a lot, but they're, uhh, the only friends I've got, a-aside from you."

She pulls her feet up onto the couch and sighs hard. "Well, I wouldn't be so frustrated if they weren't *late.* You said they'd be here like, twenty minutes ago."

"Well," I shrug. "It's not like it's my fault that they're late." I glance to the door. I am more or less used to it from them. They're often late. But Anna has never met the two of them.

"Well, you're just lucky Lorrie's going to be gone for a couple more hours."

"Anna," I sigh, gingerly shifting position to look at her. "Luck has nothing to do with it. Me and Lorrie are on the *exact* same track in college, so we share most of our classes. I know her schedule. *I'm* supposed to be in class right now." I close my eyes, exhaling hard... which I immediately regret as it aches, and I whimper slightly.

"... Issac?"

I hate being off schedule, and that's getting to me nearly as much as the stress of the situation itself. At least- At least things can get back to some sense of normality if this idea pans out. I could go home, go back to class...

God above, I don't know if I could even easily go back to my routine. This is such a *dramatic* interruption that I just feel as if I'm... metaphorically unmoored. It's going to take time to find a sense of *stability* again, once this is all over...

I'm so *tired.*

"Issac, are you okay?"

I startle slightly, looking at her. "Oh. I- Y-Yeah, I'm fine. Sorry. I just- I guess I'm just... tired..."

She offers a hand to me silently, and I stare at it for a moment, and smile slightly before taking it. She squeezes my hand slightly.

"Hey, it's okay if you're *not*; you know that, right? You're *hurt*. And like... There's that whole *thing* with Harris having murdered your parents..."

"Now," I force a laugh. "Which one of us is studying psychology again?" I jest, but she saw right through me. I do have a tendency to just... internalize when I'm suffering and try not to let it show. I've clashed with Dr. Everhart over that *a lot* in the past. I didn't even *realize* I was doing it now though...

"You're just... you're *worrying* me, Issac. I know you're hurt, but I don't know, you just seem so... closed off. Like... Is there anything I can do to help? Is there anything I *need* to do? I've- I've noticed you don't much like eye contact, and we've covered the touching thing, and you seem in general really... *nervous*, but..."

I blink a few times. She's very observant... for someone who managed to miss the trans flag hanging above my bed when we were in my bedroom. Or the Bi flag on the back of my door.

"... Ah, well..." I sigh softly. "Nervous is definitely right. I have an anxiety disorder." I start tapping my fingers on the couch beside me, staring up at the ceiling again. "And, I- uhm, I'm actually, well. I'm *autistic*, actually."

"Oh, you must be high func-"

"Do NOT finish that thought, oh my god." I cut her off, raising my voice slightly. "Functioning labels are *bullshit* and dehumanizing. *Yes*, I'm mostly self-sufficient without help, but that's after years of therapy to get me good coping skills and cultivating an environment where the people- people around me know my, uh, *quirks* let's say." I take a shaky breath.

"And *even still*, I sometimes go non-verbal when under stress, I'm really sensitive to sound and to a lesser extent light, and I have to live by really strict routines to feel at all secure... So just, don't, with functioning labels. Also, those completely disregard the other side of it; of the things that I would say are *good*. It's- It's just a different neurotype with different needs, not some scary thing that hurts the person with it like- like autism is just part of who an autistic person *is*..." I trail off realizing I rambled a little bit, and stare down at the floor. "Sorry. I just- that *really* bothers me..."

She's quiet for a moment. "No, no, it's fine. I guess I have my own blind spots, huh? Thank you, for telling me. I- I want to be able to help, if there *are* any issues, so... you know, thanks for telling me."

Before I can respond grateful in kind that she's actually being pretty cool about it, there are several impatient knocks on the door, and Anna jumps to her feet, and practically flies across the room to open the door, where Hannah and Morgan are standing. Hannah has a bag slung over her shoulder, and Morgan was poised to knock again.

"Sorry about the delay," Hannah says, skipping into the room, tossing the bag next to me on the couch. "But you said you had to leave your hiding place in a *hurry*, so I figured you weren't able to grab any of your stuff."

"*So*," Morgan continues Hannah's thought. "We took the liberty of stopping off at your house to grab some of your things. Because we're awesome friends like that." She grabs my forearms and pulls me to my feet, and I ignore the way it makes my stomach lurch from pain and just force a smile at her. "Now go change out of your PJs, you dork."

I smile sheepishly at her, and pick up the bag from the couch, trying to remain steady on my feet so I don't worry them. "Thank you."

"So, uh, you two seem to be awesome friends, but like..." Anna looks between Morgan and Hannah. "Why'd that take so long to do? His house isn't *that* far away."

"Traffic was murder, let me tell you." Morgan laughs. "I bet you've just been spoiled by Issac. F-Y-I, most mages aren't like super casters who can teleport with little tess usage."

"Oh, come on!" I say, my face heating up slightly. "I just developed a more efficient spell! It's not really that extraordinary." I huff, crossing my arms. "And I *offered* to teach it to you two. As I *recall*, you said something along the lines of '*Hannah and I don't have time for your nerd stuff, dork,*' so don't give me that nonsense..."

"Just go get dressed, dork." Morgan rolls her eyes, and gently shoves my shoulder... and I almost fall over from the gentle push, and I go as quickly as I can manage to the bathroom before she can ask why I'm so unsteady.

I have to take a moment for the intense dizziness to fade once I'm inside, leaning back against the door and breathing deeply. It's okay. I'm okay. Just... get dressed.

God, I hope they grabbed a binder... And a hat, for that matter. I haven't had my beanie since Ms. Powel took it off yesterday. I feel weird without it.

... They didn't disappoint. I dress as quickly as I can manage, being *very* ginger with the binder because I can just tell it's going to hurt with spellburn, given that *breathing* hurts a little bit... But I'm dressed, and I'm straightening my shirt collar over my sweater as I walk back out and resume my place on the couch.

"She's *really* pretty," Hannah says in a stage whisper to me, and I roll my eyes. "How did you get a prettier girlfriend than me?"

"Okay, *one*, Anna is not my girlfriend." I say sharply, and I feel my face getting hot.

I'm getting really tired of that. If... if partially because it... reminds me a little too much of when they did the exact same thing with Evan. They realize it before me *one time* and think they can joke about it for the rest of eternity...

"And *two*," I force myself to continue. "*Hannah*, your girlfriend is *right there*."

"No, no, I'll give that to her." Morgan grins. "I'd say she's prettier than me. If you *don't* date her, I might dump Hannah to snatch her up."

"You love me, and you know it." Hannah responds, and Morgan sticks her tongue out at her. "In all *seriousness* though," Hannah laughs faintly. "I'm really glad to meet you,

Anna. I'm glad Issac has another friend. Ever since he and Ev-
"

I shoot her a look, and she pauses, laughing nervously.

"E-Ever since high school, he's really only had us. I worry about him."

I didn't, ah, *mention* Evan last night to Anna, having said I hadn't made any friends since I met Morgan in the first grade... but that wasn't *quite* true. I just... don't... like to think about Evan. I always feel bad about how... abruptly I ended things... Though the way my friends keep *acting* makes it hard to not think about...

Ah, it's not important right now. It's not important. There's no need to dwell on it. Not now.

"... Yeah, he told me he hadn't made any real friends since the first grade?" Anna says quietly. "I guess he's known you two for a while?"

"I've known this boy since *kindergarten*, Anna. Oh, the *stories I could tell*." She giggles, throwing an arm around my shoulders. "Mormor is the one who met him in the first grade."

Morgan flashes a peace sign, sticking her tongue out. "He couldn't get rid of us if he tried."

"I'd shove the both of you off the couch right now if I could." I mutter under my breath.

"You can't?" Hannah tilts her head to the side. "I mean, god, I *know* if you could, you would've done so by now, but... what's up?"

"Spellburn..." I answer in just one word, and both girls wince.

"*Ooooouch.*" Morgan shakes her head. "I've heard that, you know, sucks a lot. Are you okay?"

I nod silently, pulling my feet up onto the couch and hugging my legs. I don't want them to worry too much, but I can't *lie* to them about it. "... I'm okay. I just... need time to recover. It's... painful, but I'm fine..."

I see Anna shoot me a *look* out of the corner of my eye. She knows just *how* painful this is, at least more than I'm letting on right now, but I just have to hope she doesn't say anything.

"Are you... like, did you get hurt in any other way?"

"No, he- Anderson didn't actually hit either of us." Anna says quietly. "Issac just- he just got grazed by the Spellburn thing. Uh, twice."

"*Twice?*" Hannah echoes, turning her wide-eyed gaze back to me. "Are you *sure* you're okay?"

"It was just grazing," I respond, staring down at the floor. "I'm okay, promise."

"That's... that's still a really close call. I- Come stay with us at Mor's house. You'll be safe from him in the Magic District at least."

"And bring Harris down on the two of you?" I don't look up from the floor. I'm putting them in enough danger by asking them to be *here*. I won't let Harris hurt them too. *Especially* since they both work for the school. "*Not a chance.* Besides, Anna actually had an idea."

~ Fourteen ~

Anna
September 25th, 2018

Both of Issac's friends are staring at me expectantly, and I laugh nervously, pulling on my ponytail. "Uhm, well," I bite my lip. "See, I was thinking that if magical authorities can't safely catch him anytime or, or at least not soon *enough*, then we could, well, get him in trouble with the *police*. He showed that he was more than willing to shoot at us in broad daylight in a residential area, so..."

The girl with the messy shoulder length pink and blue hair- Hannah, I guess- tilts her head to the side, and shifts on the couch to face me more than Issac. "So, you... *want* him to shoot at you in a public place, to get him *arrested*?"

"Uh, don't much like it being put that way, but yes," I say slowly. "It's not like I want to be shot at, but we have to do *something*."

"You two come into this because we need you to *stop* him from killing us." Issac speaks up, staring at his intertwined hands. "*Without* him noticing you."

"Easier said than done, Issac," the black girl dressed in all blue- Morgan I suppose- mutters, sliding down in her seat. "Anderson is like... stupidly dangerous."

"Oh, trust me I'm *well* acquainted with *that!*" Issac looks up at her, his voice pitching up, and he looks a little pained saying it. "But Anna is right. We have to do *something.* He's *too* dangerous, and inevitably going to find us again before the enforcers succeed in a capture and memory wipe. And I *really* don't want him to ambush us like that again..."

Issac shudders, and I frown at him. He really understated how much this *hurts* for him to his friends. He's... really closed off. For what he did tell me, he... didn't actually comment on the fact that he *does that.* And I'm worried about it.

"I..." Hannah sits up straight. "MorMor, forecast calls for *heavy* rain tomorrow. I think we can do this."

Morgan jumps up at that, suddenly grinning and balancing on the balls of her feet. "Ohhhh! It *is* supposed to rain real hard, isn't it! That's *perfect.* That bastard is going *down.*"

"Uh, good, but... why... does rain... in *Seattle* change your tune so quickly?" I ask, and both girls burst into giggles.

"Morgan is a Water mage." Issac answers for them. "Rain means she's very much in her element."

"What he said." Morgan says once her giggles quiet. "I *can* make water in a pinch, but it's *so much better* when nature does it for me."

"I... guess that makes sense. So now we just need to figure out *where.* Ideally somewhere the police would already be, or would get to quickly... but... like, he wouldn't expect them there?"

"Well, there's two cops who go Sal's for lunch basically every day. They're cool, for *cops* at least. And really predictable. So, like," She crosses her arms. "If the two of you went to hang at Sal's Diner for a while, the bastard will probably show up, and get his ass arrested." She flashes a lazy smile at Issac. "I can pretend to be third wheeling a date, and Hannah can watch for the guy?"

"Ah-" Issac sighs, crossing his arms. "*Minus the date thing*, yes, that works well."

Hannah shifts slightly to lean close to Issac, though she doesn't *touch* him. "Are you going to be okay by tomorrow, though? We're covering spellburn in my general education class right now, and it's *nasty*... I know, I *know* you were just grazed... but *twice*..."

"Uh..." He smiles faintly at her. "Better enough."

After a few more minutes of chitchat, the two girls leave, Morgan blowing a kiss at me as she goes, and Hannah huffing and grabbing her by the elbow to drag her out in response.

"... Your friends are kinda weird, Issac." I smile. "But I like them. They seem nice."

He laughs weakly, leaning forward with his elbows on his knees and his head in his hands. "They've been my friends most of my life. I probably couldn't lose them if I tried. I really don't like dragging them into this, but they're the only people I have to turn to..."

"They seem like good friends... Uh, but... why did you downplay how much you're hurting? I can't imagine that they'd *mind*..."

"*Mind?* No, no. They wouldn't mind. *Worry incessantly, though?* Yeah, they'd do that." He sighs. "They've... known me through some... hard times, so they tend to be a little..." He twirls his hand in the air. "*Protective*, let's say... I just, I don't want to make them worry over something that's really not a big deal, even if it hurts a lot *now*..."

Hard times? I wonder if he means when his parents died... or if there's *more*... But it's not my business to pry into it. If he wanted me to know, he'd have been more specific.

"Alright, just... don't do that to me, okay?"

"... I'll try not to," is his response, and that's... not very reassuring.

I stand up and offer him a hand to help him up as well, and he stares at it blankly for a moment, before taking it and pulling himself to his feet. He has to steady himself once he's standing, holding himself up on my forearm for a moment, but... he seems steadier than he was walking here from the park, so maybe he's getting better already...

I watch him carefully as he walks back to my room, ready to help him in an instant if he needs it, but he makes it to my door, bracing himself against it for a moment, and I hear him whimper slightly, so I *know* he's in pain... but I don't know what to do about it.

"Do you need h-"

"No- *no*." He cuts me off, shaking his head quickly, and opening the door. "I- I'm alright, but thank you, Anna. I really do appreciate that you want to."

September 26th, 2018

We're sitting in a small diner that I'd never been to, though Issac seems to be familiar with it. It's a cute little place, with a lively and friendly atmosphere, the kind of diner you don't see much anymore. The place *almost* distracts me from the fact that Issac still looks drained even after a good night's sleep.

I want to ask if he's okay, but previous experience has already very thoroughly demonstrated that he's probably going to say that he's *fine*, even if he's not. It's so stupid, like he's got a chip on his shoulder about people wanting to help him.

"Issac!" The waitress- Lizzie, according to her name tag- walks up, a big grin on her face. "Haven't seen you here in a while! Where's Morgan?"

Issac laughs slightly. "Well, you know, college keeps me pretty busy. I can't come here every Friday like I used to do in High School anymore." He pauses and sighs. "As for *Morgan*, she's late. As per usual."

"Oh, that girl," Lizzie laughs. "So, who's your friend," She nods at me, waggling her eyebrows, her suggestion plainly clear.

"It's not like that." I say before Issac can react to her, and I watch the realization of what Lizzie *meant* play across his face, followed by him groaning and putting his head down.

"Why is that the first thing anyone ever goes too..."

"Well, other than Morgan, and occasionally Hannah, the only person you've ever come here with was your boyfriend, Issac. Is it really an *unreasonable* assumption?" She giggles.

"So, unless this third pretty gal friend of yours is *also* a Lesbian."

"Lesbian? No." I shake my head, trying not to laugh with her. I've never had a waitress be this genuinely friendly before. Is this what being a regular somewhere feels like? "*Bisexual*, yes. But it's really not like that. We're just friends."

I mean I wouldn't say *no*, if he asked or whatever. He's cute, and I like to give people a chance, though it's not like I, you know, *like him* that way... *No...*

She whistles. "Issac, you sure do love your women loving women friends." She takes a notepad and pen out of her apron pocket. "So, could I start you two off with drinks while you wait for Morgan to get her lazy butt here?"

"Just a water for me, please." Issac answers quietly, and she pivots to me.

"And for you, ah, well I haven't caught your name yet, little miss?"

"The same, and I'm Anna. It's nice to meet you, Lizzie." She nods her head and skips off towards the kitchen. "... You have the weirdest friends, Issac."

"Huh, Lizzie- oh, no." He sits back up, shaking his head. "I don't know her outside this building. I just, I used to come here to study after school every Friday, so all staff from back then knows me."

"From what she said it wasn't just *studying* that you were here to do, given that you came-"

"No! No, nope! We are *not talking* about that!"

"Bad break up then?" I ask quietly. I've never had a serious relationship because I travelled so much, but I had several less serious things. Nothing that would make me react like *that*. Worst I had was Brad cheating on me, but I shoved him off his surfboard and I was happy after that. It's no big deal, so I... don't know how that goes.

"Uh, not exactly." He says, looking away. "I just... I don't want to talk about it."

"Sorry." I murmur. I should have known better than to pry, but *still*. Issac seems to have some tragic backstory shit going on. Bad breakup, *personal stuff* that affected his grades in high school, the whole thing with Harris and his parents...

He really, *really* can't have had a nice life up to now.

The tension is cut by Morgan coming in, dripping wet from the pouring rain outside, and she dashes over to our table, laughing. She pulls out a chair, spinning it around backward to sit down, leaning forward on the back of the chair. "Yo! Sorry for the delay. Hannah doesn't like driving in the rain, so she drove like a grandma over here. Stupid slow and whatnot."

"Why didn't *you* just drive?" Issac leans forward on the table, quirking an eyebrow at her. "Oh wait, that's right, it's because you *still* don't have your license."

"That's rich coming from someone who walks everywhere *despite having his license and a car.*"

"I *can* drive; I just *chose* not to because I don't like it. *You* on the other hand make your girlfriend be your chauffeur."

"Oh, shove it." Morgan laughs. "So, what have you two been chatting about while waiting for me?"

"Oh, just how all of Issac's friends are queer ladies." I smirk, and Issac groans, putting his head back down on the table.

Morgan blinks a few times. "Oh, you're queer?"

"Mmhm." I nod. "Hella Bi."

She mock sighs in relief. "*Phew*, for a second there I was worried I couldn't play matchmaker with you and Issac." She giggles. "Don't go stealing my lady though."

Lizzie skips up to the table again before I can respond, two glasses of water in hand that she sits down in front of me and Issac. "Hi Morgan. I'd ask if you want a water too, but it seems like you have plenty."

"Just," Morgan snickers. "Just get me my usual, Lizzie." She nods and walks away from the table.

Morgan suddenly looks off toward the door, and grins, watching two damp looking uniformed police officers walk in. "That's Georgie and Mike. They're cool, for like... cops. And cops are *exactly* what we need right now." She snorts. "Not often that you'd catch me saying something like that, but whateves."

I nod slightly, pulling on my ponytail as I look over at them. "At least they're here now."

"Well, yeah," Morgan shrugs. "I knew they would be. So, now we just wait for Anderson to come here after you. You guys walked here, right?"

I nod slightly. "Yeah, but we had an *umbrella,* so we stayed mostly dry."

"Umbrellas are for the weak." She responds, smiling lazily. "So, it's only a matter of time now. Anderson is *notorious*, so there's no doubt he'll show up."

"How has he never been caught before this?" I ask, forcing myself to look away from the police to Morgan. "By like, you know the *police*? He clearly doesn't care about not getting caught, given yesterday…"

"You and I aren't exactly normal by mage standards." Issac says quietly, sitting back up. "*Most* mages are very insular in their community, and so crimes against them aren't exactly *noticed* by non-magical authorities. And in the same breath, they don't spend much time in places where the police would *be*. And," He sighs. "The police aren't actually very good at *solving* crimes. This *will* probably work, but only because they're *right here*."

"Yeah, the police suck, but we can use them now." Morgan pops her lips. "Hannah is hiding outside watching for Anderson."

Issac looks out towards the window, and his gaze seems to narrow in on something that I don't see immediately. "She's not hiding very *well*. I know she's better at the sound side of sensory magic, but visual illusions fall under her specialty too…"

Morgan shrugs, and says "She's got the music in her," in a deadpan voice, before bursting into a fit of giggles. "But seriously, she's hidden well enough. He'll be so focused on tracking the two of you that he won't even notice her." She pauses. "Probably. I hope."

Issac groans, putting his head down *again*. "I'm already regretting this plan."

"Issac, *relax*." Morgan pokes him with a straw wrapper. "She's going to be fine, and even if... she's more than willing to be in a little danger to help you. You're in *a lot* of danger, and we're not gonna let that stand if we *can* help, got it?"

He doesn't say anything, sighing softly, but he does sit up, turning his gaze up towards the ceiling.

Lizzie returns with a soda and a plate of cheese fries for Morgan, then flashes a smile at me and Issac. "Sorry you two, forgot to ask if you wanted anything to eat when I was here before. I was distracted by the puddle Morgan is leaving for me to clean up later."

"Oh," I laugh slightly. "It's fine. I, uh," I haven't even opened the menu in front of me... "I'll take the same thing as Morgan, actually."

Cheese fries are good, so it'll do. And I *am* hungry. I only had cold poptarts for breakfast.

"And how bout you, Issac? Your usual?"

Issac makes a face, ducking his head and breathing out hard. "I- I'll pass, but thank you."

Lizzie makes a puzzled noise, but nods and leaves us alone again. I *knew* he still wasn't feeling well. He didn't eat anything for breakfast, either. I don't... I don't know if it's a good idea for him to be here. He's really still not okay... I just... I want to be able to protect him, the way he's been protecting me. But what the *hell* am I supposed to do? He's like, some kind of magical expert and I'm *less than a beginner*.

So, I just have to do everything *non-magical* I can for him.

"Issac, you should probably eat something." I say softly, at the same time as Morgan shakes her head.

"Issac, if you're still not better, you should *go*. Hide in the bathroom and teleport out or whatever. If you can at least. This *is* dangerous."

"I'm *fine*." He says sharply, shooting a glare at Morgan. "A little lightheaded still, that's all. *And*," he glances at me. "I really *can't*. I'm too anxious about all-" He spins a hand in the air next to his face. "*This* to be able to stomach anything. So just- just let it go, please."

Anxious? I had no idea. He seemed tired, and a little easily flustered, but... How much is he burying right now? So anxious that he can't *eat*? He... he *really* shouldn't be here if he's feeling *that* bad...

"Issac..." I stare at him, and he closes his eyes, pulling down on his hat.

"Please, don't. *Don't*. I don't want this from you too. I'm *fine*. Please just, trust my judgement on my own wellbeing. *Please*, Anna."

Morgan scoffs, crossing her arms, but she doesn't say anything.

He... He said that they knew him through *hard times*, so are extra *protective*. I have to guess that he tried to stop people from wanting to help him *then* too, given Morgan's reaction, but... he's also a bad liar, and he seems sincere. I'm going to try to trust him, but... I'm still worried.

"Okay..." I say softly. "Uh, so, Morgan," I'm trying to change the subject. "What are you doing with your life?"

"Hm?" She tears her eyes away from Issac towards me. "Oh, I'm a graphic designer. I actually work for the school, helping with their stuff for like, you know, the stuff they sell in the school store. I actually helped with Issac's jacket." She nods at him, and I glance his way, actually looking closely at jacket he has on. It just looks like a letterman jacket, blue with while sleeves and white trim, and a white sun logo on the right chest and... Oh, it says *VA* there. Vincent's Academy.

Huh. I never would have noticed that. I guess even magic schools have merchandise with their logos and stuff. It's so... *normal*. I don't know what I expected- cloaks and pointy hats?- but it wasn't that.

"You have merch from a school you didn't attend?" I tease, and he sighs.

"I'm on the *board*, technically. It's not like I have no connection to the school."

"Not to mention he's been wearing their merch his whole life." Morgan adds. "Since his dad worked there and all."

"... Yes." Issac confirms that fact, and then the lights go out with a loud crack of thunder... though I never saw a flash of lightning.

Morgan jumps to her feet, everyone in the diner reacting in surprise, with some annoyed muttering about *thunderstorms* and *power outages*. "That's our warning." Morgan hisses. "You two do *nothing*. Except like, take cover from potential gunfire."

"We know." Issac responds flatly, drumming his fingers on the table, the faint glow of his eyes once again visible in the dark. Though Morgan's *aren't* glowing, so I guess that's just an *Issac* thing, and not a Mage thing.

Weird. But he's also the only Mage I've seen whose eyes are like, *totally* purple. From what he said that purple is a sign of being a mage, but what do his eyes being like *that* mean?

Also, they're ridiculously pretty, and I'd probably stare into them way more than normal if he wasn't so uncomfortable with eye contact.

Morgan creeps away from our table, closer to the door, and I have to squint to see her in the darkness.

Little dull bursts of blue light start appearing when Issac taps his fingers, and I lean across the table towards him and whisper, "What are you doing?"

"Making it so the table will... redirect bullets around us should we take shelter behind it. Subtle protection, basically. A little tricky, for it to not be obvious visible shielding, but I'm more than capable..."

One of the officers turns on a flashlight, brightening the room a bit, and Morgan seems to be gone entirely.

"... That's actually really smart, Issac. Keeping us from being shot in a way the officers won't notice."

"It's really nothing..." he mumbles, but I think I see his face darken slightly in the dim light from blushing, and I grin at him.

"Oh, hush it, just take the compliment, silly." I lean back away, smiling at him. "It's *fine* to let people compliment you. Even your trained mage friends seem to think you're incredible, given the way they talked about you yesterday. What did Morgan call you? A *super caster*? You really are amazing."

I wish he would just... accept that he's *exceptional*. I'm really starting to get a sense of who he is. He's kind, selfless, *really smart*, but he doesn't seem to think much of himself. He seems to prioritize himself after everyone else, and doesn't want to be a burden, despite... well, being *disabled*, given that he's autistic.

And despite the stupid circumstances, I really like spending time with hi... Shit, no. *No*, I am not catching feelings. No *way*. There's way too much baggage here. I'm *thrilled* to be his friend, but...

Issac suddenly grabs my arm, and yanks me out of my chair to the ground, just seconds before a shot is fired off at where I just was. I notice Anderson standing in the doorway, though if I wasn't expecting him, he'd have been hard to recognize in the low light, and with a scarf on covering part of his face.

Issac flips the table to protect us as several more rounds are fired off at us, almost being drowned out by thunder outside.

I peek around the table and see the two officers have their guns leveled at him, and he looks pained, but still has his own gun pointed firmly at me and Issac.

I flinch back and he fires again.

Next to me, Issac is sitting with his knees pulled up to his chest, his hands are over his ears, and he's muttering something under his breath.

I... I hope he's okay. He's... *sensitive to sound*. This must be really... *AH*. Shit, I *am* starting to *like* him. Not ideal. Really not ideal. Whatever. I'll deal with *that* later.

The lights flicker back on, and Issac visibly breathes out as he lowers his hands from his ears, and Morgan suddenly sits down between us, putting a finger to her lips.

She was there the *whole time*, got it.

One of the officers comes over, asking if we're okay, and if we knew the man. I admit that I know he's a local publisher, and that he approached me recently, but I turned it down, wanting to finish school before trying to publish anything. They take him away, arranging for us to come in to give more detailed statements later, and I sigh in relief as they go.

"Ah, that mess is *finally* over..."

Issac smiles faintly, nodding. "Yeah, finally. Now I have to deal with Ha..." He trails off, his gaze fixing on something outside, and I follow it to see... Carrie Harris, standing outside, with the rain blatantly missing her entirely, and a smirk on her face

~ Fifteen ~

Issac

September 26th, 2018

I slowly open my eyes, the blurred gold and blue surroundings that are *definitely* not Sal's diner, not really coming into focus quickly enough, and I groan weakly, blinking until all the bleariness is gone from my eyes.

And it almost feels like the whole world freezes for a moment when I see where I am, and I can't breathe, just frozen, magically bound to a chair... in *his* office.

Harris.

How did I...

The last thing I clearly remember was seeing Carrie Harris outside, flagrantly disregarding concealment laws. But how-

Ah. *Ah*, the Spellburn would have ripped down my defenses. I hadn't got them back up yet, so it would have been a lot easier for her to just magically daze me. It would explain why I *can't remember...*

Has- Has he decided he's going to kill me after all? That he doesn't need me for whatever reason? No... *no*. He would have already done it if that was his plan.

But still, still I don't- I don't know what he's planning. I don't know what he needs me *for*.

And- And what happened to the others? *Anna*? She doesn't even know how to defend herself. Morgan and Hannah could have gotten away, especially given the storm, but *Anna*- I- I couldn't keep her safe- I've never felt so useless in my life, and my head is spinning from lack of oxygen.

I manage a gasping breath, just as Harris steps around in front of me. "Well, nice to see you've finally woken, Issac." His voice is cold, and slick as oil.

"Godfrey Harris," I growl with as much venom as I can muster, momentarily locking eyes with him, and he sighs overdramatically, taking a seat at his desk, and weaving his hands together and leaning forwards towards me.

"Now, now, Issac," he draws out slowly. "No need to be so hostile. I want us to be *allies*. I'm not your enemy, and you're really being quite rash. Just like you were *quite rash* in leaving here the other day. You went and put yourself in danger by hurrying out so quickly. I heard he got you with Spellburn. I can *see* it still, the edges of your reserve look a little frayed. You must be so *tired*. And for *nothing*."

I *am* still a little lightheaded and tired, but it's not as bad as he seems to think it is, and I narrow my eyes at him. What's he playing at?

"You- You *murdered my parents!* Why would I be your *ally*?!" I strain slightly against the restraints, glaring at him. "You've done nothing but make me *miserable* since you *killed them!*"

"You'd want to be my ally because you want to *live*, at least for a few more years." He pauses, studying his fingernails. "Or if that doesn't convince you; I know how little value your own life used to have to you; how about wanting your pretty little friend *Anna* to live?"

I jerk back, rocking the chair slightly, and shut my eyes tight, trying to fight back tears. Oh god, no, no, *no*- Anna, not Anna- *Anna...* I- I couldn't- I couldn't keep her *safe...*

"What did you do to her?!" I snap furiously after a moment, glaring at him through teary eyes.

"Oh, you're *very* predictable, putting more value on her life than your own. But," He smiles. "Don't you worry, she's unharmed. And will remain so, assuming you *cooperate.*" His fake smile instantly drops to a scowl, and he stands back up, walking around to this side of the desk, and leaning back on it. "Now, Issac, you *took something of mine.* I'd like you to tell me where it is. We can do this the easy way, or the hard way." He studies his fingernails again. "Up to you. The girl's life is at stake. Keahi though, hm." He chuckles darkly. "What an *interesting lineage* she has. It would be such a shame to see the Nature Specialty die so soon after its return. And with no other relatives to pick it up, either. Such a *shame...* and it'd be on *your* head."

"What's even the point?" I mutter, staring at the wall past him. "You'll kill the both of us eventually, no matter what I do. I don't know what you *need* me for, but you're not getting it. I'm not going to help you with your bullshit plan to restart the Master's Cycle."

He laughs, and steps forward towards me, putting two fingers on my chin and forcing me to look at him, and I want to move away from the contact that metaphorically burns at my skin, but I can't. "Silly boy. I'm not going to kill you until I'm done with you, unless I absolutely have to. And I don't need *any* input from you for it." He steps back. "I mean I *could* kill you, but that would make things *much* more difficult."

More difficult? What is he- What-

So- So he needs me alive, but only insofar that my being dead would make whatever he's planning *more difficult*? What is he up to?

Why'd he want Dad's research? A small voice nags in my head, and I frown.

Harris... Harris needed *me specifically* alive. Not just any Riley. *Me.* He needs *me.* Or things would be more... *difficult...*

... That Life Magic spell... I tried to analyze it yesterday, but couldn't focus much on it. Best I could tell it had something to do with manipulating a *soul*, but it was... a mess. And *way* out of his specialty, so unless he intended to get Carrie to cast it...

He needed Dad's research to cross check his own theories about the Master, probably. He found *something,* and he wanted my father's *very* thorough research to confirm it. At least, that's my best guess.

- *those darkened skies will* **return** *one day* **with us** -

My eyes jump to the Master's staff mounted on the wall as time seems to slow to a crawl.

- *until such time that they were needed again* -

No... If... If nature mages have come back, then...

Until they were needed.

No, no... I shut my eyes tight, taking several deep breaths, trying to process this without getting overwhelmed.

Based on Vincent's writings, Nature Mages and the Master would return *together-* with some sort of implied doom, but putting *that* aside...

The Master should already be back, if Anna is a Nature Mage. I open my eyes again, not taking my eyes off the white wood staff with its purple crystal mounted behind Harris.

I'd always dismissed the possibility. Thought at times that it was most likely that I just... was a sensory mage like my father, since my first accidental spells were sensory, and it did always come kind of naturally to me, so there just must've been wrong with my *Icon*, but...

But I've never hit the metaphorical wall in *any* specialty that you're supposed to hit past a certain point, if it's not *your* specialty... But, I always just put that down to hard work, dedication, and more than a little bit of hyperfixation, since magic has been a special interest most of my life.

My reserve isn't any bigger or my refresh any faster than one might expect with a *bit* of natural strength and the amount of study and practice I've put in... but... Well, it *is* a large reserve, and I know my refresh is *fast*...

Could... could it be? Is that actually possible?

The Master's Staff. It's a magic item said to only work for the Master, and it increases their already incredible power tenfold. It's been here since Vincent founded the school. He mounted above the entryway door, and it stayed there until

Harris moved it here, just... waiting for the next Master to claim it.

"I'm not giving you your journal back." I growl, closing my eyes slowly. Will this work? I don't know... It's... It's... I'm still hard pressed to believe it, but it's worth a try. "If you couldn't find it in my mind, you won't find it at all." Little does he know it's in the room, still stored away in my tessence reserve. "You're going to pay for what you did."

His hands are suddenly around my throat, and I gasp for air before he lets go, taking a step back to compose himself. "*Well*," he growls through clenched teeth. "I guess the girl dies then."

"Good job dooming the whole world then." I say quietly, taking a chance on setting him off to *keep him here*. And keep Anna safe. "Nature magic would only be returning if it's *needed*."

I see the color drain out of his face, and I know my ploy *worked*, even before he glares at me. "What do you *know*, boy?"

"I..." I stare intently at the staff, biting my lip. "I know more than you, I'm sure. You're missing pieces, I can tell." I still am too, but I'm fairly certain I know more than him, given *that* reaction. "You don't know how they're connected. You've always scoffed at a whole half of my father's research, never realizing just how intertwined it is."

"*What are you talking about?*" He hisses, his fists clenched tightly at his side. "What the *HELL* are you talking about, Riley!?"

"I-" I twist my arm in my restraint, so my hand is palm up. "I will give you credit for one thing though..." The staff flies from its spot into my hand, dissolving the magical bindings instantly, and I jump to my feet. "You figured out I was the Master *a lot* sooner than I did. Dr. Everhart is right, I really do need to work on evaluating my own self-worth."

I level the crystal adorned staff at him, the purple crystal glowing slightly, and he stumbles backward, almost falling onto his desk.

"You lack foresight." I say softly. "You knew what I was when I *didn't*, yet you still chose to trap me in the one room that had an easy way of escape. Planned for a long time how to pull off the perfect murder that looked like an accident, but wrote it all down in a book that anyone could find in your office."

I take a step back, keeping the staff pointed at him.

"I'm not even sure what you were planning. What, keep me locked up in the basement until one of your daughters was pregnant?" I shake my head. "You *have* to know that wouldn't work. I'd be missed, in both Mage *and* Non societies. You know it."

I magically pull him into the chair that I vacated, and then create force restraints to keep him there.

"You lack foresight, Harris. And that's why you *lose* this one." I shake my head. "I still don't understand you, though, really. Why did you want this- something for your non-existent *grandchildren* so badly that you'd kill your own best friend? Did my father mean *nothing* to you? After an entire lifetime as friends?"

He doesn't say anything, just glowering at me. I sigh and back out of the room. It's only a matter of time before someone finds him there, but I should have more than enough time to find Anna and get away.

And by virtue of where I need to go *now*... well, I guess I'll be going *way* over his head to get justice for my parents, as much as I don't... I look at the staff in my hands and exhale hard. As much as I don't like this, it's going to change *everything.*

I'm not sure I can handle this.

~ Sixteen ~

Anna

September 26th, 2018

The windows shatter, Carrie Harris stepping in, still staying totally dry as the wind whips the rain inside, and people are screaming. I feel Issac grab my sleeve, then a wave of *cold* slams into me and everything goes black.

Something flat is cold against my face, and, in a daze, I run my fingers across it, dimly realizing it's worn, cracked flagstone, and I push myself up to sitting, blinking blearily. The floor is old flagstone, concreted over in a few places where there was probably more severe damage, but even the concrete is cracked and unmaintained, and it's *dark*, with a few empty sconces on the worn brick wall that is *also* concreted over in several places, and just a little bit of light is getting in through a small window at the top of the wall in the right back corner. And there's no *door.*

Great, I seem to be in the world's shittiest dungeon. They can't even bother to maintain their shitty concrete patches. I bet it looked cool back when it was all brick and flagstone. It probably floods though, given the damage.

Where am I anyway? Is this the school? Can't imagine where else it could be...

How did I get in here, though? There's no *door* after all. Was I teleported in? But... I thought Issac said you couldn't teleport on and off school grounds or something? Am I *not* at the school?

I push myself to standing, and walk over to the window, going on my tiptoes to even grab the edge of the windowsill. I pull myself up, wedging the toe of my shoe onto the edge of a larger crack in the brickwork to stabilize myself as I peer through the dirty glass... *At a flowerbed*, rather effectively blocking my view of anything.

"*Shit...*" I mutter, dropping back to the ground. There has to be *some* way to get out of here. Or at the very least, find out where the hell I am.

I huff, sitting back down on the floor, my back pressed against the wall. There's got to be *something* I can do. I'm not content to sit here and be the damsel in distress. I'm an *adult*, I'm uninjured, and I'm *alone*. I can help myself, and I *have* to. This place is a wreck. There *has* to be something I can do to escape...

The window would seem like my most likely bet, but even if I *could* somehow get it out with the bricks cracked around it... but part of around the window is concreted and in a little better repair, so that would be... difficult. And I'm not exactly skinny, so I'm not sure I could fit through that tiny window anyway...

I look over the room slowly, trying to find *something* in the empty room I could use? Could I break a sconce off the wall to try to use it to make an exit or something?

My eyes jump back to two sconces, just a couple feet apart; much closer than the others, and I stand slowly. The bricks aren't cracked between those two...

I walk over to it, tracing my fingertips along the barely noticeable divide of these bricks in better repair, and the rest of the wall. This... This is the door.

I take a step back, staring at it. Well, if I was going to attack anywhere, that would be my best bet, but I'm not sure *how*...

How did they even do this, turning the door into the brickwork? Was it magic?

I close my eyes. How did this work... I... Try to... Try visualizing *life energy*, right? I sit down in front of the not-door, crossing my legs and taking a few deep breaths, just... trying to focus on *myself*, on my own *life*... And after a moment, purple colors the world again, like before.

It's *so much brighter* this time, and I gasp, barely stopping myself from opening my eyes. It's hard to discern *anything* with just how much tessence there is here, but... after a few minutes a lot of it fades into the background, and I'm aware of it... flowing past me. Is... Is this a *leyline*?

Weird.

There's still a lot of tessence lingering around, even once I can filter out the line, but I *can* pinpoint a concentrated spot of it in the shape of a door in front of me.

Okay. Cool. I can... I can do this. Just... try to pull it out Anna, shouldn't be too hard... I extend my hand, palm out like before, pushing quintessence towards the door, but then I *immediately* have to retract it, gasping in pain, as the leyline tried to rip the tessence away from me. Or, like, at least that's what it *felt* like.

It's ripping past me at high speeds and pulling any even slightly loose quintessence with it.

Ouch.

Okay, I guess- I guess I don't have enough control for that. I need to- I need to try something else.

I go over to the window again, pulling myself up, trying to see if there's *anything* that might be able to help me, but it's hard to tell past the mums growing in front of it...

There's a cute little bird there now, and it turns to peck at the glass.

"Hello little Birdie." I say quietly, smiling a bit despite myself. "You wouldn't happen to have a way to get me out of here, would you?"

The bird pivots to face me immediately, like it heard me through the glass, and pecks at it again, right in front of my nose.

... Okay. That was weird. It tweets and pecks at the glass again.

"Window doesn't open, little buddy. Sorry." I say softly. I can't believe I'm actually talking to a bird, while clinging to a tiny windowsill with my foot wedged on a crack in the wall to support me. Is this what my life has come to? *Really*?

The bird pecks again, then plucks off a flower petal with its beak, dropping it in front of the window before pecking hard at the window again.

If I didn't know better, I'd think the bird is trying to tell me something. But that's absurd. I do wish there was some way I could just break open the wall at this window.

The bird pulls on a stem from the mum, fluttering its wings before pecking on the window again.

"It's not like I can break it with *flowers*..." I mutter, about to jump back down to the floor when I freeze. Wait- *Could I?* I'm uh, a nature mage, right? That would apply to flowers, right?

Does it apply to *birds* too? Is that what just happened?

Could I... Could I somehow use the flowers, though? The bird tweets then flies away, and I take a deep breath, closing my eyes again. I can't keep control of my tessence over the leyline to try to pull on the tessence from the door, but maybe I could... *push* tessence. There's certainly plenty of it around.

It's easier each time to bring the purple light to my closed eyes. Tessence is life energy. Does that apply to plants too? I focus on the mum outside, and *slowly*- agonizingly so- the mana defines itself, outlining the plant clearly in my mind's eye, from the flowers to the roots into the soil, and I breathe out hard.

Okay, I... I can do this. I can do this.

If ripping tessence away, or even just blocking it off is harmful, then *giving* tessence has to be *helpful*, right? Not wanting to risk it being pulled away from me by the flow of the leyline again, I try to focus on moving the tessence around me, and I think I see it... flutter, but I can't make it properly *move*.

Gritting my teeth, I try a different tactic, just pushing my own tessence as hard as I can at the plant, hoping it won't be pulled away. It... just spreads out in the soil, and ebbs away over the next few moments, and I sigh.

I press my hand flat against the glass, leaning as close to the window as I can without losing my footing on the crack, and try again, pushing the tessence as hard as I can while focusing intently on the roots of the mum and other plants in the flowerbed, successfully feeding at least... *most* of the tessence into the roots, and... it *works*. The mum starts to grow dramatically as I force the tessence into it and the other plants around, and the roots grow out quickly, and *CRACK-*

I jump back from the wall, coughing slightly as the pressure from the fast growing and now unnaturally large plants broke it by the window, sending a cloud of dust into the room.

I close my eyes again, trying to give more tessence to the plants, to do more, even as my head starts to spin a little, and the wall is crumbling by the time I have to stop. I take a long moment to catch my breath, blinking light spots from my vision, like I'd been staring into the sun too long.

I frantically pull at the cracked and crumbling concrete and brick, using a now free brick to break out the window so I have a wide enough gap to crawl out through the dirt and past the now giant mum, and out into the evening sunlight.

Who needs rescued? *Ha.*

Now... to find Issac. I get to my feet, fruitlessly brushing dirt off my sweater, and look around. This *is* the School, so... I guess if Harris is the reason we're here, I'll just *make* Harris tell me where he's keeping Issac...

~ Seventeen ~

Issac

September 26th, 2018

I walk slowly through the entrance hall, twisting the staff in my hands, and not looking at anyone as I walk purposefully out.

Find Anna. Get plane tickets. Go to D.C. before Harris can stop me. I repeat these three things like a mantra as I walk out, to try to keep calm despite how *not calming* the present situation is. Or really, how *not calming* the rest of my life is going to be given this... I look at the staff clutched tightly in my hands, and take a shaky breath, almost stopping in my tracks, but I force myself to keep going.

Find Anna. Get plane tickets. Go to D.C. before Harris can stop me. *Find Anna. Get plane tickets. Go to D.C. before Harris can stop me.*

Stopping outside the doors in the warmth of the evening sunlight, I pause for a moment to just make myself *breathe. Calm the fuck down, Issac.* Find Anna. A- A simple location spell ought to do it, with this staff in hand. It can easily get through whatever divination blockers Harris might've put up.

He probably didn't bother with much, since the divination specialty was lost a few generations ago. There *are* no mages who are particularly good at that anymore, so protection from them isn't as important. But... But if I'm the *Master*, it should be no trouble, and I know a handful of divinations in *theory...*

Ah. I'm over thinking it. I can do just about anything with this staff. I twist it in my hand, closing my eyes and taking several deep breaths. *Stay calm.*

Before I can do anything, a pair of arms are suddenly thrown around my shoulder, and my next breath catches in my throat as my eyes shoot open, but... then she pulls back, and I realize it's Anna, all the panic evaporating in an instant.

She's... she's completely lacking the normal ambient quintessence that surrounds all untrained mages, and there's no trail showing where she came from. She... She must have escaped on her own. Her reserve is *completely* tapped; I have to pay close attention to even tell that it's *there*, but... that's not a surprise, really. She's only been *taught* how to do *one thing* magically, and I had no time to go over how to do *anything* efficiently. And on a line... half of anything she tried would have been pulled away, with how shaky her control would be.

It's remarkable that she was able to accomplish anything. She's probably going to be a powerful mage with a little bit of training, if that's any indication.

She's also covered in dirt, and she's looking over me with wide eyes, her hands still hovering around my shoulders, but she's not touching me. "Are you okay? Did Harris hurt you? I didn't know where you were, or what happened. I just- I woke up in this crappy like, dungeon room-" She pulls her hands away, tugging on her ponytail. "I mean, I *escaped*, and they didn't even have a guard to anything at least not at the window." She laughs weakly, shaking her head. "But it was. Uhm. Very not good, and I just improvised a thing where I made the plants outside the window super grow so they would damage the wall around the window, and I did enough that I could get out..." She pauses, looking down at her dirty and slightly scraped up hands. "But I did it! I escaped on my own. And I did it with *magic*! And I figured it out on my own!"

I manage a faint smile. She has no *idea* just how incredible that is. How incredible *she* is. If I'm reading her right, she really proud of having done *any* magic on her own... but what she just described is nothing short of amazing for a beginner, and for her to have figured it on her own...

"I'm going to have to teach you how to *properly* channel quintessence someday." I say softly after a moment. "Your reserve is almost completely empty. What you did was *great*, but, ah, not very efficient." I twist the staff nervously in my hands, and her eyes jump to in before going back to my face.

"What's up with the stick thing?"

"Staff," I correct softly, then glance nervously over my shoulder. "Can I get you to wait a few minutes on the explanation for us to get out of here?"

She nods slightly, and I hurry forward, trying to get off school grounds as *quickly* as I can. I could probably- I could probably teleport past the wards with the staff, but I'd rather not. It could damage the wards, and those are there for the safety of the student body...

"We have to get to D.C." I mutter as we walk, and I hear her make a puzzled noise, but I keep my gaze forward.

"Why? That's clear across the country, unless you're about to tell me you can teleport *that far*?"

"Oh, *god no*." I shake my head, then glance down at the staff in my hands. Well, ah, *maybe*, but I'm not going to risk that if I don't have to. "Not with any *accuracy*, at least. I was thinking of a more mundane method of transport. A *plane*."

She snorts. "Yeah, I guess that makes more sense, but still? Why? Or is that waiting a moment?"

"Waiting a m-" My words are cut off by Hannah throwing her arms around me in tears.

"Oh god, oh god," she sobs, clutching me tightly. "We were so scared! Carrie got the both of you- *your defenses were down!!!* I-I was sure you were goners!!"

"I- I need to breathe Hannah-" I gasp softly, and she pulls back, and I see Morgan standing there too, a couple feet back, with her arms crossed behind her back.

"Did you steal the Master's Staff?" Morgan asks slowly, eyeing the staff in my hands, and I flinch, holding it close. "Why would you...?"

I shake my head quickly, taking a shaky breath, and offering a hand to Anna. "I- I don't have time, I'm sorry." Anna takes my hand, and I take off *running*, just trying to get off the grounds. He might be able to trace the teleport if he gets to it in time, but hopefully, hopefully we'll be in the airport by then, and even he wouldn't dare attack us in an *airport*.

"When- When are you going to *explain*?" Anna says, her voice raised slightly.

"*Airport!*" I answer with just one word, struggling to breathe as we run. With how much I've been *running* lately, I probably should have forgone the binder; dysphoria induced anxiety be damned. This *can't* be good for me, to be straining to breathe from running against the binder so often like this...

Finally, we get off school grounds, and I pause just a moment, leaning forward with my hands on my knees to try to catch my breath, the staff clutched awkwardly at a horizontal angle.

"Okay," I stand back up straight, still struggling to breathe. "Okay, we can- we can teleport from here." I offer my hand to her again, and she sighs, immediately taking it back.

"We teleporting straight to the airport?"

"Nearby, yeah," and I whirl us away, reforming near the Seattle-Tacoma International Airport. "We can't- We can't teleport directly in; there are too many cameras. And Harris might get to that in time to trace it, so we need to keep moving." I start walking as quickly as I can manage while still breathing evenly enough.

"Uh, so are we just going to look totally suspicious walking into an airport with no luggage or anything?"

"We'll be fine," I mutter, "It'll suck, but we'll be fine."

"What," Anna jogs to catch up with me, then slows to match my pace, "hate flying?"

"Ah, no," I sigh and shake my head. I've flown plenty of times; travelling with my dad. "It's *security* that I hate..." I absentmindedly pull on my binder strap, then shake myself. We're not doing anything illegal, so we'll be *fine*...

"Oh, well, I guess, yeah, airport security can be annoying, but I don't think it's *as* bad as people make it out to..." I glance at her, biting my lip, and she pauses, blinking a few times. "Wait do they not like...?"

"Mm." I scowl. "But a few minutes of invasive security is a necessary evil at the moment, I suppose."

"How are we even going to get tickets?" She asks. "Aren't last minute plane tickets really expensive?"

"Well, we can stand to wait a bit once inside. We'll be safe from Harris there. If there's anything you can say about an airport is that it's pretty damn secure. Even Harris wouldn't dare attack us in front of so many cameras..." I pause. "Also, money is no object, really."

"Wait- *Wait*, are you *rich,* Issac? I know you have a nice house but that was just like, upper middle class wealth, not *'money is no object'* wealth."

"*Ah*, yeah." I laugh, glancing sidelong at her, worried about her reaction. "Old money in the mage community. I try not to touch it, and usually just use the money from my *job*. But emergencies are emergencies."

I always feel weird when I think of how much money my family actually has. I know there's a lot of good I could do with it, but it's... a little tangled up with secrecy laws, since if I tried to do anything with it to meaningfully help people it could *draw undue attention.*

So, it just... sits. Someday I'm going to find a way to actually *help people* with my third of it. It's not my decision what my siblings do, but I'll find a way. I don't need that kind of money, generally speaking...

"... Okay, I don't know how to feel about that." She says softly. "I never imagined I'd h- be friends with a member of the *aristocracy*."

I momentarily come to a stop, laughing into my hand. First time I've ever been called an *aristocrat*. "*Involuntary* member thereof. Trust me, if it was *my* choice entirely, most of it would have gone to reputable charities years ago. It's a mess with the secrecy laws though."

Anna slows down to a stop, grabbing my wrist to stop me. "Please tell me why we're going to D.C., Issac?"

"Once we're inside. I just, I want to be sure we're sa-"

"You are *infuriating*." Anna laughs slightly. "Just *tell me*." She takes a step closer to me, standing right in front of my face. "And I'm not taking a step further until you *tell me*, no matter how much I *really* like you."

"It's kind of com-" The words die on my lips as her last words hit me. "*Really like me*?" Why would she say that? It's kind of a strange way to note that she does consider me a friend. "What's that supposed to mean?"

"Oh, honestly..." She sighs, then puts her hands on my shoulders, going up on her tiptoes and gently pressing her lips to mine. And everything seems to freeze.

... I... *holy shit*.

She drops back down, staring at me expectantly, and I just blink at her dumbstruck.

She just- She-

"Well, why are we going to Washington D.C.?"

"I- you- you-" I gasp, staring up at the sky. "Harris- I- Master- *Ah!*" The words leave my mouth in a jumbled mess, and I twist the staff nervously in my hands as I struggle to gather my thoughts while still metaphorically in free fall after *that*. Wait- I look at the staff. Ah. That'll never get through security without questions. I turn it to tessence and store it away in my reserve.

"Going to use actual sentences any time soon, Issac?"

"Y-You kissed..." I make a strangled noise, clutching my head. "Wasn't expecting..."

She laughs weakly, looking at the ground. "Sorry. Never had a relationship I intended to take *seriously*, so I don't really know what I'm doing. You don't have to feel the same way, or anything like that..."

I shake my head quickly. God, are all my- I mean, it was the same with Evan. *It was the exact same with Evan.* He totally blindsided me too, down to my friends teasing me about it, because they noticed before I did.

Maybe it's me. I must be bad at picking up at the cues that someone likes me in a romantic sense. Or that I might feel the same.

"That's not- Anna- I *just*..." I hide my surely very red face in my hands. "I *wasn't expecting that.* Can- can we please *walk*, I need- need a minute. I'll explain in- in a minute..."

Anna gently takes my hand and starts walking. I exhale slightly, letting her slowly tug me along as I try to collect myself in silence.

~ Eighteen ~

Anna

September 26th, 2018

We sit down after getting through security, and Issac still frankly seems a little dazed, but I'd really like some answers, and we have awhile yet before our flight leaves. "So... are you going to finally tell me why we're going to D.C.?"

Issac blinks quickly a few times, looking furtively around the mostly empty area before sighing and tilting his head back to look up at the ceilings. "To do the only thing that will keep us safe from Harris indefinitely." He groans slightly, closing his eyes. "I..." He hesitates, biting his lip. "I figured... I figured something out while he had me; it's... it's what allowed me to escape..." He leans forward, taking off his hat and running his hands through his hair. *Whatever* this is, it's clearly stressing him out. "Harris had already figured it out, and was just... counting on me not... doing... so..."

I lean close to him, lightly putting a hand on his knee-ready to pull it back in an instant if he seems uncomfortable. "What is it? What did you figure out?"

His gaze flickers to my hand, and he smiles faintly before sighing again and looking away. "I told you what the Master was, right?"

"Uhm," I bite my lip, trying to remember *exactly* what it was other than something related to our shared family history. "The Master is... the mage who could cast any spell regardless of specialty, and the last one was Vincent, and just... stopped along with nature mages?"

He nods slightly, then breathes out hard, closing his eyes. "Ah, yeah. Came back with them too." He reopens his eyes and turns that intense violet gaze of his to me, biting his lip.

It takes a moment for the implication to hit me, and I gasp before bursting into giggles. "I *said* that! I said that it could be you! And you told me I was being silly!"

"Oh," His face is red, and he looks away from me with a huff. "Oh, shut up. But, ah, the various seats of magical government have all had something set up for centuries for the next Master to register who they are and that they exist. Basically skeleton crews at this point, but..." He sighs. "We have to go to D.C. to do it in the US though..." He wrings his hands in his lap. "Frankly, I'd rather *not*, because it's going to bring... a lot... of attention... but it's not only... the right thing to do, it's a surefire way to make something *stick* to Harris. It's about as far over his head as I could possibly go..." He smiles slightly at me. "Also, you need to be instated as a magic citizen, which will be a bit of a *hassle* given your specialty..."

I pull on my ponytail. "I guess that makes sense. And hey, if anyone tries to bother you about this, just blow them off honestly. No one is entitled to your time due to some stupid circumstance of your birth."

He laughs slightly, muttering something like *"yeah, right..."* under his breath, leaning forward on his knees, with his face in his hands. "I'm sorry about all this, though. I wish it wasn't all so," He pauses, twirling his hand in the air as he seems to fish for the right word. *"Chaotic."*

"Issac, don't apologize." I say immediately. "It's not *your* fault." He looks up at me, clearly surprised at my words. "You've done nothing but try to help me since we met, even when we were total strangers."

"... I'm afraid it only gets worse from here." He says softly, putting back on his hat, sniffling like he's on the verge of tears. "Both the Master and Nature Mages were said to come back when they were *needed*, so I can't fathom we have good times ahead of us..."

"So, what, are we the chosen ones?"

He blinks several times before leaning forward with his face, his hands again, with his elbows resting on his knees. "I *guess*," he peers at me through his fingers, "but it's really more so just that you're descended from the last Nature mage, and just happened to be alive at this time. And the Master reincarnates, so if *I'm* a chosen one, so was every other Master in history."

"Yeah, sure they were. And destiny still landed on me in this generation, so I'd say it counts." I laugh lightly, reach to grab one of his hands, pulling it away from his face, squeezing it gently. "And if more crap is coming, it's going to have to get through us. Together. I'm with you, alright?"

This is all just... a fucking lot, and I have no clue what I'm doing, but I know damn sure that I'm not leaving him to deal with it alone. I've grown way too fond of him, way too fast for that.

Though... I'm not really sure how he feels about *me*. His reaction to me kissing him wasn't super clear. He was just *shocked*. Which, I mean, I don't blame him. It was a bit of an impulse thing on my part, but...

He smiles at me, then sighs, closing his eyes and leaning back in the airport chair. He seems really tired, so I don't really want to bug him, and... *Ah*, he hasn't eaten all day, and I haven't eaten since breakfast.

"Get up," I jump to my feet. "We're going to find someplace good to get food here. Because you haven't eaten *all day*, and I haven't eaten since Breakfast."

"Oh, I'm not really hungry-"

"*Nope*, none of that. You need to eat something, Issac. Come on." I pull him to his feet despite his reluctance, and we go to find some place in the airport that serves halfway decent, if overpriced, food.

September 27th, 2018

It's past midnight by the time our plane takes off, and Issac doesn't say anything on the plane, just quietly staring out the window, and he ends up falling asleep there. I should try sleeping too, but I'm not good at sleeping on planes. Something I figured out on my initial flight from Honolulu to Seattle, because I *tried*.

I don't really sleep much on this flight either, just nodding off a few times, and it never lasts more than a few minutes, so I spend a lot of time just watching Issac sleep. He looks younger when he's asleep, like he could still be in high school, frankly. It's horrible how much the anxiety and stress visually weighs on him.

And then the plane lands, and that wakes Issac up, and he blinks blearily, looking out the window at the runway as the plane comes to a stop.

"What- What time is it?" He yawns. "I can't do time zones first thing upon waking..."

"It around eight, I think." I say softly, and he nods before yawning into his hand. "How are you doing? Are you okay?"

"Oh," Issac laughs faintly. "Not remotely." He sighs, ducking his head. "I'm *afraid*, Anna. I'm terrified of how what happens next is going to change my entire life."

He takes a shaky breath, weaving his fingers together and leaning on them, his knuckles against his lips, and he's staring at the back of the seat in front of him with wide eyes. His hands are shaking as he leans into them, and his brow is furrowed. I can *tell* that he's afraid.

"After... After this..." he continues in a quieter tone. "My life just... it won't be *my* life anymore. Absolutely everything will revolve around me being the Master, and I don't... I really don't know if I could handle that. I- I don't do well with *attention*..." He sighs, his hands dropping to his lap. "I guess I'm just glad it wasn't discovered when I was child- as- as much as I would have expected my father to..." He shakes his head. "My point is that I'm glad that, you know, at least I was able to grow up normal, relatively speaking..."

I offer him my hand, and he hesitates a moment, but does take it, smiling at me. "It's okay to be afraid. But just, please remember that you're not alone. Things may change, and *drastically*, but it doesn't change anything for me. And it won't change anything for Ethan and Lexi. Or Morgan and Hannah. The people who actually *matter* won't care."

He looks away, but squeezes my hand. "Thank you, Anna."

We don't have any more time to talk before it's time to get off the plane, and he doesn't once let go of my hand as we exit out into the airport.

"So where to next?" I ask.

"Capitol Building." He walks purposefully out, and I have to jog a little to not be dragged, as my legs are still a little stiff from the five-hour flight, and I wasn't prepared for him to speedwalk.

"So, uh, what's this going to be like?"

"For me? Ah," he breathes out hard. "A bureaucratic nightmare. For you, the same, but to a lesser extent, and a whole lot of school."

"Fuuuun," I mutter sarcastically. "So, what, do we just walk in and you announce yourself as the Master?"

"More or less." He says, "I'd need to supply some proof, but the Master's staff working in my hands should be more than enough."

"The, uh, white stick with the purple crystal that you vanished? You still have that?"

He made it disappear, so...? But maybe this is a magic thing he hasn't explained yet.

"It's just in my reserve. I turned it into tessence; the same way I do to *us* when we teleport."

"Wait, that's-" I blink at him, just *astonished* for a moment. "*That's a thing you can do*? Do all mages have their own personal hammerspace, or is that an *Issac Thing*, like your way of teleporting?"

Issac stops walking for a moment, laughing into his free hand.

"*Like my teleporting*," he says slowly, "it's a trick I copied and adapted from Wizards. Any mage *could* do it. Most everything Wizards can do is applicable to some degree, but you'd be surprised how most mages turn their noses up at them." He rolls his eyes. "It's ridiculous."

"*Sounds* ridiculous." I chuckle, shaking my head. "You've got to teach me some of these tricks of yours later."

"I'll be sure t-" He skids to a stop, staring down the exit hall we were about to walk out of, at... *Shit*, Kaitlyn Harris standing there, waving at us. Issac winces and spins around, dragging me with him towards a different exit.

The next exit has a very bored-looking Carrie Harris outside of it, studying her nails with a bored expression on her face.

"*No no no-*" Issac turns away, hiding his face in his free hand, visibly trembling a little.

"Issac, if they're blocking every exit, what are we going to do?"

His hand drops from his face, and he throws a furtive look around. "Something not entirely *legal*." He mumbles under his breath before tugging me into the nearest girl's restroom. For a second, I'm shocked by him not even *hesitating* to charge into a girl's room, like most guys would... but, well, I guess he's probably been in girl's restrooms thousands of times before he transitioned...

He doesn't pause at all once inside, just tugging me into a stall before anyone can notice us.

"I *hate* doing magic in public..." he mutters, and then without warning turns both of us into tessence and teleports us away.

We reappear a ways outside the airport, and he quickly starts walking.

"I thought- I thought you said there were too many cameras to do magic stuff in the airport?"

"Well," he laughs, a clear nervous edge to it, and he looks up at the sky. "I did say it wasn't entirely *legal*. Though going into the bathroom at least made it so no cameras actually saw us vanish." He shakes his head. "But attention damping spells don't affect cameras, so it's still possible that it could be noticed, so... I'm... going... to have to report that so it can be dealt with, just in case..." He shakes his head. "Whatever, we need to get to the capitol building."

"Right. So, we get there, you prove you're the Master, and our problems with Harris disappear?"

He twirls his free hand, light coalescing in it, forming into a leather journal. "They disappear because he's going to be arrested for his crimes. This journal is good as a signed confession for his having killed my parents. And we're *way* over his head here, so he can't make it go away."

"And then we can go home to Seattle, no Hunter or Evil Headmasters to worry about." I smile, squeezing his hand. "And screw anyone who wants to get in the way of us returning to our lives."

He chuckles. "You're a lot bolder than I am, Anna..." He vanishes the journal away into light, just like he did the staff, so he must be storing it in his reserve... He seems to notice me watching him, and smiles at me. "I, in general store, important things in my tessence reserve. I'm the *only* person who can access it, so it's a very handy trick."

"You definitely need to teach me that later." I giggle, and we walk in silence, still holding hands, and we eventually board the metro to get closer to our destination.

Issac is clutching my hand like a lifeline on the train, squeezing my hand so tight that it honestly kinda *hurts*, not that I'm going to tell him that.

"Issac... Are you okay?" I ask softly, and he inhales sharply through clenched teeth and shakes his head.

"Can- Can we just not talk until we're off this train?" He hisses through his teeth, and I shut up real quick.

I can't blame him for being... *tense*. I know he doesn't like being touched, and the train is crowded by people on their morning commute and such. I wonder though, why we couldn't just teleport straight there? Is it warded like the school is? Are there laws against it? It must be something. I can't imagine he'd subject himself to this crowd for no reason...

The train starts moving, and I squeeze Issac's hand to try to reassure him, when a large man backs into me, knocking me over and ripping my hand away from Issac's, which earns *me* a lot of dirty looks, despite it being the guy who backed into me's fault.

I quickly get back up, looking wildly for Issac so I can take his hand again, but he's nowhere to be found, and the extremely *rude people* around me aren't exactly helping me find him.

And then I hear a scream somewhere out of sight. It's quickly cut off, but I *know* that- that was *Issac.*

No- No *No No Nononono-*

~ Nineteen ~

Issac
September 27th, 2018

I wake up, black spots spinning in my vision, my head is pounding, and I'm bound tightly to a chair with rough rope that cuts into my skin.

Shit. *Shit*, oh shit. What happened? *What happened!?*

I gasp for air, the dimly lit room seeming to spin around me, and I shut my eyes to try to find some sense of stability. We- We were on the Metro, and there were too many people and I felt like I could barely breathe, and then someone knocked Anna away from me, ripping away my... only point of reference...

And then... ah... I... *think* someone shoved me? Maybe? I'm not sure. I was having a hard time discerning what touches other than Anna's hand were, even before we were separated... It was so difficult to process *anything* with so many people in close quarters.

I test the ropes, and inhale sharply in pain at just how tight they are, and I immediately stop, wanting to prevent breaking skin if at all possible. I open my eyes, studying the rope visually. They... look to be an older but fairly standard braided rope, clearly well used but not to the point of fragility. Unfortunately.

But if I can move my hands... I flex my fingers gingerly, and it hurts a bit where it strains against the ropes, and my fingers are a little numb, but I can still move them, so...

I try to pull tessence from my reserve to burn off the rope, and I almost double over in immediate pain, only not because my torso is also tied to the chair, and I barely don't scream as the *agony* of that rips through me like metaphorical fire through my veins, and my vision almost blacks for a moment and my stomach lurches.

Shit, shit- Spellburn. A fucking *Hunter* got me? Anna wasn't trailing, still recovering tessence after her escape, so the only way a Hunter would have known we were there is if they were just... *on the Metro* and watching for mages. *Fucking hell...*

Ah, ah, it's okay. It's okay, I can just... I can just pull tessence from around me, it's *fine...* It's fine.

Fucking wish the hidden magic wing of the Capitol building wasn't teleport warded though, *god.*

I take a deep breath, and it's *painful*, but I need to just *focus*, gathering ambient tessence around the ropes on my wrists, wincing slightly as I actually take in just how *empty* my reserve is. It's almost completely depleted, the *only* remaining tessence being my stored objects, which I can't tap on without destroying them.

God, I was hit *hard*. My reserves have *never* been this low. The nausea gets worse as I dwell on it, so I shake myself for try to take a few more deep breaths, despite how each one aches.

I twist one hand around so it's palm upward- pushing through the burn of the ropes as each rough fiber of them digs into the flesh of my wrist in the movement, and I have to take a moment, just breathing raggedly as it starts to ooze blood around the rope.

Don't- *Don't dwell on it Issac. Just keep going, lock control on the tessence...* I clench my hand into a fist, pulling the gathered mana tight around the ropes, and then I snap my fingers- a difficult task with the slight numbness- on my other hand to just ignite the tessence with a small spark on both ropes and... nothing.

It doesn't catch; the tessence being *completely* unreactive. *Basic* wizardry didn't work. One of the *easiest* things- No... no no *nonono*- I start to breathe quickly and I can hear my heart thundering in my ears, and I close my eyes, throwing my senses out and... *no no*- All the mana in my immediate vicinity is still and muted... but fizzing and pulsing just a few feet away at the edge of an...

I'm in an anti-magic field.

This isn't just a Hunter, but a *powerful* one. Only one or two hunters have *ever* been known to be able to create an anti-magic field. No- *no*-

I-I can't dwell on that. I need- I need to find a way out of here. I have to find a way out- *the staff.* If I could just get it out, it could probably overwhelm the field. I can- I can do this.

Clenching my jaw, I turn my focus on my own tessence reserve, isolating the staff.

Oh god, this is going to *hurt...*

Even mentally prodding at the bright spot of mana that is my staff twinges pain in my core, the energy rippling uncomfortably along the edges of my frayed reserve, but I- I can't stop just because it hurts. I might not survive this if I don't escape now. So I push it to coalesce in my upturned hand, the travelling tessence like fire ripping through my veins.

Light in the shape of the staff does start to form hazily in my hand, but it's hard to keep control of it as the field tries to force it back in, and my control slips, and it *violently* shoots back into my reserve/ I let out a strangled scream and I literally can't *breathe*, the chair rocking slightly with how hard I jerked back in pain.

My scream turns into sobs and I gasp for air, straining against the ropes as I instinctively try to curl in on myself.

Oh god, oh god, no, no, no- Oh- *fucking hell-*

I'm going to die here. I'm going- I'm going to die here. I have- I have no means of escape- I'm trapped- trapped by a hunter- an *incredibly dangerous* hunter- I- I'm going to- I'm going to die- No no no *no nonononono-*

My vision is more black spots that not, and I'm dimly aware that I'm crying, but what does it matter? I-I'm going to *die-*

The sound of a door creaking open comes from somewhere behind me, and I blink dazed, trying to look over my shoulder, but even what little I can see, I can't process, just being vague shapes in my head.

"Hm. It's a shame I can't kill you yet."

Kevin Anderson's deep and imminently recognizable voice sends a cold chill down my spine, and a burst of clarity despite the pain I'm in. I suck in a sharp breath, closing my eyes. How is he *here*? We *got him*. He was taken away in handcuffs before Carrie showed up. I'm *sure* of that much, and I doubt he would have been able to get out on bail, at least not so *quickly*...

He walks up directly behind the chair I'm in, and crouches so he's hissing in my ear. "You almost got me, boy." He chuckles, gently pressing a knife on the side of my face. "But lucky for me, that *Harris* is a fool."

"No arguments there." I croak out, and my voice just sounds *hollow*. And tired. "*You* were foolish enough to shoot at us in a public place in front of police officers and you have more foresight than him."

Harris must have gotten him out. To try to use him against me. Wait- *Anna*- What- *What about Anna?* Is- Is she okay?

"Oh," Anderson laughs. "Yes, the fool thought he could make a pawn of me. Definitely lacks, ah, *foresight*, yes. And I won't ever make a mistake like I did with you again. I'm not used to *degenerates* like you feeling so comfortable in the real world." He traces the edge of the blade gently up my jaw. "You certainly are *interesting*."

"Let me guess," I mumble, "You're using me to lure him in, and then you're going to kill us both."

"Oh, and that little girlfriend of yours too, Riley. You might have saved her once, but you won't be alive to do it again."

No no nono- *not Anna*. She has- she has to survive this... She has to...

"So, you figured out who I am, then?" My voice shakes slightly, and he snorts, walking around in front of me, while spinning the knife in his hand.

"It wasn't easy." He crosses his arms behind his back. "I never would have expected someone with public school records all the way back to kindergarten to be one of you abominations, let alone the most unnatural of them all, according to Harris." He laughs.

"You're even attending a normal college, and work a normal job. It's like you're trying to copy a real human being. I never would have noticed you, had you not charged right into my office to save the girl. *She* was easy. I've never seen one of you that was so easy to track, leaving a trail of your evil power wherever she goes. And homeschooled her whole life too. It's like she *wanted* to be caught. It's funny though," he laughs again. "I actually didn't know she was one of you until she walked into my office."

"Actually, her homeschooling had nothing to do with magic..." I mutter, feeling the need to correct him, though it doesn't really matter.

"Hm? Don't try to trick me, *Isabelle*-" I wince at the use of my deadname. "Nothing you say is going to change this. You're only still alive because I need you to get Harris and his brats." He pauses. "After I kill them and you, and that girl-friend of yours... I'll be paying your siblings a visit. Ethan and Alexis, isn't it?"

My blood runs cold, and for a second, I legitimately *cannot* breathe before a sob painfully rips through me, followed by many more. "No no- *please don't*- please- just- just leave them out of it- *please-*"

They're all I have left. Lexi and Ethan are all I have left. They can't- They can't die- They can't die because of me-

"Aw, look, the abomination is pretending it can feel love." He puts the tip of the knife up my chin and forces my head up to look at him. "I told you not to try to trick me. You *Mages* are soulless degenerates who harvest life energy to do the devil's work. You don't feel love. You don't feel *anything.*"

He pulls the knife away from my face, gently caressing the side of the blade, and then he smiles.

"Hm, well, I might not be able to *kill* you yet, but I can certainly punish the wicked while it lives."

~ Twenty ~

Anna

September 27th, 2018

I pace on the platform, ignoring everyone around me as my only thoughts are focused on Issac and his *absence*. I let myself get knocked away from him, and *something happened!* I *heard* him start to scream before it was cut off.

Something happened. I can't just stand here and be useless. There *has* to be something I can do. Someway I can *find him.* Just- *think...*

He's rescued me enough times. I need to rescue *him* now.

But... *what?* What can I do? I have no sense of where he is, or really where *I* am, even. I've never been to DC before, and my maps app isn't really helpful given that I have no clue where I'm going. Should I continue to the capitol building to tell someone what happened? Ah, that doesn't sound wise, since I have to assume there's some secret magic door or something to separate mage stuff from the congress...

But I have to do *something.* I can't just let some untold fate happen to my... boyfriend? Friend? Magic Guide? *I don't know.* It doesn't matter. He's important to me, and I *have* to help him. I can't just sit around and hope he escapes on his own.

I'll find Harris or... his daughters... My eyes trail over to Kaitlyn and Carrie Harris over by a wall, whispering to each other. People are milling around them like they aren't even there. I might not know much magic, but my Dad made sure I knew how to physically defend myself, so maybe I can *beat* the answers I need out of them. Too many people around for them to do magic after all.

It's either that or start crying because this is just- it's *too much*, and I'd rather do something that can actually *help*. Crying can *wait* until I know he's safe.

I march over to them, my hands clenched into fists at my side, and they both stop whispering at once when they notice my approach. Kaitlyn winces and takes a step back, pressing her back against the wall, and Carrie scoffs, rolling her eyes.

"You're dumber than I thought." Carrie sneers. "I don't know what I expected from some Non-raised savage, but just walking dire-"

I swing and punch her right in her stupid jaw, sending her staggering backward, and... no one notices it. *Excellent.* Racist bitch. I was going to punch her either way, but then she dropped *savage*, like *wow*. Calling an indigenous girl *savage...*

"You *barbarian!*" She hisses, standing back up straight, her hand on her jaw. "Resorting to physical violence?!"

I grab her by her shirt, pinning her against the wall. She's shorter than me, and very thin, so it's not difficult to do at all. "How about you tell me where Issac is, and I *don't* give you a concussion?" Dad wouldn't be proud of me for this, with how gentle he tends to be, but I'm going to do whatever it takes to help Issac. And if it takes blunt force; blunt force it is. "Does that sound good to you, Harris?"

"You seem to be forgetting something." Carrie hisses, and I roll my eyes.

"What? The people? It's clear that they aren't noticing us right now. It's like the two of you- and now me too- aren't even here."

She snickers. "No. I mean Kait."

Without letting go of Carrie, I turn halfway around, grabbing Kaitlyn by the wrist before she could attack me, and she just freezes, yelping slightly, and sinking down to the floor with her free arm over her head to try to protect herself.

"She doesn't seem like she wants to help you." I say, letting go of her wrist, and she quickly pulls it close to her chest, whimpering quietly. "You can't hurt me without breaking out magic, and there are cameras here. You wouldn't *dare*." Issac said attention damping spells don't affect cameras, after all.

"Maybe we should just tell her." Kaitlyn says quietly from the floor. "I was *just saying* I think Daddy went too far. And-And she's *right*. There would be *serious* trouble for obviously doing magic on camera, especially *here in D.C.*"

"I won't tell this trash anything." Carrie spits. "She's not one of us. I'm-" She puts her hand on my arm, and a black aura flashes around her hand and... my arm suddenly stops working and drops limply to my side. "I'm going to kill this worthless piece of trash, then force her corpse to devour her stupid boyfriend alive! Issac had *hiiiiis* chance, and she doesn't deserve one!"

She extends her arm towards me, that black aura still surrounding her hand, and I feel my feet leave the ground as something cold tightens around my chest.

"Carrie!" Kaitlyn sounds on the verge of tears as she scrambles to her feet, and I'm struggling to breathe as the cold seeps into my skin and I feel like my *lungs* are going numb. "Carrie, Carrie, you *can't*-"

"I can and I *will*!" She growls, and the feeling on my chest tightens more, and I just *can't breathe* at all.

There are two flashes of light at once, a purple flash that comes with a high-pitched tone that knocks Carrie back with the force of the *sound* and a light blue flash that coats her in a thin layer of ice, pinning her there.

And a wiry young man catches me as I fall, and he sits me down gently.

He's an Indian guy, looks about my age, with thin framed glasses and messy black hair. He flashes a smile, revealing teeth with lines of blue banded braces; a surprise on someone my age. "Sorry, Ma'am, this must be very confusing-"

"Stop right there Buddy, I know about Magic." I say, a little breathlessly as I get to my feet.

He blinks a few times, squinting at me before, "Oh!" He chuckles. "My bad. Your reserve is fairly empty, so I didn't notice it at first. I imagine the *actual* authorities will be here soon. I was just in the area, and it looked serious, so I thought I should intervene and stop this chick from killing you. What kind of first responder in training would I be if I didn't, you know?" He glances at Kaitlyn. "Glad to see that you did something too, though maybe you should have acted *sooner*?"

"I didn't expect her to try to *kill* anyone!" Kaitlyn says, throwing a panicked look at her sister. "We just- I- *I'm sorry!*" She hides her face in my hands. "I didn't sign up for *this...*"

I scowl, turning my attention to Kaitlyn. "Pull yourself together and *tell me where your father took Issac.*"

"I don't know- He- He got Anderson out to-"

My blood runs cold, and I take a shaky breath, shaking my head quickly. Harris got a *fucking Hunter* to go after Issac? *What the fuck!*

"Wait, their father *kidnapped your friend?* Oh dear, you *really* need the authorities..."

"Yeah, no kidding." I glare at the girls. "We were *so close* too... *fucking...*"

"My father will be able to make this all go away." Carrie hisses. "You have nothing on me!"

The guy scoffs and rolls his eyes. "Ma'am, come off it. You *blatantly* did magic in a crowded non-magical location *with cameras*, and nearly killed this woman. I don't *care* who your father is; there's no *making this go away.*"

"My father is Godfrey Harris! Headmaster of Vincent's Academy for Magic! You can't touch me!!" She strains against the ice, cracking it slightly.

The guy nonchalantly waves his hand, resealing the cracks, the pauses, looking at me with a frown. "... *Vincent's...* Hey, I'm sorry, this is kinda weird, but is your friend Issac *Riley,* by any chance?"

I blink at him several times, unable to form words for a moment. "*How did you-*" I mean- I- I guess if his family is *old money* and an ancestor of his founded a famous school, he might be like, well known, but still this is *weird*...

The guy laughs weakly, clearly not at all amused. "Uh, Issac is," He rubs the back of his head. "He's a friend of mine. We met online, a- a few years back. I'm Doug. Doug Misra."

"... I'm Anna Kahale." I say slowly, frowning at him. Issac told me that he only had two *friends*... Oh! But he did mention a fellow mage in his D&d group. I think he even said that they were in *D.C.*

That must be Doug here, then.

Suddenly all the Nons freeze in place, though *most* of them hadn't noticed us; just a few who had been staring in confusion, and several people dressed in dark purple uniforms push through over to us.

"Okay," One of them says, "What happened? We got a report of a masquerade break, specifically with life magic."

Doug, I, and Kaitlyn all immediately point towards Carrie, pinned to the wall with ice.

Doug then bows slightly to them before quickly standing back up straight. "I do apologize, for having to magically restrain her and protect Ms. Kahale here."

The guy who spoke double takes at Doug, and sighs heavily. "*Misra*. You know damn well that it's permitted in an emergency. You don't need to apologize for it."

He shrugs. "Sorry, Joseph. I'm not a certified responder yet, so I thought it best that I do so. *However*," He gestures at me. "Ms. Kahale here needs your help rather immediately."

Joseph looks at me, raising an eyebrow. "What is it then?"

"My friend, Issac Riley-"

"Riley," Another one of the men whistles. "That's a name we haven't heard in a while."

"He was *kidnapped*," I continue, more than a little annoyed at being interrupted in something so *important*. If they didn't seem like Official People, I'd snap at them. Thankfully, they completely focus on me with the word *kidnapped*. "Right here on this subway, and it was arranged by these girls' father. And done by a *Hunter* that their father- Godfrey Harris- had specifically gotten out of being *arrested* to do so. *Right*, Kaitlyn?"

Kaitlyn nods, whimpering a bit. "I- yeah, yeah. It's Kevin Anderson, a- a really dangerous Hunter from the Northwest. My father somehow convinced him to track and abduct Issac."

The guys in purple hurry into action, taking Carrie away... and Kaitlyn too, to get as much information from her as they can, I guess.

Doug gently puts a hand on my shoulder. "I might be able to help find him. I'm a water-social mage, and with the two of us both having a personal connection to Issac... I *miiiight* be able to make a social-based tracking spell work. Figure out where he's at; and tell the responders if we find him first? If it's a *Hunter*... Time is very much of the essence, and... it can't hurt anything."

I nod quickly. I'm not going to argue with *anything* that might be able to help. If I can help save Issac, I'm *going to*.

~ Twenty-One ~

Issac

September 27th, 2018

I'm faintly aware of a loud crash somewhere nearby, and I lift my head slightly as Anderson stares over me towards the door behind me.

I only know he's gone because I hear the door close behind him, the physical pain just an all-encompassing blur over my consciousness now. I can't discern much else, but... it couldn't be much worse than this, since I can hardly tell that he *stopped*...

But I'm... I'm alone again. I have to try to... ah... I duck my head again, letting out a ragged breath, trying to think through the agony spread in a hundred small cuts all over my body, each burning like my own blood is acid soaking my skin.

I can't figure out the source of the commotion I feel like my brain is short circuiting. It- It sounds both incredibly close and far away as my head spins wildly, and all my senses are deadened as my mind just won't process any of it.

Fuck- why- why couldn't he just *kill me*? That would be infinitely preferable to *this*... Dying wouldn't be so bad. I almost did it to myself back in high school, so I accepted it a long time ago.

Anything but this.

My eyes, blurred and spotty as my vision is, zero in on the knife, left on a table against the nearest wall, just a few feet away from me.

If... If I can... If I can get to it, I might be able to... to cut the binding and escape. If... If I could move the... move the chair...

I shake myself, trying to think through the pained haze over my mind, and I close my eyes.

My eyes immediately shoot back open, and I suck in a sharp breath. The anti-magic field is gone. It must have a range around him, and he- he moved too far away. If I can...

Focusing on it, the tessence is clearer to see than... actually seeing with my eyes right now, and I take several deep breaths, pulling some into my reserve, which is like a fresh wave of fire, but I need the strength boost, as temporary as it is.

I only have a moment to act before the tessence escapes out of my *beyond* damaged reserve, so I use the moment of strength to pull the staff from it. It properly coalesces in my hand this time, and I barely feel it leave my reserve, the agony from before hardly noticeable amongst my more *tangible* injuries from that maniac.

Squeezing it tight, aggravating a small wound in my palm- I will the binds to fall away, and instantly the ropes fall away as if cut.

Ok... okay... Using the staff, I push myself to my feet, putting most of my weight on the spiral carved piece of wood, but I only make it a couple steps before I hit the floor, and just start to *sob*.

What am I supposed to- *What can I-*

I hear the door open, and I curl in on myself, anticipating Anderson, but the touch that comes is very gentle, stroking my hair, and it's a female voice, but I can't... I don't know what she's saying... I don't...

Anna? I shift as much as I can manage to look at her, and my vision is very blurry, but... I think... I think it's Anna.

A spark of clarity hits me, and I take a shaky breath, grabbing her arm with my free hand. "*Help me up.*"

"... Issac..."

"*Honestly*, Issac," another voice says, and it's familiar but I can't place it, and I'm not taking my eyes off Anna. "You're-you're in bad shape, just-"

"Help me up." I repeat, trying to sound as firm as I can, but I can't muster much strength, even in my voice, staring intently at Anna, and she frowns, but nods slightly, standing up. She helps me to my feet a second later, not letting go of me, and I fix my gaze on the door, able to peg the sounds of the *fight* out there a little better, and I point the staff, knocking the door off its hinges, revealing the conflict with D.C.'s responders out there.

My focus zeros in on Harris, and I level the staff at him, sending him flying back with barely a sluggish thought from me. Everyone turns to look my way, clearly shocked, and I see Anderson smirk. He's probably confident that he weakened me too much to be effective.

Not with this staff.

Before I can do anything about Anderson though, Harris is staggering back to his feet, glaring daggers at me, and I focus back on him, about to do *a lot* worse than just knocking him back, when someone gently pries the staff from my hand. With it gone, I almost hit the floor, even with Anna's support, but the person who took my staff helps catch me, sighing my name softly, and then I black out.

September 29th, 2018

I awaken to the sterile white of the hospital, and some medical equipment beeping, though I can't really place it as the world comes into focus.

I jolt upright, looking around the room, trying to take in my surroundings and my own condition. *Ah.* My reserve is still good as empty, and... probably *can't* hold anything at the moment, but... I'm alive. I'm *alive.* And... I look down at my arms and hands. My physical wounds seem to be mostly healed, with some new scars joining the others I already had. Ah, it's fine. I tend to cover up a lot, anyway. A few more scars aren't the end of the world.

"Issac! You're awake!"

My gaze snaps to Doug, and I laugh weakly... which still aches a little, but it's *fine.* "*Doug?* What- What are you doing here?"

"Issac!" Anna shouts from the doorway, and I look over at her just in time for her arms to loop around me tightly. *Painfully*, in fact, the contact sending sharp shooting pain down my back and shoulders, and I gasp.

"Anna, *Anna*," I mumble, feebly hitting her shoulder. "Please let go."

"Oh!" She pulls back quickly, staring at me with wide eyes. "Did I hurt you?"

"A bit." I squeak. "What... What happened?" I clutch my head with one hand. "I'm still finding it a bit difficult to think clearly. *What happened*? With- with Harris and Anderson? What's Doug doing here? Where's-" I look around the room wildly. "Where's my staff?!"

"Calm," Doug brushes his fingertips across the back of my hand, and I involuntarily let out a breath as the world softens a little. "Responder Joseph has it. I took it and turned it in; seemed like you were about to kill Harris with it."

I blink several times, and exhale hard. "I probably was, honestly. I- ... thank you for stopping me. But what are you doing here?"

"I ran into your girlfriend on the Metro." He nods at Anna. "Carrie Harris was trying to kill her, though from what she says, it was because she was totally kicking Carrie's butt before that. And then I helped her find *you*. We actually got there before the responders and enforcers, since we told *them* where to go."

I blink several times, processing all that. "Girlfri..." *Is* she my girlfriend? I glance at Anna, who just shrugs. That's not helpful.

Doug looks between the two of us. "Oh, I'm sorry. Am I wrong? I just sort of assumed, based on the way she's been acting. She's been completely losing her mind the past couple days, waiting for you to wake up, and hugged you like *that* without even hesitating, and you wouldn't take your eyes off her when we rescued you..."

"Well, uhh, uhm, there was... a... thing at the airport, but we haven't exactly *talked* about..." I mumble, staring at the bed next to me, my face almost certainly going red.

Wait, *a couple days*? I glance at the patient whiteboard on the wall and exhale hard, seeing the date there. The *Twenty-ninth*. It has been two days. The last time I had my wits about me it was *morning* on the twenty-seventh...

"Oh," Doug laughs. "Okay then. I guess that explains why it never came up then." He pauses. "I suppose the craziness that led to you being *here* is why you went off the grid for a bit there?"

"Oh, ah," they noticed? I guess I did miss a session through all this... "Yeah, sorry. Things were... chaotic for a while there, but I didn't think anyone would care."

"*Issac*," Doug sighs, and I look at him as he's shaking his head. "Of *course* we cared. You're our friend."

"W-What-?" I shake my head. "We just play tabletop RPGs online, why... why would you care about *me*? This is the first time we've even met."

"*Issac*." Doug huffs. "Dude, don't do this. It's 2018. Friends *online* is a perfectly normal thing. We've been friends for *three years*. It doesn't *matter* that you live clear 'cross the country."

I manage a faint smile and look away. I just... didn't think Doug and the others actually *cared* about me. I was just... the party's paladin. It's nice to know that they do care, I guess...

A responder in a slightly rumpled purple uniform, like he's been working for far too long, comes in, with a middle-aged woman dressed in a prim black pant suit right behind him, my staff in her hands.

She steps around the responder, walking up to my bedside.

"You are Issac Joan Riley, correct?" She asks smoothly. "Son of Steven Daniel Riley, and direct descendant of the last known Master, Vincent George Riley?"

I nod slowly, but I'm not looking at *her.* My gaze is focused sharply on the staff in her hands.

"Responder Joseph here, along with a number of other Responders and Enforcers report seeing you use this staff effortlessly to perform magic, whilst Spellburned to an extent that should have rendered even the most basic magic close to impossible. Is this correct?"

"Well, my memories of that are a bit hazy, but yes. I did, in fact use that staff. The thing you're slowly leading to? It's why I'm even in D.C."

Her mouth thins, and her grip on the staff tightens. "Mr. Riley, may I please view your Icon?"

"Go nuts." I sigh, and she holds out her left hand, palm up, with her fingers curled upward. A yellow aura forms inside her hand, a blue aura inside of that, and a second later a spinning image of a light blue star surrounded by smaller twinkling stars appears, and I'm hit with a pang of sadness.

My father's magic aura was yellow, so this is a lot like the first time I ever saw my own Icon, and I have to wonder... Did he *know*? There's no way he didn't. He'd been studying the Master longer than I was *alive.* If anyone would have been certain about what that *meant...* it'd have been *him.*

But... why... why wouldn't he *tell me*...? God, I wish Doug had let me... I don't know, I just, Harris deserves to...

Stop it, Issac. Stop. Revenge is a useless idea. It doesn't matter how much he hurt me; nothing would have justified killing him. I'm *glad* Doug took the staff from me. But it's hard to tell my feelings that.

"Well," the woman says sharply. "That's plain as day, isn't it? I'm not sure why it took *twenty years* for you to get out here, especially given your father's work compiling and analyzing data on previous Master's, but that's certainly *clear*."

"I can't answer for my dad. And you can blame *Harris* for him not being able to answer for himself." I pull the journal from what little remains of my reserve, ignoring the shockwave of pain that comes with that. "He wrote it all down here himself, if you needed..." I exhale hard, waiting a moment for the burn of that to die back down. "... I only just figured out I was the Master myself the day before coming out here."

She doesn't say anything for a moment, taking the journal from me, and flipping through it, and then she *immediately* hands it to the Responder. "File that as evidence in the Harris case." She focuses back on me. "Fine though, at least you came here immediately once you did." She sits the staff down on the bed next to me, then crosses her arms. "We have a lot of work to do once you recover, *Master* Riley."

The title shift is a little unnerving, but I grab the staff at once, the rush of magical power taking the edge off the ache from spellburn.

~ Twenty-Two ~

Anna

October 5th, 2018

"And you're *absolutely certain* that you're a nature mage?"

I groan, putting my head down on Government official-#5-who's-asked-me-that-question's desk. Why do I keep getting shuffled around to twits who ask me the same damn things...

I huff, and sit back up, glaring daggers at the man. "*No*, as I've told *every one* of you people. I have *no clue.* This is all super new to me. But *Issac* is pretty damn certain, and he actually knows things." I cross my arms. "Have you talked to *him* about it at all?"

"Master Riley is busy with other matters." He says shortly, clearly as impatient with me as I am with him.

"He *should* be left alone to recover, but I know that's not what you people are doing." I scowl, crossing my arms. He only got out of the hospital *two days* ago, and I haven't seen him even once since because they won't leave him alone.

#5- as if I could be bothered to remember his name- sighs, leaning forward on his desk toward me.

"Ms. Kahale, *Master* Riley is *the Master*, one of the most important figures in the magical world, and has been gone for *three* centuries. *Ergo* there is a lot of work to be done. He was discharged from the hospital, and that should do, should it not?"

"Well, *last I checked*, he's still in a wheelchair because of something the bastard that *you people let get away* did, so I'm of the opinion that no it should not do, but I know *my* opinion doesn't *matter* at all."

#5 is silent for a moment, scowling at me. "*Look*, Ms. Kahale, let's try this from a different *angle*." He forces a smile that looks more like a grimace. "What magic have you actually *done*?"

"Well..." I pause, briefly considering telling him to fuck off, but decide *not* to piss off the Government guy anymore that he already is. "Mostly making a bunch of things flying at me accidentally, but I think I might have accidentally controlled the weather once? Then following Issac's instructions, I temporarily cut someone off from their natural tessence or something. Then I made the roots of plants grow to break the wall of a dungeon Harris put me in." I pause. "Oh, and maybe that bird thing was something... I don't know."

He sighs. "Yes, that... That undeniably matches up with what little information we have on Nature Mages." He shakes his head. "We'll get you into general magic classes, but there's not really any way to teach you your specialty. You have to figure that out on you own. Which is... far from ideal."

"Can it wait?" I frown. "I'd really like to go *home*." Pausing, I tilt my head to the side. "And like, couldn't I take these classes *in* Seattle?"

"Well, Ms. Kahale, we'd much prefer to keep a close eye on you, and to keep you and Master Riley toge-"

"But Issac needs to go back to Seattle too! He's his younger sibling's guardian, and they're there. Plus, both of us are enrolled in college there, and I don't know about him, but I have missed *far* too many classes as is."

He groans, his head in his hands. "If that Non degree is *truly* important to you, we could arrange for you to attend a closer university. Perhaps an online one. As for Master Riley's family, they could *easily* be moved out here, but that's not what we're here to talk ab-"

The door to his office opens, and a girl with springy red ringlets pokes her head into the room.

"Mr. Davids, sir? Akerman wants to see Ms. Kahale. They say it's urgent."

#5 huffs, but waves me out.

Whoever this Akerman is, they must be his boss.

I hop to my feet, eagerly following the redhead to wherever. Probably better there than with #5, who's been the most annoying of them all.

She stops outside a door. "Enter and have a seat Ms. Kahale. Mx. Akerman will be here shortly."

I shrug, and walk in, before stopping dead in surprise, seeing Issac already at the small circular table, rolling a pencil back and forth.

"Issac!" I pull up a chair next to him, and he looks up at me, a wide grin spreading across his face.

"*Finally.*" He laughs lightly, shaking his head. "I've been telling them to stop shuffling you around for the past week."

"Do you know who Akerman is?"

"Oh, Jay. Yeah. They're the only person here who hasn't annoyed me to no end. I've known them since I was a kid though, having come here a few times with my dad..." He sighs quietly. "They just went to grab some papers, I think." He smiles, leaning back in his chair. "Maybe we're finally going to go *home.*"

"Well #5- uh, I mean Mr.... Davids? Was acting like he'd sooner have our whole lives moved out here than let us go back to Seattle."

Issac snorts, shaking his head. "Nah. That wouldn't happen. They can keep us stuck here for a while, but they can't force us to stay." He flashes a grin at me. "We're still free citizens."

I manage a smile back. "It hasn't felt that way." I laugh weakly. "But if you say so."

"Sorry about all of this." he sighs. "I had wanted to help you be a little more accustomed to the Magic world before you had to do all of this." He gestures vaguely around the room. "It would've made it a bit easier." He runs his hands through his hair, and leans forward on the table, his head in his hands. "Everything just got to be such a *mess...*"

"I'm *fine,* Issac." I shake my head, my eyes flitting to his wheelchair. "You don't need to worry about me. But..." I bite my lip. "Are *you* doing okay?" My eyes flit down to his chair again, and he sighs, pinching the bridge of his nose.

"Yeah. I'm *fine*." He closes his eyes. "I just... can't stand up for more than five minutes without getting intensely dizzy." He starts rolling the pencil again, his eyes still closed. "The doctors say it will get better on its own with time. I was just the first mage to be alone with a Hunter *that* long and live, and treatment for spellburn is... well it *exists* but very limited, so there's not much to be done but wait. I mean, I'm lucky really, that I even lived." He wrings his hands. "It's still difficult to even channel tessence without the staff, but you know. I'm fine."

"Issac..." Hesitantly, I reach forward and grab his hands in mine. "You don't *have* to be fine. Not for me."

He takes a shaky breath. "I *am* fine Anna. I'm by no means *good*. But I'm *okay*." He sniffles. "I just... I just want to go home. I don't really *care* if I never recover fully. I just want to go *home*."

I'm silent for a moment, just holding his hands, not sure what to say. "I... I want to go home too, Issac. I really do."

He opens his eyes, smiling at me. "We will. *Soon*. I'm sure of it."

"Issac. Are you *sure* you're doing okay?" I ask one last time, and he sighs.

"Anna." He turns his chair to face me. "*Really*, I am. Stop worrying about me."

"I'll try." I smile at him, and the door opens, someone who I presume to be Jay walks in with an armful of papers.

"Hello!" they chirp, dropping the papers on the other side of the table. "You must be Anna! I'm Jaydyn Akerman, but you should just call me Jay!"

They look to be in their late thirties, with a thick shock of black hair, thin framed round glasses, and dressed in a light grey business suit.

"Uh, nice to meet you Jay." I smile slightly, and they beam back.

"So *terribly* sorry about your past week or so Anna. *Everyone* wanted a say in what happened to you, and it took *forever* to get you classified in association with Issac so I could get you out of it." They practically fall back into their chair before rocking forward, and leaning towards us, their elbows on the table. "But that's all settled now, and just a few things need taken care of before I could get the pair of you on a plane to Seattle by the end of the day!"

"Wait, woah, really?" I lean back in my chair, startled. "That fast? Nice! I like you already!"

They laugh, grinning at me. "Two centuries of nothing means the Master's division is all of two people, so I've got a lot of swing. Me and Ms. Dorian are all there is, really. You'll be seeing a lot of us, I'm sure. But, I managed to convince her that it would be best to allow you to go to a more comfortable and familiar environment. Especially since I think, after your ordeal, both of you just need rest and relaxation. And *not* this. Am I right?"

"Definitely." Issac murmurs, weaving his fingers together. "Home would be wonderful right now. Just a little bit of *normal.*"

"Yeeeeeaaah." They say slowly, looking at Issac, their brow furrowed. "I know messed up routines suck hard for you, and you two have been all..." They tap their fingers on the table, seeming to struggle for the right word. "... offset for weeks now." They fiddle with their papers. "We just need to establish a few things. Immediate way to get in contact if needed, Ms. Kahale's education, protections placed on both of your homes- Oh! Ms. Kahale, would you like your room-mate informed on what has transpired? It's entirely up to you, but there's another form that needs filled out if you do."

"Uh, yeah." I pull on my ponytail. "It'd probably be best to tell Lorrie, since I don't know how I would explain other-wise."

They nod. "Noted. Glad I grabbed that form. There's also a bit of paperwork to do so the effects on your college classes are negated. You'll have to catch up on the work still, but we can make sure that as far as the systems- and your pro-fessors- are concerned, you two didn't miss anything." He smiles. "So, let's get started! I imagine you both want this done as quickly as possible, so you can *finally* go home."

I share a look with Issac, and we both laugh.

"Hopefully this doesn't take *too* long." I murmur, smiling.

~ Twenty-Three ~

Issac

December 18th, 2018

"Issac! Hurry up!" Anna bounces on her toes like ten feet ahead of me. "It's been over five months since I've seen my dad, and I have a lot to make up for!"

The temperature is warm, much warmer than I'm used to this time of year, and much sunnier too. I look up at the mostly clear sky, and then back at Anna, chuckling. You'd never guess it was *December* based on this weather.

"What, am I not allowed to appreciate the scenery? This is my first time ever in Hawaii after all!" I flash a quick grin at her, and she stomps back and grabs my free hand.

"Scenery appreciation can wait." She huffs. "Now come on!"

She pulls me forward faster than I can walk, and I almost fall, barely holding myself up on the staff that I've taken to using as a walking stick, with how hard it is to stay balanced anymore.

"Anna. Anna. I can't walk that fast anymore." I shake my head slowly. "I was *uncoordinated* before, and you expect me to be able to speed walk *now*?"

She winces, taking a step back. "Sorry sorry sorry..."

I sigh, shaking my head. "Don't be." I right myself, standing up straight. "You're fine. Just keep in mind that I can't exactly keep up with you."

"Are..." She bites her lip, looking away. "Are you ever going to get better?" Her eyes widen. "N-not that it's a problem if you don't!"

"Anna." I shake my head. "You know I was disabled before my... ordeal with the Hunter, right?" A mental disability, but still. Not being able to function as an abled person would isn't *new* to me. "You don't need to trip over yourself to be sensitive about it. But honestly, no clue." I shrug. I was getting better for a while; but eventually my recovery just plateaued, and I'm left still easily dizzied and with extremely poor balance. Not to mention the ache that settles over my whole body when my staff isn't in hand, but...

It's... frustrating, certainly. Dizziness can make my sensory problems a lot worse, but it's not the end of the world. If I never get better from here, I'd be *fine*.

Besides, Dr. Mendoza still has me on the one medication proven to help with Spellburn, so he still has some hope for it getting better.

"When no one even knows *exactly* what's wrong, it's really hard to say if it'll get better." I pause for a long moment. "*Frankly*, I'm lucky. If it wasn't for the extremely skilled life mages of the D.C. Mages hospital, I wouldn't have survived at all."

Anna is silent for a moment. "I still can't believe he got away..." She kicks at the ground. "What if he comes back for you?"

I'd be lying if I said that Anderson being out there still didn't haunt my nightmares. Extensively, as much as I actually remember them. But I have to remind myself that I'll be *fine*. I lift the staff slightly, smirking. "I'd like to see him try."

She blinks several times, then starts laughing into her hands. She takes a step forward and kisses me. "I love it when you get cocky." She murmurs, then takes a step back.

I feel my face heat up, and she giggles. "Now come on!" She bounces on her toes and bounds forward again, clearly unable to contain her excitement.

I chuckle and follow her as quickly as I can. It's weird, honestly. Just a few months ago I was almost certain that I was mostly worthless in magic no matter how hard I studied because I couldn't figure out my specialty, and now... Now I have to remind myself that I'm technically the most powerful mage in existence.

At least... I am so long as I'm holding my staff. Without it, my ability to channel tessence is still shot. I can do it, but it's quickly depleted and can be downright painful if I try to channel too much.

So, I keep a hold of the staff and remind myself that I'm literally *the Master*. If I come off as cocky... then so be it.

She's waiting just in front of the house that was at the end of this path, grinning widely with her hands clasped together, and bouncing on her toes.

I chuckle. "You know, for someone who was refusing to talk to their father a few months ago, you've made an awful lot of progress."

Her grin fades, and she smacks me upside the head. "Issac! We're on break! Don't go Psych Student on me!"

I laugh. "What, am I allowed to when we're actually in Scho-"

"No!" she cuts across me, scowling. "Never! Damn it. I get enough of that from Lorrie. I don't need it from my boyfriend too!"

She grabs my free hand and tugs me up the steps to the door.

"Okay, so my Dad tends to be rather exuberant at ti-" The door opens behind her, and there's a man with short curly black hair and thick-framed glasses, almost with a Hawaiian Clark Kent look going on about him.

He beams and picks Anna up from behind, hugging her and spinning her around.

"Daaaad." She groans as he puts her down. "Don't do that!"

He laughs and ruffles her hair. "I'm sorry, I just missed you so much Anna!"

"I-" Anna looks away, wincing, and seeming to fight back sudden tears. "I missed you too, Dad. So much." She throws her arms around him. "I'm sorry."

He hugs her back, murmuring something to her, and I look away, feeling like I'm intruding, and my heart aches a little.

My parents would have liked Anna. They would have treated her like she was part of the family instantly. My mother would have fretted over whether the lightning had any long-term effects. My father would have been more help than I am for her learning how to control her magic...

But there's no point to dwelling on it. The man who killed them was charged and is awaiting trial, and I'm going to finish my father's research if it's the last thing I do. I'm okay, and right now I'm supposed to be meeting my girlfriend's father. And that's what matters *now*.

I'll probably never completely understand why any of this happened. Anderson refuses to talk about it, to admit what he's done. I'll never have the closure... but it doesn't really matter, does it?

Anna pulls away from her dad, wiping at her eyes. "Uhm." She clears her throat. "Dad, this is Issac Riley. My boyfriend. I've told you about him... Somewhat."

He glances at me momentarily. "You told me that he existed and that you would tell me more in person."

She laughs nervously. "Yes. Yes, I did. Uh. Let's go inside before he gets distracted by actually warm weather again."

I blink a few times, then huff, crossing my arms. "Hey! It's *weird* for it to be this warm in December!"

"He's lived in Seattle his entire life." Anna says immediately, laughing at me. "He's used to just cold and rain."

"Oh, so I imagine he doesn't get much sun either, huh?" Her dad laughs and motions us inside.

"It's not like it rains every day in Seattle..." I grumble, walking in past him. "We get sunlight... And it warms up in the summer... And we're on the water so it's not even *that* cold for being so far north..."

He follows us in, staring oddly at my staff.

Anna noticing him staring too. "It's a walking stick." She says immediately. "There was an... incident a few months ago, and he needs it to walk."

"Huh? Sorry, it just... looks familiar."

I stand bolt upright, staring at him with wide eyes. "How so?"

"Just... an old thing of Anna's mother's..." Anna frowns at him, her brow furrowed, then glances at me and shrugs. He sighs. "I'm sorry. I shouldn't have brought it up. It's something she got from her father when she was about Anna's age... I suppose... But I'm not the one who should explain it..." He fiddles with his glasses. "I'm not even sure how I would..."

I exhale slowly. "Mr. Kahale-"

"Please, call me Kai."

"Uhm." I bite my lip. "Kai, is this item by any chance... a locket?"

His eyes widen, and I know I'm right. "H-how did you...?"

I laugh weakly, pinching the bridge of my nose. "Anna already knows most of the story, now, actually."

"Anna doesn't know about the locket." She pipes up, and I laugh.

"Vincent gave it to Leilani. It was his mother's before that."

Kai looks between the two of us. "You... already know about the magic stuff?" He shakes his head slowly. "I never knew how to..."

Anna waves her hand through the air, a trail of glittering green light left in its wake. It's become a fast favorite of hers as far as 'neat magic things' goes. "Yeah. I know about magic stuff. Kind of surprised you do, since it's most of what I wanted to talk about in person."

"Your Mother..." He shakes himself. "Wow, it's actually back..." He closes his eyes, shaking his head. "Your Mother told me that her family was magic, but was... cursed? To lose that magic, and it would only come back when the world needed it."

"Yeah, I already know I'm a chosen one or something." She smiles awkwardly. "It happened when I was struck by lightning."

Kai shoots a glance at me. "Wasn't he the one who helped you to the hospital?"

"Fate is weird." Anna murmurs.

"Actually, I have a theory on that, and it's not just 'Fate is weird'." I smile nervously. "I believe our close proximity to each other in that moment, or maybe right before when we met at the library, is what caused your magic to unlock then, and the energy of that drew the lightning to you."

Anna scowls at me. "I'll stick with 'Fate is weird' Mr. Brainiac." A moment later, she chuckles. "But really, it's cool. I've learned so much in the past few months..."

"Uh." Kai looks between us. "So... so what is exactly is his connection to this whole thing?"

I spin the staff in my hands. "My ancestor, Vincent Riley, he was close to Leilani Keahi. What limited records there are, have him having lived with her from roughly age nine to age nineteen, after which he moved far away from both of his previous homes in Pennsylvania and Hawai'i, to found a school in the area that would eventually become Seattle. Where his descendants have been ever since."

Kai sighs, hanging his head. "This is all even more complicated than I thought, isn't it?"

Anna pats her Dad's back. "Don't worry. You get used to it."

"He better." I say softly. "Because something tells me it isn't going to stop anytime soon."

THE LICENSE

Shared Open Universe License, version 1.3

By exercising the Licensed Rights (defined below), You accept and agree to be bound by the terms and conditions of this Shared Open Universe License ("the SOUL"). To the extent the SOUL may be interpreted as a contract, You are granted the Licensed Rights in consideration of Your acceptance of these terms and conditions, and the Creator grants You such rights in consideration of benefits the Creator receives from making the Original Work available under these terms and conditions.

Statement of Purpose.

The SOUL is intended to protect and promote the rights of fans of creative works to create and Share Fan Works derived from the Creative Content in the Original Work, including for commercial purposes, but without infringing on the original creator's exclusive rights to publish the Original Work and control how it is Shared. In turn, the requirements for the Fan Works being released under the terms of this licence is intended to allow different fans and the original creator to build upon each other's ideas as each desired.

Section 1 – Definitions.

1. Fan Work means material subject to Copyright and Similar Rights that is derived from or based upon

the Creative Content in the Original Work in a manner requiring permission under the Copyright and Similar Rights held by the Creator. Material that does not add new Creative Content is not considered Fan Work.

b. Copyright and Similar Rights means copyright and/or similar rights closely related to copyright including, without limitation, performance, broadcast and sound recording, without regard to how the rights are labeled or categorized. For purposes of the SOUL, the rights specified in Section 2(b)(1)-(2) are not Copyright and Similar Rights.

c. Effective Technological Measures means those measures that, in the absence of proper authority, may not be circumvented under laws fulfilling obligations under Article 11 of the WIPO Copyright Treaty adopted on December 20, 1996, and/or similar international agreements.

d. Exceptions and Limitations means fair use, fair dealing, and/or any other exception or limitation to Copyright and Similar Rights that applies to Your use of the Original Work.

e. Original Work means the artistic or literary work, database, or other material to which the Creator applied the SOUL.

f. Creative Content means the characters, settings, events, objects, groups and other narrative elements and ideas expressed a work. For purposes of the SOUL, text and images are not inherently Creative Content.

g. Licensed Rights means the rights granted to You subject to the terms and conditions of the SOUL, which are limited to all Copyright and Similar Rights that apply to Your use of the Original Work and that the Creator has authority to license.

h. Creator means the individual(s) or entity(ies) granting rights under the SOUL.

i. Share means to provide material to the public by any means or process that requires permission under the Licensed Rights, such as reproduction, public display, public performance, distribution, dissemination, communication, or importation, and to make material available to the public including in ways that members of the public may access the material from a place and at a time individually chosen by them.

j. Identifying Elements means the title, logo and other elements unique to and identifying of the Original Work.

k. You means the individual or entity exercising the Licensed Rights under the SOUL. Your has a corresponding meaning.

Section 2 – Scope.

1. License grant.
1. Sharing Fan Works. Subject to the terms and conditions of the SOUL, the Creator hereby grants You a worldwide, royalty-free, non-sublicensable, non-exclusive, irrevocable license to exercise the Licensed

Rights in the Original Work to produce, reproduce, and Share Fan Work.

1. For the avoidance of doubt, the Creator does not grant You the right to Share the Original Work, in whole or in part.

2. Using Identifying Elements. Subject to the terms and conditions of the SOUL, the Creator hereby grants You a worldwide, royalty-free, non-sublicensable, non-exclusive, irrevocable license to utilize the Identifying Elements in the Original Work in the process of exercising your Licensed Rights to Share Fan Work, subject to Section 2(a)(7).

3. Exceptions and Limitations. For the avoidance of doubt, where Exceptions and Limitations apply to Your use, the SOUL does not apply, and You do not need to comply with its terms and conditions.

4. Term. The term of the SOUL is specified in Section 5(a).

5. Media and formats; technical modifications allowed. The Creator authorizes You to exercise the Licensed Rights in all media and formats whether now known or hereafter created, and to make technical modifications necessary to do so. The Creator waives and/or agrees not to assert any right or authority to forbid You from making technical modifications necessary to exercise the Licensed Rights, including technical modifications necessary to circumvent Effective Technological Measures. For purposes of the SOUL, simply making modifications authorized by this Section 2(a)(5) never produces Fan Work.

6. Downstream recipients.

1. Offer from the Creator – Original Work. Every recipient of the Original Work automatically receives an offer from the Creator to exercise the Licensed Rights under the terms and conditions of the SOUL.
B. Additional offer from the Creator – Fan Work. Every recipient of Fan Work from You automatically receives an offer from the Creator to exercise the Licensed Rights in the Fan Work under the conditions of the version of the SOUL You apply to the Fan Work.
C. No downstream restrictions. You may not offer or impose any additional or different terms or conditions on, or apply any Effective Technological Measures to, the Original Work if doing so restricts exercise of the Licensed Rights by any recipient of the Original Work.

7. No endorsement. Nothing in the SOUL constitutes or may be construed as permission to assert or imply that You are, or that Your use of the Original Work is, connected with, or sponsored, endorsed, or granted official status by, the Creator or others designated to receive attribution as provided in Section 3(a)(1)(A)(i).
b. Other rights.

1. Moral rights, such as the right of integrity, are not licensed under the SOUL, nor are publicity, privacy, and/or other similar personality rights; however, to the extent possible, the Creator waives and/or agrees not to assert any such rights held by the Cre-

ator to the limited extent necessary to allow You to exercise the Licensed Rights, but not otherwise.

2. Patent and trademark rights are not licensed under the SOUL, except as stated in Section 2(a)(2).

3. To the extent possible, the Creator waives any right to collect royalties from You for the exercise of the Licensed Rights, whether directly or through a collecting society under any voluntary or waivable statutory or compulsory licensing scheme. In all other cases the Creator expressly reserves any right to collect such royalties.

Section 3 – License Conditions.

Your exercise of the Licensed Rights is expressly made subject to the following conditions.

1. Attribution Requirement.
1. If You Share Fan Work, You must:
1. retain the following if it is supplied by the Creator with the Original Work:
1. identification of the creator(s) of the Original Work and any others designated to receive attribution, in any reasonable manner requested by the Creator (including by pseudonym if designated);

ii. a copyright notice;

iii. a notice that refers to the SOUL;

iv. a notice that refers to the disclaimer of warranties;

v. a URI or hyperlink to the Original Work to the extent reasonably practicable;

B. indicate the Original Work is licensed under the SOUL, and include the text of, or the URI or hyperlink to, the SOUL.

2. You may satisfy the conditions in Section 3(a)(1) in any reasonable manner based on the medium, means, and context in which You Share the Original Work. For example, it may be reasonable to satisfy the conditions by providing a URI or hyperlink to a resource that includes the required information.

3. If requested by the Creator, You must remove any of the information required by Section 3(a)(1)(A) to the extent reasonably practicable.

b. In addition to the conditions in Section 3(a), if You Share Fan Work You produce, the following conditions also apply.

1. You must apply the SOUL to Your Copyright and Similar Rights in the Fan Work.
1. The license You apply must be the version of the SOUL applied to the Original Work or a later version.

2. You must include the text of, or the URI or hyperlink to, the version of the SOUL You apply. You may satisfy this condition in any reasonable manner based on the medium, means, and context in which You Share Fan Work.

3. You may not offer or impose any additional or different terms or conditions on, or apply any Effective Technological Measures to, Fan Work that restrict exercise of the rights granted under the version of the SOUL You apply.

Section 4 – Disclaimer of Warranties and Limitation of Liability.

1. Unless otherwise separately undertaken by the Creator, to the extent possible, the Creator offers the Original Work as-is and as-available, and makes no representations or warranties of any kind concerning the Original Work, whether express, implied, statutory, or other. This includes, without limitation, warranties of title, merchantability, fitness for a particular purpose, non-infringement, absence of latent or other defects, accuracy, or the presence or absence of errors, whether or not known or discoverable. Where disclaimers of warranties are not allowed in full or in part, this disclaimer may not apply to You.

b. To the extent possible, in no event will the Creator be liable to You on any legal theory (including, without limitation, negligence) or otherwise for any direct, special, indirect, incidental, consequential, punitive, exemplary, or other losses, costs, expenses, or damages arising out of the SOUL or use of the Original Work, even if the Creator has been advised of the possibility of such losses, costs, expenses, or damages. Where a limitation of liability is not allowed in full or in part, this limitation may not apply to You.

c. The disclaimer of warranties and limitation of liability provided above shall be interpreted in a manner that, to the extent possible, most closely approximates an absolute disclaimer and waiver of all liability.

Section 5 – Term and Termination.

1. The SOUL applies for the term of the Copyright and Similar Rights licensed here. However, if You fail to comply with the SOUL, then Your rights under the SOUL terminate automatically.
   b. Where Your right to use the Original Work has terminated under Section 5(a), it reinstates:
1. automatically as of the date the violation is cured, provided it is cured within 30 days of Your discovery of the violation; or
2. upon express reinstatement by the Creator.

For the avoidance of doubt, this Section 5(b) does not affect any right the Creator may have to seek remedies for Your violations of the SOUL.

c. For the avoidance of doubt, the Creator may also offer the Original Work under separate terms or conditions or stop distributing the Original Work at any time; however, doing so will not terminate the SOUL.

d. Sections 1, 4, 5, 6 and 7 survive termination of the SOUL.

Section 6 – Other Terms and Conditions.

1. The Creator shall not be bound by any additional or different terms or conditions communicated by You unless expressly agreed.
   b. Any arrangements, understandings, or agree-

ments regarding the Original Work not stated herein are separate from and independent of the terms and conditions of the SOUL.

Section 7 – Interpretation.

1. For the avoidance of doubt, the SOUL does not, and shall not be interpreted to, reduce, limit, restrict, or impose conditions on any use of the Original Work that could lawfully be made without permission under the SOUL.

   b. To the extent possible, if any provision of the SOUL is deemed unenforceable, it shall be automatically reformed to the minimum extent necessary to make it enforceable, taking into account Creator's Statement of Purpose. If the provision cannot be reformed, it shall be severed from the SOUL without affecting the enforceability of the remaining terms and conditions.

   c. No term or condition of the SOUL will be waived and no failure to comply consented to unless expressly agreed to by the Creator.

   d. Nothing in the SOUL constitutes or may be interpreted as a limitation upon, or waiver of, any privileges and immunities that apply to the Creator or You, including from the legal processes of any jurisdiction or authority.